SPECIAL MESSAGE TO READERS

THE ULVERSCROFT FOUNDATION
(registered UK charity number 264873)
was established in 1972 to provide funds for research, diagnosis and treatment of eye diseases. Examples of major projects funded by the Ulverscroft Foundation are:-

- The Children's Eye Unit at Moorfelds Eye Hospital, London
- The Ulverscroft Children's Eye Unit at Great Ormond Street Hospital for Sick Children
- Funding research into eye diseases and treatment at the Department of Ophthalmology, University of Leicester
- The Ulverscroft Vision Research Group, Institute of Child Health
- Twin operating theatres at the Western Ophthalmic Hospital, London
- The Chair of Ophthalmology at the Royal Australian College of Ophthalmologists

You can help further the work of the Foundation by making a donation or leaving a legacy. Every contribution is gratefully received. If you would like to help support the Foundation or require further information, please contact:

THE ULVERSCROFT FOUNDATION
The Green, Bradgate Road, Anstey
Leicester LE7 7FU, England
Tel: (0116) 236 4325

website: www.ulverscroft-foundation.org.uk

AN ANGEL'S WORK

England, 1941. As nurse Jo Brooks arrives at Mill Road Hospital, a ward takes a direct hit from a bomb. Pulling herself from the rubble, Jo's first priority must be her patients...but she can't stop herself frantically searching for her friend Moira. When she eventually finds her, Moira is barely clinging to life. Jo makes a solemn vow: she will do whatever it takes to help the Allies win the war, even if it means sacrificing her own safety.

But when Jo makes the acquaintance of a handsome American soldier, she feels her heart skip a beat, and all her promises are put to the test. Because sacrificing everything is so much more difficult when suddenly you have so very much to live for...

KATE EASTHAM

AN ANGEL'S WORK

Complete and Unabridged

MAGNA
Leicester

First published in Great Britain in 2020 by
Bookouture
London

First Ulverscroft Edition
published 2021
by arrangement with
Bookouture
London

A catalogue record for this book is available from the British Library.

ISBN 978–0–7505–4925–7

Published by
Ulverscroft Limited
Anstey, Leicestershire

Printed and bound in Great Britain by
TJ Books Ltd., Padstow, Cornwall

This book is printed on acid-free paper

For Joe

We never know how high we are
Till we are called to rise;
And then, if we are true to plan,
Our statures touch the skies —

Emily Dickinson

Prologue

The English Channel, June 1944

'What's that?' screamed Jo, clutching her metal seat as a loud explosion rattled the frame of the C-47 Dakota. Her orderly shouted something about German anti-aircraft guns at Dunkirk. She tried to answer but her mouth was bone dry and her heart was thumping against her ribs.

Count backwards from ten like you used to at home when thunder rumbled across the fells, she instructed herself, as relentless explosions continued to burst around them. Ten, nine, eight, seven... A heavy thud caused the plane to lurch violently, making her shoot up from her seat and grab a handhold. Six, five, four, three... She forced back the tears that were stinging her eyes and started from ten again as she clung to the fabric of the plane, shivering in her unwieldly Mae West and oversized battledress tunic that prickled her skin through the man's shirt that she wore underneath. As the aircraft pitched and equipment slid across the cabin floor, she wondered if maybe the pilot had been right when he'd shouted before take-off that he didn't want any woman on board his plane because it was bad luck.

Instantly, her mother's broad Lancashire voice was in her head: *Don't be daft. That's superstitious nonsense. Besides, you're as good as any man and damned near as strong.*

Jo glanced at the wiry figure of the orderly oppo-

1

site, whom she'd only met as she boarded the plane, and he motioned for her to hold fast. 'I was the same on my first mission last year,' he shouted above the roar of the engines. 'You'll get used to it.'

Jo nodded and held on tight. At least if they got hit on the way to France, she could use her parachute, but on the way back, the air ambulance nurses had been told that under no circumstances could they bail out. If the plane was going down their duty was to stay with their patients. The rest of the crew could evacuate, but the nurses' parachutes would be locked away. She shuddered.

Ten, nine, eight, seven, six ... she counted slowly as, at last, the Dakota levelled up and her heart began to steady. She breathed out, feeling the euphoria, letting go of her handhold and pitching unsteadily towards the orderly. He turned from the window and beckoned for her to come and stand beside him.

'Will you look at that,' he said, his voice husky with emotion.

Jo pressed close to the glass and for a moment all she could see was white cloud. Then, through a break in the cover, she saw the Normandy beaches laid waste below — cut open with shell holes, churned up and littered with scattered equipment and burnt-out tanks. Abandoned landing craft lay like toys in the surf. She felt her breath catch as she held on to the orderly's arm and remembered the reports of the D-Day landings — of the sea stained red with men's blood. All those soldiers who had given their lives fighting on the beaches to push the enemy back.

Nobody had told her during basic training that crossing the Channel would be so terrifying, and very soon they would be landing at a temporary airbase where wounded men lay waiting to be evacuated from casualty clearing stations. Each Dakota would be taking at least fourteen stretcher cases and six walking wounded. She'd worked at a military hospital and seen what horrors war could inflict; she knew that some of the injuries would be severe. And this time she would be on her own with no support from a doctor — she would have to be strong. The injured men that were waiting for her had fought hard on the Normandy beaches; she would fight equally hard to keep them alive as they made their journey home. It felt like a mission of mercy.

★ ★ ★

Mac filed up the gangplank of the *HMS Duke of Lancaster* with the rest of the army nurses; all fully kitted out with tin hats, kit bags and rattling billycans. 'Come on Vera,' she urged, pulling her new friend in close beside her. She forced a brave smile to try to reassure her, all the while hoping to God that the sea would stay as calm as it was right now.

As their ship gathered speed and they began to feel the swell of the English Channel, a whole convoy of vessels of varying sizes surrounded them: some carrying troops, others supplies and there was even a tank carrier. The whole convoy moved together as one.

'We really are part of something now,' Mac murmured, tears welling in her eyes.

Close to the Normandy beaches, the sea was choppy. They were ordered to climb down onto the landing craft that would take them ashore. Ungainly and off balance in her lifejacket and with heavy equipment on her back, Mac moved first. But before she could reach the side of the ship, she heard the screech of a missile and then, terrifyingly, a loud explosion so close it made their ship lurch from side to side. The women grabbed each other for support.

'It's a supply ship,' shouted one of the crew. But Mac knew that there would have been sailors on board. She gasped as a tower of flame shot up towards the sky. She was sure she could hear screaming, but maybe it was inside her head. In minutes, the vessel had sunk.

'Come on, we need to move. Now!' yelled one of the crew. Mac took a deep breath and forced herself to the side of the ship — unless they wanted to risk joining the list of killed in action, there was no choice, they had to move, and she seemed to be leading the way. With a nod to the grim-faced seaman giving her rapid disembarkation instructions, she slipped over the side of the ship and found a foothold on the rope netting. She tried to smile back up to the stricken faces of her fellow nurses who'd moved to the side and were peering down at her. In moments, she was scrambling down the net, wondering how the hell she'd ended up doing this first.

When she reached the bottom, she clung there, soaked in cold spray from the sea.

'Just fall back! Let go and fall back! We'll catch you!' A man's voice was yelling from below. She fought the urge to climb straight back up the netting. But when she looked down, she saw a piece of wreckage from a ship bobbing on the water and knew that she needed to act.

'Go!' she shouted, but she found herself still cling-ing to the net, unable to move. She glanced down to the water again and saw an army boot ripped wide

4

open, caught in the swirl of the sea. It filled her with horror, and in a split second, almost involuntarily, she growled and then screamed out loud, 'Go, go!' She pushed herself off from the side of the ship and flew backwards, landing heavily against a sailor with very strong arms. He laughed as he caught her and said, 'Well done,' before setting her on her feet. She went straight back to wait for the next nurse and shout encouragement.

'You can do it, Vera,' she called as her friend edged tentatively down the scrambling net.

The landing craft were rushing; fearful of losing any more ships, they didn't want to wait for the tide to go the whole way out. So, the nurses were ordered to disembark and wade to dry land. Mac tried not to think about the thousands of soldiers who had landed here under heavy fire less than two weeks ago. So many killed, so many wounded. A cold shudder went through her.

Mac led the way again, walking down the ramp and into ice-cold water, gasping when her foot slipped on shingle and caught against something hard and metallic. She stood firm so that she could guide Vera, who was so petite that Mac had to hold her steady as the rough water came up to her thighs.

'Come on,' she gasped, hauling her along. 'We don't want you to drown before we even get started.' Vera was soaked right through to the skin and Mac had to drag her through the water. But she could do it; she seemed to have extra strength. And for God knows what reason, it felt right that they should wade ashore where the men had fought, tasting the salt and feeling the same sand and shingle beneath their feet. These were not clear waters — they were strewn with

shell cases and discarded equipment. A tin hat rid-
dled with bullet holes bobbed in front of her and she
had to push past it.

Tears filled her eyes but this was no place for crying; she had to keep going through the water, glancing
behind to check that all of her fellow nurses were
making their way safely to shore. Stern-faced Senior Sister, Marsha Lloyd, was at the head of another
group, gamely striding through the sea with her chin
set in a determined line, and the sight spurred her on.
Older than the rest, Sister Lloyd had served during
the last war. No one dared trifle with her.

Once ashore, they clambered unsteadily up the
beach, just ahead of the tank-landing ship that opened
its doors and started to discharge its load.

'Keep moving, nurses,' called Sister Lloyd, seeing
them distracted by the spectacle. With her boots and
battledress heavy with water and sand, it wasn't easy
to walk, but Mac led the way, up over a beach that
looked like a deserted battlefield. The tides that had
ebbed and flowed since the fighting had smoothed the
sand, but chunks of jagged concrete, twisted metal
and smashed landing craft remained.

Mac could almost feel the battle and hear the
screams of men. She forced herself to keep walking,
to keep pulling Vera towards the lorry that waited
for them on a rough track. She felt her legs suddenly
heavy as a wave of sadness swept through her, and she
knew if she let it, it would drag her to her knees. If she
hadn't needed to help Vera, she might have slumped
to the ground.

A group of soldiers were digging a trench beside the
track. They all looked up at the same time and one of
them yelled, 'Blimey! The women have landed!'

'We are not women, we are Queen Alexandra's Imperial Military Nurses!' shouted Sister Lloyd instantly, and the whole group of men cracked up laughing, shaking their heads and shouting bawdy, good-natured comments.

Mac found herself holding back the laughter, and as she felt that moment of light-heartedness, the tightness in her chest began to ease. And then Vera was laughing and blowing kisses to the soldiers as they passed by. What else could she do, after what the men had been through?

Hearing a light aircraft overhead, Mac looked up to the bright blue sky. Sunlight glinted off a small aeroplane, making it seem like some heavenly body. It made her think about her friend, Jo, who'd joined the Women's Auxiliary Air Force to be a Flying Nightingale. She imagined her up there, in the blue sky, and it made her spirits soar.

1

Mill Road Hospital, Liverpool, May Blitz 1941

It was evening in the Nurses' Home. In the days before the war this had always been a settling down time, an unwinding from the busy wards. But since August last year when the bombs had started falling on Liverpool, there was something else that came when the city started to darken — a sharp edge of expectation that rested, unspoken, amongst the nurses. It surfaced in the restless murmurings of conversation that came from the rooms down each side of the long corridor, and it rose in the high-pitched laughter of those heading into the city. More nurses were going out in the evenings, making the most of their time off, seeking distraction. No one knew what might happen next. There hadn't been a raid for five days, but all the time the question hung in the air — would the bombers come tonight?

Jo yearned for the time before the war, when she could slip into her flannelette pyjamas straight from a good soak in the bath and then spend an untroubled evening quietly chatting to the other nurses or curled up with a book. She never gave voice to it, but she found the fear that had engulfed the city exhausting. And her roommate, Mac… well, it was as if she'd been gripped by fever; she was out every night. It seemed like she couldn't bear to waste a single moment. Jo had started to worry about her friend; despite her seemingly boundless energy, she had dark smudges beneath her eyes and sometimes she tripped up on her words.

Tonight Jo had taken a stand with her, though. They'd both finished a late shift and Mac had gone straight to their room, unpinning her red curly hair as soon as she was in through the door and pulling her best frock out of the wardrobe — desperate to get out into the city for a couple of hours before the door to the Nurses' Home was locked shut at eleven.

'Look, Mac,' Jo had said, standing square in front of her. 'You're exhausting yourself. I know how busy you've been on the maternity ward today. When I walked through, there were at least three women ready to give birth.'

Mac flashed her bright blue eyes and started to laugh. 'But that's exactly why I need to go out. I've been with women thrashing around in labour all day long. I just need a break from it.'

Jo stood her ground as Mac turned away and started to pull more clothes out of the wardrobe. 'I'm worried about you.'

Mac spun round to confront her with a too-bright smile. 'I'm sorry that you're worried, but I think that's partly because you're a stay-at-home, that's why you mither so much.'

Jo frowned, but she knew her friend was right. 'I know I can be a worrier, but Mac, we've not had an attack for days and days, and you know what that means — the Germans will be back soon. And if you're out there, you might not be able to find a place of safety. The city is in ruins and now the docks have been blown up, and only last week Saint George's Hall took a hit and even the Liverpool Royal Infirmary ...'

'Oh, stop it. I'll be safe in some man's arms. You know I will,' she crooned as she stooped down to rummage through the array of underwear and scarves stuffed into the bottom of her wardrobe.

Jo knew that she needed to change tack. She softened the tone of her voice and made herself smile. 'Why don't you stay in with me, just for one night? We never get the chance to have our long chats any more. Not like we used to.'

'But I *have* to go out,' muttered Mac, still searching around the bottom of her wardrobe.

Jo breathed out a small sigh of exasperation.

Mac paused and glanced up, her eyes shining. 'You know that airman, Don, the one I met last night, well —'

'But you told me you're not seeing him until Saturday. Remember?'

Mac gave an anguished cry and straightened up from the wardrobe with a lacy suspender belt in her hand. 'Yes, I know, but he might be out again tonight in The Crown. I might bump into him… He had the most gorgeous dark brown eyes.'

Jo was standing firm and shaking her head. 'You'll see him again on Saturday, it's only two nights to wait. You need to rest up for one night. And if a raid does come, you'll be needed on the wards.'

'I'll be back by then, they don't usually start bombing till after ten, do they?'

Jo sighed heavily.

She saw Mac tip her head ever so slightly to one side and then glance at her reflection in their shared dressing table mirror, using a hand to brush her hair back from her face, as if deciding what style to wear it in. Then she turned with her mouth drawn down in

10

mock sorrow and threw the suspender belt onto the bed.

'Oh, alright then, Stay-At-Home, you win... But you have to let me try out some new make-up on you.'

Jo never enjoyed Mac's beauty sessions but tonight she had no choice. 'It's a deal,' she said, instantly relaxing knowing that Mac would be safely home with her and not in some rowdy pub or wandering the bomb-damaged streets, at least for one night. She gave a cheeky smile. 'Now, I'll just change into my pyjamas and I'll make us both a nice cup of cocoa.'

'As if that's the biggest treat in the world,' Mac said, laughing. She grabbed a cushion from her bed and threw it across the room to Jo's side, where she stood carefully removing the starched collar and cuffs from her uniform before taking the clips out of the neat bun that held her long hair tidy at the nape of her neck.

'I need to see what I can do with your hair,' cried Mac, crossing the space between them to take up a generous handful of locks from each side and hold both together on top of Jo's head. 'You have such gorgeous hair, Jo, it's so soft and shiny — it's almost black in this light. You should make more of it.'

'Oh no, don't fuss,' Jo replied, gently removing Mac's hands before shaking her hair loose and stepping away. 'I just like to wear it straight down or pulled back in a ponytail when I'm off duty.' Reaching up, she took two blue-patterned cups from the top shelf of her own wardrobe.

As she nosed out of the door on her way to the kitchen, she was almost knocked down by Myfanwy Jones and Ruth Lee striding along the corridor, heading out dressed in their finest. 'Good night!' called

Myfanwy, turning with a smile, a haze of black, pin-curled hair encircling her face. Myfanwy was from their set of probationers. Jo had always liked her, but she wasn't altogether sure why she'd started spending all her time with Ruth Lee. Ruth glanced back but didn't smile. Serious and uncompromising on the wards, she had a reputation for sometimes being a bit cold with the patients. But perhaps Myfanwy had found something in her that no one else had. Maybe that was it.

Jo stood in the kitchen with her pan on the gas burner, waiting for the milk to boil. She heard a quiet voice behind her and turned to find Amy Goodwin. With her small face and pale brown hair, Mac always referred to her as, 'Little Miss Mouse, the founding member of your pyjama-clad gang.'

'Hello, Amy,' she smiled. 'Busy day?'

'Oh yes,' she sighed, pushing her round metal-rimmed specs up the bridge of her nose. 'I'm still on the military ward. You know what those young soldiers are like, always up to something and playing pranks. Today, one of them thought it would be amusing to pretend to be in excruciating pain, and he lay on his bed, curled up and crying out. I spent a whole five minutes trying to work out what was wrong before I realised he was quietly laughing his head off. And in the meantime, I've got Sister breathing down my neck and then Deputy Matron.'

Jo stifled a giggle and reached out a hand to her, 'Oh no. Poor you. Those lads have always had a reputation around the hospital, but I must admit, some of the stories are funny.'

'Yes, I suppose so, they can be. And they've all been through so much, they need to let off steam. But I do wish they wouldn't put lemonade in glass urinals and pretend to drink it.'

Jo clapped a hand across her mouth to stop herself from laughing out loud. 'I'm so glad I'm still working between Female Surgical and Theatre,' she said. 'It's a bit strange, working in the basement, but at least when I see any of those young men, they're about to be put to sleep. It makes for a much quieter life.'

'Lucky you.' Amy sighed, pushing her specs back into place with one hand and shooting an arm out to grab Jo's pan before the frothy, boiling milk surged over the sides.

'Oops, nearly did it again,' Jo laughed, a little too loudly, carefully negotiating the pan from Amy. 'I've done that so many times. Sometimes I'm just stand-ing here thinking about goodness knows what, and over it goes.'

'We're all a bit distracted, aren't we? What with…'

'Yes, that's true,' Jo replied hurriedly, not wanting to give Amy the chance to name the threat that hung over every man, woman and child in the city.

With the cocoa made, she stood in the corridor out-side her shared room with a cup in each hand, waiting for admittance.

Staff Nurse Josephine Brooks

Staff Nurse Moira MacDonald

She read the nameplate over and over to distract herself from looking at the empty single room next door. It had been Nurse Lomax's, during the months when she was desperately trying to continue work-ing after her mother and eleven-year-old brother had

13

been killed in an air raid a few days before Christmas. Home Sister had moved her to their floor, hoping that it would be quieter, but in the end it had all been too much for the poor girl and she'd had to leave. Jo felt her stomach clench when she thought of the nights that she'd woken to the sound of Nurse Lomax sobbing through the thin wall. A number of times she'd gone out into the corridor and knocked gently on her door, but the young nurse would never answer — she would simply go quiet. In the end Jo had stopped knocking; she wanted the girl to be able to cry for as long and as hard as she needed.

Staff Nurse Josephine Brooks... Staff Nurse Moira MacDonald... She read the nameplate once more before tapping more urgently at the bottom of the door with her foot. At last, she heard a muffled voice and Mac swung the door open.

'Sorry about that, I was trying out this new Revlon lipstick — what do you think?'

'Yes,' she replied, never knowing quite what to say about make-up or hairstyles or anything like that. 'It makes your lips look more ... red.'

'My friend sent it from America. I'll try it on you.'

'Alright,' she said, trying to sound enthusiastic.

'Do you want some of this to pep you up?' called Mac, fishing in the large red leather bag that she used to stash her gas mask when she was going out. 'A drop of the strong stuff.'

'No thank you,' she grimaced, 'I never adulterate my cocoa.'

'Ha! Only you would say something like that, it must be all those books you read.' Mac laughed, pouring a good glug from the hip flask into her own cup. 'You don't know what you're missing.' And then she

14

got down onto the floor and began rummaging in the box of goodies beneath her bed. 'But I bet you won't say no to one of these,' she cried, brandishing a full packet of custard creams.

Jo gasped. 'How did you —?'

'I know somebody who works at the Crawford's factory. She has a secret stash.'

She took one, savouring the sweet smell before dunking it. And it was so nice to have Mac in the bed next to her, propped up on pillows, sipping cocoa and stretching out a bare foot to reveal bright red toenails.

'It's called Fifth Avenue Red,' she said when she saw her looking, 'matches the lipstick.'

'Mmmm.' Jo sighed between bites of custard cream. She was now so relaxed that she almost volunteered for a trial of the nail polish as well. Then glancing down at her own feet in their sturdy dark brown carpet slippers, she started to giggle.

'What you giggling at, Brooks? You won't be laughing in a minute when I get the make-up out.'

As they sipped their cocoa, she saw Mac reach for her flask once more and empty the dregs into her own cup. She could feel her friend's restlessness; it was hard for her to stay in, especially when she had a man in her sights.

'How did you meet him then, this new one?' she asked, feeling a little guilty now for putting pressure on her not to go out.

'You mean Don?' Mac grinned, leaning up on one elbow with such a glint in her eye. 'Well, I was going to the Dance Hall, like I said, but I was running late because of the day I'd had on the ward. Anyway, as I'm on the approach, I see this man leaning against the wall in a Royal Air Force uniform. I saw him look up

15

and then he looked back down again, but I knew that he'd clocked me. As I got that bit closer, he tapped a cigarette out of his pack and pulled out a silver lighter; he didn't light up straight away, he paused for a few seconds before he leant in. And then he looked up at me again, breathing out smoke just like an American movie star — like a young Clark Gable. Something in the way he did that made my knees go weak. And I was just standing there, staring at him…' Mac rolled onto her back and heaved a sigh. 'It felt like magic, like it was meant to be. You know what I mean?'

'Mmm, not really,' Jo replied, scrunching her brow as she tried to make sense of it. All she'd ever had was a shy smile from a red-faced farm boy. 'So, neither of you had even spoken a word?'

'Well, not until I asked him to the pub and he pretended to think about it for a few seconds, then he straightened up and he said yes. In the end we didn't even get to the pub, we just walked around chatting and then one thing led to another, if you know what I mean.'

Jo cleared her throat. 'I see,' she murmured, feeling her cheeks flush pink, knowing full well that if she'd seen a strange man leaning against a wall lighting a cigarette she would probably just have averted her eyes and gone straight in through the door of the Dance Hall.

'Anyway, come on,' said Mac, rousing herself. 'I won't be seeing him until Saturday night now, so we might as well get on with our make-up session.'

Jo sat down patiently in front of the mirror with her face turned to the light and tried not to flinch as Mac perused her skin. 'You have a lovely complexion,' she murmured. 'A bit dry in places — you should use

16

some more of that Ponds cream I gave you. And we could do with covering this scattering of freckles on your nose with some powder.'

'No, not the face powder. It makes me sneeze,' she said, groaning as Mac reached for her compact and flicked open the lid.

'You promised.' Mac grinned as she used the pad to apply the powder liberally.

Jo grimaced and sneezed loudly. 'Maybe I should have let you go out and look for your airman after all.'

'Maybe you should. But it's too late now.' Mac laughed as she selected an eye pencil. 'Hold still, you pest,' she ordered, 'this is hard to do on someone else.'

When she'd finished putting on the eyeliner, Mac urged Jo to look in the mirror. Jo gazed in horror at the pale cream powdered face with drawn on eyes staring back at her.

'I wish I had big grey eyes like you,' Mac murmured, 'they're amazing when you get some definition on them. You are so lucky you've got long, dark eyelashes — not like me with my colouring.'

All Jo could offer was a wan smile as she sat staring at the mirror. She didn't know what to say. 'Is that me done?'

'Oh no, my beautiful friend, we have the mouth to do and then some preening of your hair to give the final finish.'

As Mac applied the lipstick, Jo couldn't help but admire the concentration on her face. She had such focus. This was the side to Mac that made her an excellent nurse in whatever area she worked. She could pick up new procedures and practise them so easily. It was almost pleasurable to feel the sureness of her hand as she smoothly applied the lipstick first to each side of her upper lip and then, with precision, from side to side on her bottom lip.

'Now smudge it together,' Mac ordered, before taking a breath and standing back.

Jo did as she was told and glanced back to the mirror. She was shocked to see her mouth so full and crimson red. The skin felt heavy and swollen. She didn't look or feel like herself any more.

'What do you think?'

She had no words to describe it — she didn't think she liked it, but it gave her a tingle of something quite unexpected. Something that she knew might well lead her to the Dance Hall with Mac one of these nights.

'It's a good colour isn't it?' Mac urged, desperate for some feedback.

'Yes, it is,' she replied at last, looking up to her friend's eager face. 'I think it's better on you though, with your hair and everything...'

She tried to get up.

'Not yet,' insisted Mac with a grin, 'we still need to fix your hair — pile it up on top like this. Yes?'

Jo held back a groan and nodded.

It didn't take Mac long; she was an expert. And when Jo looked once more to the mirror, she could see what a difference the finished look made. Her neck was pale and slender, her face belonged to somebody else and that hairstyle was something that she'd never seen before.

'Well?' said Mac, standing back with her hands on her hips.

'Yes, I like it,' she said, making herself smile.

Jo admired Mac's persistence with the make-up sessions, but she had to fight the urge to find some cotton wool and go straight to the pot of cold cream and wipe it all away. It just wasn't her style, but it was only fair to wait the required time, out of respect for Mac's skilful work. So she went back to her bed and took up the book she was reading, whilst Mac switched off the light, opened the blackout curtain and pulled up the bottom sash of the window to lean out for a smoke.

'Ahhh, I can hear it all going on down there,' she called back over her shoulder. 'It sounds like they're dancing in the street.'

It was too dark to read now so Jo put the book face down on the bed. As she rested on her pillow, she caught the whiff of fresh smoke drifting back towards her. Even though she'd never once inhaled a cigarette, she didn't mind the smell. She breathed it in and it made her feel calm and a little bit edgy, all at the same time. She leant up on one elbow. It was a warm May night and the sky was clear. If she was at home she'd probably be sat out at the back of the house with a cup of tea, looking up to the—

'Air raid!' screamed Mac over the mournful wail of the siren, falling back into the room so fast she banged her head on the window.

Jo leapt up from the bed, sending her book flying to the floor, as Mac slammed the window shut and dragged the blackout into position. They both knew the drill — all state-registered nurses to the wards to prepare for incoming casualties. She ripped off her pyjamas and struggled into her royal-blue uniform, all fingers and thumbs with the fiddly buttons and studs. Then she had her starched cap on her head, perched on top of the new hairdo, as Mac scrabbled for her shoes.

They ran together down the corridor — already

hearing the dull thud of explosions in the distance as the attack began — meeting wide-eyed Myfanwy and Ruth running in the opposite direction, desperate to get into their uniforms.

'We'll tell Matron you're on your way,' Jo shouted.

They felt the walls shake as another explosion sounded much closer to the Nurses' Home. Mac was already out of breath and struggling to keep up, and, desperate not to leave her behind, Jo grabbed her hand and hauled her along the corridor and then down the stairs, their feet pounding in time with the many other nurses who were running full pelt towards the hospital wards.

2

Mac clung to Jo's hand, grateful for her friend's lithe step and physical strength, imagining that if she did let go, she might never get to the wards. Her breath rasped sharp in her chest and she could feel her shoes rubbing sore patches on her heels — there'd been no time to scrabble around to find her thick black stockings.

'Nearly there,' called Jo over her shoulder. What would Mac do without her, this friend of hers, who, quiet as she was, never gave up on anybody or anything.

At last they were in the waiting area outside Casualty, the place designated for the trained nurses to gather in the event of an air raid. Deputy Matron, Rose Jenkins, stood tall in her starched cap which rose sharply from her forehead, and she indicated for them to form a circle. Mac was still doubled over and gasping for air, but she managed to straighten up with Jo's assistance, hastily trying to push back the strands of hair that she could feel escaping recklessly from her nurse's cap that was no doubt skew-whiff on her head.

Jo gave her hand a squeeze as they all stood to attention in their white starched aprons. She glanced at her friend and noticed she was still wearing full make-up — hopefully no one would notice. But she knew that Deputy Matron would not fail to spot her own bare legs that could only look like two milk bottles next to the others, who all seemed to have effortlessly slipped into their regulation black stockings, even in an emergency.

Matron Jenkins narrowed her eyes and scanned the group. Feared even by the senior physician, she stalked the hospital like a bird of prey. Mac groaned inwardly as she saw her lower her eyes to bare leg level, knowing that a penalty might mean being grounded for a week. *I'm for it now*, she thought, as Myfanwy and Ruth pushed into line next to them. Matron adjusted the ornate buckle on the belt around her thin waist, a sure sign that she was about to deliver a warning. Ludicrous as it seemed, though they were in the middle of a raid, with bombs falling on the city, Mac knew that she would still uphold their strict uniform code.

Matron took in the two new arrivals and nodded her approval but then switched her gaze back to Mac. 'Nurse MacDonald,' she said, simply, and then pursed her lips.

Mac opened her mouth to speak, 'I didn't have time—'

Whump! A bomb fell so close it shook the building to its foundation. As the nurses composed themselves after the shock, a man covered in dust ran in through the main door, dragging another who had blood streaming down his face. They had their first casualty. Mac seized the opportunity and moved instantly to assist.

'I'm blind, I'm blind,' screamed the man, as his rescuer shouted that he'd been hit by a falling slate right outside the hospital, and then hastily retreated. 'I need to go,' he called. 'My family are in a shelter. I need to be with them.'

Mac spoke softly to soothe the man and took his arm, guiding him carefully past the wooden benches waiting to be filled by more casualties. She continued to speak to him as they walked, telling him that he was in hospital, she was a nurse and they were going to help him. When she glanced back, she could see Matron Jenkins holding the rest of the staff at bay with a raised hand. All thought of a reprimand for any of the nurses now gone, Matron was straight to business, her eyes bright as she shouted her orders. Mac was pleased when she heard her direct Jo towards Casualty. They always made a good team when they worked together.

Her patient mumbled that his name was Bill and as he lurched sideways, she had to grab him with both arms to steady him. Casualty Sister came running towards them, rustling with starch, but quickly headed back into the treatment area when she realised that Mac had the situation under control. She couldn't help but wonder how Sister Lydia Reynolds managed to move so fast in her stiff uniform; even her navy-blue dress was lightly starched. Not only that, but by Mac's standards, Sister was old. Rumour had it that she'd been working at Mill Road since the time when nurses wore uniforms with leg of mutton sleeves and skirts down to the ground.

Another loud explosion cracked outside the walls of the hospital and Bill grabbed hold of her very tight. She felt some grit fall onto her starched cap. 'Come on, we're alright, we're still standing,' she murmured as she gently urged him to move so that she could guide him to a seat inside the treatment area. As the casualties continued to stream in, they would be assessing and treating people on stretchers and on the benches in the waiting area, sending those who needed emergency surgery straight up to the top floor where they had two wards of casualty beds standing ready and waiting. But for now, there was room enough to take him straight through.

By the time she had him seated, Jo was at her side. 'I'll get a dressing and bring a bowl of water so we can start to clean him up.'

'I'm blind,' Bill sobbed.

'You've blood in your eyes from a wound on your head. They always bleed a lot, try not to worry,' Mac soothed. Carefully, she used a large cotton swab to clean his face as Jo applied a dressing to the deep gash on his scalp. Her stomach clenched with anxiety, hoping to God that it was just blood from the wound and not some horrendous injury. She could manage most other things in her line of work but not eyes. As she cleaned, all seemed to be well and there was no serious injury. Dabbing a clean swab in some more water, she was able to give a final wipe.

'Open your eyes,' she said gently. As he blinked, she held her breath. She gave another wipe with the swab.

'I can see,' he murmured, and then more loudly, 'I can see!' It felt like a miracle as Bill's rugged voice broke and he started to cry. He grabbed hold of Mac and pulled her towards him. 'Thank you, nurse. Thank you.'

She smiled. 'Steady on, you still have a wound on your head, we don't want to dislodge the dressing.'

'But I can see, I can see!'

'Yes, you can see,' she said, laughing. 'Now let's get you a cup of sweet tea whilst we wait for the doctor to take a look and then we can get that wound on your head stitched up.'

Minutes later she was standing beside Jo as they both washed the man's blood from their bare hands.

'I'll replenish those swabs before we get more patients,' Jo murmured but before Mac could reply there was another shout for help. They both wiped their hands quickly and ran into the reception area to meet an ambulance crew in their tin hats, one each end of a stretcher, covered in dust and out of breath.

'It's hotting up out there, tonight,' gasped Bessie Wright, the broad-shouldered ambulance woman at the head of the stretcher. 'We pulled this one from a pile of burning rubble on the street — some young lass making her way home, must have come out of one of the pubs. She's breathing but not showing any sign of coming round yet. Obvious fracture to her left humerus; we've applied a sling, and she has small superficial cuts to her hands and face. We've no name for her, nothing in her pockets and her bag and gas mask must have been lost in the rubble.'

'Bring her through,' ordered Mac as they all walked together into the treatment area, moving as one to transfer their patient onto a narrow bed in one of the curtained cubicles. 'Grab yourselves a cup of tea before you go back out there,' she called. But the ambulance crew were already on their way. 'Not yet,' Bessie shouted as they trotted towards the door with their stretcher. 'It's hell on earth out there and we need to get the ambulance down towards the docks. They're catching the worst of it, as always.'

Mac pulled a clean blanket over the casualty before checking her breathing and taking her pulse. The young woman was wearing a torn blue dress, but her hair still held its style beneath all the dust and debris. She could see the remains of bright red lipstick on her mouth. Jo was already gently cleaning with a damp flannel to remove the worst of the muck. Mac saw

25

her look up, and with the set of her mouth, she knew exactly what she was thinking. She gave her friend a quick smile.

'It's a good job you persuaded me to stay in. But I will still be seeing Don on Saturday night, just so you know.'

Jo sighed. 'I suppose there isn't any way I can stop you, is there?'

She knew that it wasn't fair to lie, so she shook her head. 'I'm sorry, Jo. But who knows where these bombs are going to fall anyway. It's pot luck. I might stay in with you and then we'd be running to the hospital and boom—'

'Don't say that!'

'I'm sorry, but you know it's true. We're not exactly running to safety when we come here, are we?'

Jo gave her a solemn look and shook her head. 'They wouldn't bomb a hospital,' she insisted, gathering up the bowl and the towels before walking away with her shoulders held square.

'I hope to hell you're right, Jojo,' Mac replied under her breath. But she'd seen enough of what had happened since the Blitz began last year to know that anything was fair game. They all needed to live life while they had it, that was her motto.

The injured young woman gave a groan and started to move her head from side to side.

'Hello. Can you hear me? Hello.'

The girl groaned again and opened her eyes.

'You're safe now; you got caught by some falling debris, but you're going to be just fine.'

The Casualty doctor, Steven Hedley, was there now, his face creased with concentration as he picked up the woman's wrist to check her pulse.

26

'Help!' A man's cries came from the waiting area. 'Please God, help me!'

Mac ran, closely followed by Jo. The man stood swaying unsteadily, covered in dust, with a child in his arms. Jo took the child, who was unconscious but still breathing and at first glance didn't appear to have a life-threatening injury. Mac grabbed the poor man before he collapsed to the ground.

'It's alright, we've got her. We're going to look after her.'

'She's my daughter, she's all I have,' he sobbed.

It was as if the man and his daughter had opened a floodgate of casualties. Others were now limping or staggering through the door and the night was in full flow. Mac quickly settled the girl's father on a bench and, calling for a doctor, went to tend to the next in line, expertly casting her eyes over each patient in turn, assessing those who could wait and those who needed urgent treatment.

Outside, the bombs continued to fall, and from time to time the lights dimmed or the foundations of the hospital shook so hard that it seemed like the end of the world was coming. All the staff could do was keep going, keep working, as parts of the city disintegrated around them.

3

Don stayed at the bar even after the air raid siren had sounded. Why run to some sweaty shelter and squeeze in with the rest when the chances are you might get hit anyway? If your number was up, that was it, as far as he could see. He'd rather die here at the bar, in his aircrew uniform, with a pint of best bitter in his hand, thinking about the girl he'd met last night, than squashed up with strangers in a pit beneath the street. As he looked around the empty pub, he liked the idea of being the only man standing. It's a good job his mother wasn't still alive though, he knew that she'd have been horrified and given him a right telling off when he told her the story.

'Here's to you, Ma,' he called to the empty room, lifting his glass to toast her. 'And you'd have liked this one, if I'd brought her home,' he murmured, unable to stop thinking about the red-haired beauty he'd met only last night.

Well, at least he knew now that she definitely wasn't coming. She'd told him about the air raids and what the hospital staff had to do when the siren sounded. All hands on deck. She would be on the wards. And it had only been an off-chance anyway. Even so, he'd made sure to wangle another night away from the base, hoping that he might bump into her again before Saturday. He'd never felt like this before about any woman. She was breathtaking. His mates had teased him all day for being distracted, but he didn't care.

Don heard the door opening behind him and he

turned, just in case it was her after all. But it was just some fella out of breath and running for cover. He raised his eyebrows when he saw the young man's brand-new uniform: a smooth blue jacket, complete with brass buckle and a peaked cap with gold braid, plus a full set of wings above his breast pocket. Don knew instantly that he was well and truly outranked; this fella was a pilot. But pilot or not, he was still holding onto the back of a chair, trying to get his breath back.

Don slipped from his stool ready to offer a salute. But the pilot was crouching and when he straightened up, he seemed distracted, taking off his cap and walking towards the bar shaking his head. Don wasn't sure what to do, so in the end he simply lifted his glass in greeting. 'Fancy a pint?'

The man looked up and smiled, his eyes were bluer than his uniform. 'I don't know about that, but I sure could do with a Scotch right now,' he drawled, dusting grit from his shoulders.

'You're a Yank! Why are you wearing one of our uniforms?'

The man ran a hand through his light brown hair. 'Have you heard of the Eagle Squadrons?'

Don thought he had heard them mentioned somewhere.

'We're American pilots recruited to join the RAF. Help you fellas out, until it's our turn to join the war.'

'Ah, yes, that's it… I have heard of the Eagles but I never thought I'd actually meet one. So, welcome to Liverpool, and please feel free to join me for a drink at what is, at least for now, my very own bar.'

The American gave a diffident smile. Don liked him already.

'Come on, sit yourself down,' he said laughing, before another bomb fell close by and a big chunk of plaster dropped from the ceiling, crashing onto a small table near where the pilot had just been standing.

The American ducked instinctively. 'Is this OK? I mean, should we not be going to one of those air raid shelters or something?'

'Nonsense,' said Don. 'Me and you, we're the "who dares" squadron tonight. And, for all we know, this might be our last night on earth. So, come to the bar! What do I call you?'

'I'm Zachary Taylor — friends call me Zach.'

'Hello, Zach. I'm Don Costello, trainee aircrew, posted to RAF West Kirby, just finished my initial wireless training at the seaside town of Blackpool.'

'Black Pool, hey, I think I've heard of that,' he said, reaching out to shake his new friend's hand before placing his cap on the bar and sliding onto a stool.

'Now what can I get you? This is Scotch whisky,' Don shouted, raising his voice above the noise of anti-aircraft fire as he leant across the bar to grab a bottle. He then picked up a half-drained glass of something and emptied the dregs onto the floor. 'And I think you'll agree that this glass will do.'

Zach laughed and nodded. Once they were settled with their drinks, elbow to elbow at the bar, they had a kind of companionship unique to their situation. As the air raid continued, there was little space for conversation; they simply ducked when a big bomb fell close, weathered the drone of the bombers and the constant *ack ack* of the anti-aircraft guns.

'Why are you here tonight?' Zach shouted.

'I was hoping to meet Rita Hayworth,' he shouted

back.

'Ha! Aren't we all, buddy?'

Don laughed. 'Well, she isn't actually Rita Hayworth but I've never met a woman who looks so much like her.'

Zach nodded. 'Lucky man,' he shouted, reaching for the bottle to fill his glass with more whisky. 'I had a sweetheart back home, but she went off with my best friend.' Don patted his arm in sympathy. 'Oh, I'm over it now,' he grimaced. 'I only joined the British RAF to get away from the situation.'

'Bit drastic.' Don's pint sloshed at the crack of another loud explosion a bit too close for comfort.

'Yep!' Zach was clinging to the bar now as the whole building shook to the foundations. 'I'm inclined to agree with you.' He dusted some debris from the shoulders of his jacket.

'Where you from?' asked Don.

'Long Island, New York.'

Don grinned and punched his arm. 'I've been there!'

'Whoa! Really?'

'Before I joined up, I worked as a steward on the transatlantic crossings, Southampton to New York. The Queen Mary. I loved it.'

'So why the RAF? Surely you'd have been a cert for the Navy.'

'I can't swim... so I figured this was safer!'

Zach started laughing. 'Well, who knows what's best? I can swim like a fish, after school I worked at Coney Island as a lifeguard. But I've always wanted to fly, ever since I was a boy. On Long Island we're famous for our airfields — Charles Lindbergh took off from there on his non-stop flight to Paris and we saw Amelia Earhart take to the air. I'd already had some flying lessons so when my love life went down the pan, I thought, why not follow your dreams. So here I am, just sailed into Liverpool yesterday, dodging U-Boats all the way. Went to the collection point to register and get fitted out for this fine uniform and now I'm meant to be taking a train out to RAF Church Fenton, near Tadcaster in Yorkshire... You know it?'

'Well, Yorkshire's not too far, just the other side of the Pennines, but I've not heard much about the base. Let's face it though, they're all the same. They find somewhere flat and clear a space so they can send men into the sky. Cheers to that!'

As they laughed and chinked glasses, the 'all clear' sounded.

'We'll just top these up, before the others come back from the shelter.' Don said, his voice a little slurry as he filled their glasses once more before pouring the rest of the whisky into a large hip flask.

The hatch to the beer cellar lifted and the bad-tempered landlord struggled up the steps, brushing debris from his hair and coughing on dust. He shook his head in disbelief when he saw them propped at the bar, and they knew that it was time to leave.

'Why don't we call by the hospital,' slurred Don, 'See if we can find my Rita Hayworth.'

'Sounds like a plan.'

* * *

All the benches in the casualty waiting area were packed full of people covered in dust, spattered with blood and wearing an assortment of bandages. Jo

32

came out to check on the condition of those who were still waiting.

As she scanned the patients, her sharp eye caught a change in an elderly man lying on a stretcher furthest away. She stepped nimbly across and crouched down beside him. 'Mr Watson,' she called, gently at first and then more loudly, 'Mr Watson!' His colour had drained even further. She felt for his radial pulse and lifted her fob watch to check the rate. The pulse was so weak and thready, it was impossible to count. He didn't have any injury beyond cuts and bruises and the ambulance crew had said it had been a miracle that he hadn't been flattened by the house. He was frail and suffered from heart failure; he'd been too weak and breathless to make it to a shelter, so he'd hidden under the stairs. 'Can you hear me, Mr Watson?' she called again, giving his shoulder a gentle shake. He groaned quietly and then opened his watery blue eyes. He tried to smile but the effort seemed too much for him.

'I'll be alright, nurse,' he whispered, so quietly that Jo had to lean in close to catch his words. 'I was just thinking about my Martha, wondering when she'll be home. We've only been married a few weeks...'

Jo had admitted him, and he'd been coherent when he'd come through the door. She felt for his pulse again and it was extremely weak now. Maybe Dr Hedley had been right when he'd stood over Mr Watson's stretcher, solemn-faced in his white coat, shaking his head. He'd taken her aside to tell her that there was nothing they could do for the poor old chap, he was very frail and most probably dying from his heart condition and the shock of the explosion. With all the other casualties desperate for attention, Mr Watson was way down the list.

She gave his hand a squeeze and then murmured a few words of comfort. She would come back to check on him soon, but right now she had to go to a young man who had started to panic because his dressing had slipped. Blood was running down his face. She took one of the spare bandages that she carried in her pocket and went straight to him.

'You're alright,' she soothed. 'Now just sit down and I'll fix this for you. These head wounds always bleed briskly, try not to worry. We'll get you stitched up just as soon as we can.' She had the roller bandage applied and secure in a minute. As she straightened up, she saw the door open again and two men in RAF uniform walked in. She looked them up and down, assessing them — no sign of any injury whatsoever — but the shorter one with black hair and what looked like an aircrew uniform looked a bit drunk. She noticed the taller one holding back. He stood at the door in his tailored blue-grey uniform and met her eyes with his own, which were startlingly blue. For a few seconds she felt hypnotised by him. The spell was broken when the other one, who looked a bit like a young Clark Gable, started to call out for Rita Hayworth, wanting to know if she was on duty.

Jo moved quickly in his direction. She couldn't have this disruption in a room full of injured patients. 'I need to ask you both to leave,' she ordered, firm but polite.

Clark Gable had just removed his side cap and now stood swaying with a lock of black hair falling rakishly onto his forehead. He grinned at her, flashing his deep brown eyes. She took his arm, feeling the rough fabric of his thick tunic, and insisted that he

34

move, right now.

'We are members of the air fosh,' he said. 'This man here, heesh come all the way from America and heesh a pilot. I'm just a trainee aircrew, I work the radio. But heesh...'

'Sorry, Miss, he's had a little too much to drink.' She heard the American's polite voice and looked towards him. He removed his peaked cap, revealing short-cropped hair with a side parting, and gave an apologetic smile, but she felt irritated by them both now. She just needed to get them out through the door as quickly as possible.

Then she heard Mac's voice behind her. 'Don? What the hell are you doing here?'

'Rita,' he called, 'My Rita... Come with me, come now.'

Already the American had replaced his cap and moved to Don's other side and was trying to help him. 'Come on, fella. We need to get you out of here.'

Mac took over, talking to Don quietly. Jo could see him nodding and then he tried to kiss her, knocking her nurse's cap askew. He was apologising profusely and then, at last, he was moving away. Mac walked towards the door with the two men to see them out and Jo left her to it. She went back to the stretcher on the floor to check on Mr Watson.

He was lying perfectly still, his face serene, almost smiling. She knew instantly from the lack of rise and fall of his chest that he wasn't breathing. She knelt beside him and took his hand, saying a silent prayer, hoping that he was now reunited with Martha. Then, the young man on the bench was calling her again, rising panic in his voice, and she had no choice but to gently pull the stretcher blanket over Mr Watson's face and go back to her duties. As she turned to leave him, a middle-aged woman sat at the end of a bench, her arm in a sling, crossed herself and gave Jo a grateful smile.

The young man was becoming agitated; she thought that he might be showing signs of concussion or, far worse, a bleed on the brain. She would need to get him through as an urgent so that Dr Hedley could check him over. As she tried to gently persuade him to come with her into the treatment area, Mac appeared and slipped around to the young man's other side. 'Now, what's your name?' she said. The man stared at her blankly.

'He told me earlier he was called Frank,' said the woman who had been sitting next to him. 'But he's not making much sense now.'

'Come on, Frank,' urged Mac, using exactly the right tone to get the man moving.

Once they had him settled on a chair between two cubicles with Dr Hedley in attendance, Jo and Mac both went to wash their hands together at the sink before going back out to find the next case from the waiting area.

Jo looked over at Mac, and she was grinning from ear to ear. She was glowing.

'So that's Don then, is it?' she whispered.

Mac nodded. 'Isn't he gorgeous? I know he was a bit drunk, but fancy him turning up here to look for me. He must have remembered what I said about our emergency procedures.'

'He is good-looking, yes,' said Jo firmly, as she dried her hands with vigour. 'But when you see him on Saturday night you need to remind him that he can't just call by the hospital whilst we're on duty. Thank goodness Deputy Matron wasn't on the prowl.'

'I'll make sure to keep him at bay. But what about that American fella in the Officer's uniform with the gorgeous blue eyes; he seemed to be looking in your direction.'

'Don't be ridiculous, Mac. You must be as drunk as Don.'

A patient screamed from behind a screen and Jo ran over. A junior staff nurse was struggling to apply a collar and cuff sling to a terrified teenage girl with a fractured clavicle. Jo took hold of the girl's hand and spoke gently to her, 'Take a few deep breaths. That's it. It will hurt as we fit the sling but once we get it secure it should settle and we'll give you a couple of aspirin to help with the pain.'

Then, turning to the staff nurse, she said, 'Let me show you. It seems tricky if you haven't done many of these before, but you'll soon get the hang of it.'

Jo and Mac continued to work steadily until the last of the casualties were safely treated and the inevitable exhaustion began to creep in with that familiar swimming feeling in the head. In the early hours, Night Sister appeared. 'We'll clear up now, you two get yourselves back to bed,' she urged. Jo looked down to her dusty, bloodstained apron and felt no urge to insist that she stay on longer. She would be up first thing for an early shift so she needed all the sleep that she could get.

'Come on, Mac. Let's get going,' she said. As she looked at Mac, she gasped and clapped a hand over her mouth when she saw her friend's bare legs. 'You're not wearing any stockings!'

Mac cracked up laughing. 'I know, I couldn't find the bloody things and I didn't have time to fiddle about looking for them. So I came without… And do you realise you're still wearing a full face of make-up? Granted, most of the lipstick's rubbed off, but you're still sporting plenty of eye liner.'

'Oh no! I wondered why Night Sister gave me a funny look, but she didn't say anything.'

'Come on, it's too late to worry now. We've worked damned hard tonight, that's all that matters.'

They walked out in the early morning light. Numerous fires were still burning, lighting up the skyline. Down the street Jo could see firemen silhouetted against the yellow glow, pumping water onto a pile of smoking rubble that used to be a building.

'Hell's bells, look at this,' Mac exclaimed. Broken glass littered the ground and crunched under foot as they walked back to the Nurses' Home.

Jo couldn't speak, all she could do was think about what Mac had said earlier. That one day, it could be them, it could be the hospital that was hit. How would the planes be able to tell from the darkness above that it was a medical facility? There was no red cross on the roof, nothing, to show that it wasn't some other building.

As they walked, they caught up with Myfanwy and Ruth. They were both exhausted — Myfanwy had delivered two babies on Maternity and Ruth had ferried the more mobile patients down to the basement and then back up again. And she'd helped in theatre as the supply of patients needing surgery came through. Before they reached the door to the Nurses' Home, Amy Goodwin sprinted past them. 'Goodnight,' she shouted, opening the door with vigour and disappearing inside.

'How the heck does she do that?' muttered Mac,

shaking her head. Jo started to smile and linked her arm. 'It must be all that cocoa she drinks.'

'Ha! Maybe I should join your pyjama gang after all.'

They walked quietly up the stairs with the other two nurses and headed to their respective rooms.

'What a night, hey, Jojo,' murmured Mac as she flopped down onto her bed. 'I don't think I can even get myself undressed. I'll just lie here, like this. I'm on a late tomorrow.'

Jo picked up the jar of cold cream, removed the remains of the make-up from her face and quickly slipped into her pyjamas. Then she took the spare knitted blanket that she always kept neatly folded on the chair next to her bed and gently covered Mac with it, before crawling into her own bed. 'Goodnight,' she called. But all she could hear was the sound of gentle snoring from the next bed.

4

When Mac woke the next morning, she felt groggy, like she'd been drugged. Forgetting she'd been at work until the early hours, she tutted to herself, thinking that she'd had one too many the night before. But as soon as she sat up and looked down at the stained uniform that she'd slept in, she remembered. She glanced at Jo's bed; it was empty, and the alarm clock was telling her it was nine in the morning. She'd be back on the maternity ward by one o'clock. She needed to get up, have a bath and go out into the city, just for a break.

Coming down the stairs that led from the Nurses' Home into the outside world, Mac felt a tingle of goosebumps. Out of the corner of her eye she saw her, the little girl with tousled hair sitting on the bottom step. She'd seen her before, the girl, and she knew that she wasn't real. But Mac knew from the first sighting that it could have been her — all the hours she'd spent sitting on the cold step of the children's home, waiting for her mother to come. Even though she'd been told over and over that she had no family, and that she'd been found by one of the nuns on the front step, wrapped in a blanket, one chilly November morning.

It didn't worry her, seeing this apparition — if that's what it was. She'd heard plenty of stranger stories from other people. But even so, she never told anyone, not even Jo.

Instinctively, she reached up to feel the shape of the silver locket that she always wore — the one they'd given her when she came out of the children's home. They'd told her that it must have been placed around her neck by whoever left her on the step; a token of the life that she might have had, Mac had thought wryly. A water-stained photo of a man in uniform inside the locket was her only connection to that life, but she'd never been able to make out his face, not even with a magnifying glass.

She glanced back before opening the door. A weak ray of sun highlighted the spot where the girl had been, but, as always, she was gone. Mac emerged into the light and then slipped a pack of cigarettes out of her pocket. Pausing to light up, she tried to rid herself of the feeling that she always had after seeing the little girl — that there was someone breathing down the back of her neck. She took a deep drag and breathed out the smoke.

As she walked she could see fires still smoking and the street ran with water from the hoses. Some men and women were using stiff brushes to sweep up broken glass and debris, and they seemed remarkably cheerful given the dire situation. As she passed by a terraced house she even saw a housewife wearing a turban and a flowery apron cleaning her front window.

The world felt upside down and inside out. She took another drag on her cigarette. She wasn't sure where she was heading but she seemed to be going in the direction of the docks — maybe to see if there was anything left standing, she thought with a wry twist to her mouth.

It took a moment for her to realise that someone was calling her name and she turned on her heel to see Don running towards her. The cigarette fell from

41

her hand as he picked her up and swung her around, losing his cap with the effort. By now she was shrieking with laughter. But when he put her down, his face was intense and his eyes burnt into her. She had no choice, all she could do was kiss him, right there in the middle of the street. His unshaven chin bristled against her, sending tingles through her body. He tasted of stale beer but it didn't matter, his lips were firm and he knew how to kiss. It made her head spin. She reached up to put her arms around his neck and she could feel him pulling her close, crushing her body against the fabric of his uniform.

The sound of a male passer-by cheering and a loud wolf whistle from another broke through at last and she gasped and stepped back.

'Rita,' he murmured, trying to pull her close once more.

'Come on,' she said, 'let's go for a walk.'

He stooped down to pick up his cap, then he put an arm around her shoulders, pulling her tight against the side of his body as they walked.

He leant in to whisper in her ear. 'Will you marry me?'

'Not likely, not till you've earned your stripes.' She laughed, still heady from that kiss. 'But shouldn't you have gone back to your base by now? Won't you get court-martialled or something?'

'Hopefully not, but only because I'm between things at the moment. There's been some mix up so I'm still waiting for gunner training and then, after that, I'll be posted. But I sent a message to say that I couldn't get back because of the raid, which is true. And, the truth is, I don't remember much from last night and if it hadn't been for my kind American friend putting me up in his lodgings, I don't know where I'd have ended up.'

'Yes, he was nice, and he had such lovely blue eyes...'

'Hey, watch it,' he warned playfully, but Mac could see that he was a little bit rattled.

'Do you remember showing up at the hospital?'

'No, but Zach told me this morning. I'm so sorry about that, hope I didn't get you into any bother.'

'Well, thankfully Deputy Matron wasn't in the vicinity but I did get a bit of a telling off from my best mate, Jo. She's what you might call "straight down the line". But she did have a point — we were packed out with casualties...'

Don was shaking his head and she felt the arm around her shoulder give her an extra squeeze. 'I'm sorry, I won't do it again... I just couldn't keep away from you. And Zach agreed, he thinks you definitely look like Rita Hayworth.'

'Nonsense,' she said, but inside she smiled. About the only thing in the world she could be sure of was that she had a good set of cheekbones. 'Well, your American friend was probably nearly as drunk as you. What's he doing here anyway? America isn't even in the war.'

'He was jilted by his sweetheart and so he signed up to a special squadron of pilots serving with the British Army. They're called the Eagles...' He leant in to whisper playfully in her ear. 'This is what you women drive us poor men to do.'

'Ha!' Mac laughed out loud. 'You've not seen anyth—'

She fell silent as they turned a corner and saw two firemen pulling the body of a woman out of a collapsed building. Her clothes were torn to ribbons

43

and her chestnut hair splayed out as they placed her carefully on a stretcher, next to another that bore the outline of a much smaller bundle, undoubtedly the body of a child.

'Oh, Don, that's so terrible,' croaked Mac, tears springing to her eyes. He pulled her closer and she buried her face in his shoulder. She could tell that he was holding his breath as he guided her past.

She gave a sob and wiped her eyes. 'Isn't it strange,' she said, her voice unsteady, 'I see death on a regular basis in the hospital, and only last night a dying child was brought in. It was so sad because the ambulance crew took us aside to tell us that both her parents were killed outright in the explosion, but all she kept asking was when were Mummy and Daddy coming. So we told her that they were on their way, they wouldn't be long... just so that she stayed calm and she could die peacefully.'

Don was looking at her intently, his eyes full of tears.

'And I coped with all of that. But seeing it out here, in the raw, it seems to have hit me.' She pressed a hand over her heart.

Don didn't speak but he kissed the top of her head and held her fast as they continued to walk.

As soon as she could smell the salt air of the docks and hear the cry of the gulls, she began to feel a bit better. She pulled away from him and took his hand, turning to give him a smile so that he'd know she wasn't drawing away, she just needed some space to breathe. As they came closer to the docks, they saw a pall of black smoke from the fires that still burnt. And then they turned into a small terraced street that had taken a direct hit. Some walls of the houses were still standing; there were stairs in one and a fireplace in another and a selection of random door frames suspended in mid-air. But everywhere were piles of broken brick, glass, and in the middle of the street, the mangled metal of some vehicle with one twisted wheel poking out of the debris.

People stood in forlorn groups or sat on broken chairs outside the remains of their homes. 'They must be waiting for evacuation,' Mac said, almost in tears once more when she saw the sticks of furniture and meagre, dust-covered personal belongings that each group had gathered from the debris.

'It's unbelievable, isn't it? What one bomb can do...'

She took his hand and pulled him along, moving down the street as quickly as they could. Who knew what tomorrow might bring for any of them? It made her aware of the breath moving in and out of her lungs, of the feel of his hand in her own, making her skin prickle with sensation. And she had no more than two hours with this beautiful man before she would have to go back to work. If there was an air raid tomorrow night, she might not even be able to see him. She couldn't spend any more time in these ruined streets; she needed to find somewhere private, where they could be alone together, whilst they had time.

They turned the corner of the street and Mac saw a bombed-out house that still had all four walls. There was a hole in the roof and some of the front wall had collapsed revealing a dressing table and a bed still made up with a white camberwick bedspread. As she walked closer, she could see that the front door was splintered and hanging loose in its frame, its blue paint peeling. Clearly the house was empty. 'Come on,' she said. 'Let's see if they've got a room.' She knocked politely, as if she were an invited guest not entirely sure of the welcome she might receive. Don cracked up. She turned, grinning. 'Well, you never know, somebody might still be in there.' When there was no sign of anyone coming to the rickety door, she pulled it open and listened for a moment.

Don was still laughing, so she urged, 'Be quiet,' and grabbed his arm. 'Come on.'

He burst out laughing again when they tried to close the door with a piece of debris.

Mac looked around. 'This will do, I suppose,' she said, even though the kitchen sink now rested in the hallway and the remains of the stairs were hanging loose from the floor above. She'd seen a door to the right, no doubt the closed entrance to a parlour. It was a bit stuck but when she used her shoulder, the door burst open to reveal a room littered with broken pottery and covered with a thin layer of dust, but otherwise surprisingly intact. A sofa rested at an angle as though it had been hastily pulled away from the wall. Above it hung a lopsided tapestry in a frame: There's No Place Like Home. She carefully picked her way through shards of pots and discarded magazines to open the blackout just a sliver so they had a bit more light. As she stepped over a broken mirror, she crossed herself.

Taking hold of the loose blanket that covered the sofa, she pulled it away to reveal reasonably clean fabric beneath. The disturbed dust made them both cough and Mac started to giggle. Don threw himself down onto the sofa and bounced up and down, making the springs squeak loudly. They laughed even more. Then he went quiet and he held his hand out for her to join him. She grasped his hand readily, feel-

46

ing the warmth of his skin. She was already starting to breathe more deeply. In the next moment, it didn't matter where they were, and the thought that somebody might come in through the battered front door of their refuge, only added to their excitement.

'This is our house, just for now,' whispered Mac, as she undid the metal buttons of his tunic and then started to remove his air force issue tie. 'I hope you like the décor.'

'We can redecorate next spring,' he said, kissing her hard on the mouth and then sliding a hand inside her blouse. Her skin was alive with sensation, her body craving his touch. She couldn't think about anything else other than satisfying the need that coursed deep inside her body. She pulled up her skirt, revealing stocking tops and suspenders.

It felt like the most natural thing in the world to be doing this on a sofa in some stranger's home in the middle of a bombsite. And when she felt his bare skin against her own, she gasped with pleasure. She wanted him and she knew that nothing was going to stop that from happening.

Afterwards, as he lay full length on the dusty sofa, he murmured sleepily, 'You'll have to marry me now.' His air force issue shirt with starched collar was now lined with creases and gaping open to reveal a white vest and dog tags on a cord around his neck.

'I will not,' she said playfully, grasping her silver locket and tucking it safely inside her petticoat before buttoning her blouse and standing to pull down her creased skirt. 'And although you are adorable,' she murmured, leaning over to give him a lingering kiss, 'right now, I need to get going. I'm due on the ward in less than an hour and I need to

47

get my uniform sorted.'

'Don't go, don't leave me,' he begged. 'What if there's an air raid tomorrow night and I can't see you? What if I never see you again?'

'Well, that's life during a war, kiddo,' she said, pushing him back and slapping away his hands when he tried to pull her down onto the sofa again. 'And look at the state of this place, you should clean up before I visit next time.'

'No, please don't go. Stay with me here, forever, in this house with a crooked door. I'll give you all of my worldly goods — these dog tags, after the war you might get a bit of money for 'em, they're stamped RAF, see here,' he said holding them out towards her.

She shook her head.

'Well what about these?' he cried, producing a cheap lighter and a packet of Woodbines from his pocket. 'Or this tinny, fake watch... Nurse Rita, I lay these treasures before you.'

She raised her eyebrows and gave him a cheeky grin. 'Come on,' she said, holding out his uniform jacket. 'Time for you to go back to war.'

As they walked through the streets arm in arm, she tried to hold onto the feelings that she'd had in the house. For a brief time, she'd felt content, happy even. But they were out in the ruined streets again now, and even though she could feel the strength of Don's arm through his uniform, that familiar restlessness was coming back. All she wanted was to get back inside the hospital and work, keep working. And she knew that once she was off duty again, all she would want to do was go out and see Don. She wasn't sure what was ruling her at present but all that seemed to hold her together was her work. And of course, Jo; she would struggle to cope without Jo.

When the Nurses' Home came into view, Don groaned. 'I don't want you to leave me.'

'Well, I don't think Sister Codey would be too pleased if I turned up with you in tow on Maternity. And what would you do in a room full of women about to give birth.'

'I suppose you're right, Nurse MacDonald,' he murmured.

'Stop right here,' she ordered. 'We can't go too close to the Nurses' Home, I don't want to get a black mark if I'm seen kissing some random man in the street.'

'Random man! I'm a member of the Royal Air Force, as you well know. Look at the blue uniform, all the ladies love it.'

'Oh they do, do they? Well, that's because they don't know that you're just trainee aircrew.'

'I'll be airborne in the very near future.'

'Mmmm, well, the way you looked when you came into Casualty last night, you might be better staying on the ground.'

'That was your fault,' he said, grabbing her around the waist and pulling her towards him. 'I was pining for you.'

'Well, me being late to the ward won't help, I'll be grounded if I'm not careful,' she said, giving him a kiss on the cheek and trying to pull back.

He pulled her close again and as he did so, she saw Deputy Matron stalking by on the other side of the road. 'I need to go,' she said, pushing away from him. 'See you tomorrow night, all being well.'

5

Jo's stomach rumbled as she stood at the top of Female Surgical, scanning the beds down either side of the long ward. Wartime rationing barely touched the healthy appetite that she'd always had and given that she'd already used up her fortnightly egg, monthly orange and small cube of cheese, there was little to look forward to at lunch, bar a Spam sandwich made with dripping. Checking that everything was in order after a busy morning's work, before the Consultant Surgeon and his entourage of white-coated medical students arrived for their round, she was pleased to see a settled ward.

With all the curtains drawn back, light streamed in through the high windows. She glanced to Sister's table to check that all the mercury thermometers had been replaced in their jars of pink antiseptic, and then her eye followed the pleasingly precise line that demarcated the shiny dark green paint at the bottom of the walls from the cream above. She breathed in the smell of polish from the newly cleaned wooden floor as she made sure the cast iron hospital beds were freshly made up, with the opening of the pillowcases facing away from the door and the bed wheels pointing in the same direction.

She gave a sigh of satisfaction. Only the nurses knew how much work went into the rendering of this scene and it was always a special time of day, particularly for someone as meticulous as Jo. In this calm, light-filled space with patients chatting quietly from bed to bed, staff finishing their tasks, and a couple of vases of flowers set on the long table down the middle of the ward, she might even have been able to forget that there was a war on. One thing snagged her eye though: a first ward probationer had arranged the flowers and she'd mixed red and white blooms. Nurse Lucas must not have been told about the superstition — the mixing of red and white flowers was bad luck, something about blood and bandages from the last war, or so she'd been told. She'd have a quiet word with Nurse Lucas to let her know. The last thing she wanted for her timid first warder was to face the wrath of sharp-faced Sister Marks. She ran a tight ship, which suited Jo, but she was incredibly strict with the probationers.

As Jo walked briskly down the ward to deal with the flowers, her black lace-up shoes sounded satisfyingly on the wooden floor. She glanced from side to side to check on the patients as she went, noting that an oxygen cylinder sitting by the bed of their most recent post-op would need changing soon. Just as she picked up the flowers, Sister Marks called down the ward, 'Staff Nurse Brooks, you're needed urgently in the basement theatre. Go now.'

Jo signalled that she was on her way. But she did take a few seconds to switch the red and the white blooms into separate vases. She told herself that it was because she didn't want her new probationer to get into trouble but, in truth, even though it was only a superstition, she didn't want to take any chances.

She ran along the corridor, pulling off her starched cuffs to save time in the changing room. As she slipped them into her pocket, she saw Amy Goodwin coming in the opposite direction, single-handedly steering a trolley with a barely conscious theatre patient aboard,

51

one of her soldiers by the look of the army cap and badge that lay at his feet.

'Can you manage?' she shouted, knowing that she hadn't time to stop and assist but she could send someone out to her if required.

'Still not enough porters, never will be in this damned war, but I can manage,' Amy replied breathlessly, her small frame braced against the weight of the trolley.

'Good work, Amy,' she called, disappearing down the steps and into the basement.

She went straight to the small changing room next to theatre. Removing her starched cap, she grabbed a clean white cotton gown with long sleeves, pushing her arms through and fastening it down the back. Then she put on a soft white hat that fitted like a turban to cover her hair and grabbed a cloth mask from a wooden box, pulling the string ties tight as she walked into theatre. She was happy as always to feel the green linoleum underfoot, to catch the familiar smell of carbolic acid sterilising fluid and anaesthetic gas, and pleased to see the shining metal instruments laid out in order on a white linen cloth.

An unconscious male patient with a worryingly pale complexion was on the operating table as the anaesthetist — white-haired, unassuming Dr Langley — applied a rubber oxygen mask.

'Good morning, Nurse Brooks. Thank Christ it's you,' shouted the surgeon, Mr Angus Dunbar, twisting around from the sink with his bright eyes almost burning as he hurriedly and vigorously washed his hands. 'The last scrub nurse I had was slow *and* forgetful. A dire combination.'

'Good Morning, Mr Dunbar,' she said, her voice

steady. She didn't make any comment about the poor nurse; she'd already heard the rumour about him throwing an instrument at her during an operation. She didn't want to give any encouragement to the young, flame-haired surgeon, who was fast getting a reputation for being difficult. She joined him at the sink and grabbed a bar of carbolic soap and a stiff nail brush.

In his characteristic rapid-fire style, he began telling her about the patient. 'We have a Mr Lawrence Fisher, aged fifty-nine years, travelling salesman, a visitor to Liverpool, found trapped beneath a wall after rescuing a dog. Sustained a head injury, fractured ribs and a compound fracture of the right humerus. Appeared stable but is now presenting with rapid pulse and unreadable blood pressure. His abdomen is rigid. Undoubtedly an internal haemorrhage. We've put up some plasma and ordered some blood but if we don't get in quick to tie off whatever is bleeding, he won't stand a chance.'

Mr Dunbar shook his hands and then dried them on a clean towel. Jo held the tops of his sterile rubber gloves one at a time as he plunged first one hand and then the other into them. She quickly donned her own and joined him at the table. With a nod from Dr Langley, the surgeon took up his scalpel and prepared to make the first incision. Jo checked the table at her elbow and the bowls on the floor to make sure that they had all the instruments and equipment they needed. As soon as Dunbar had made his first incision through skin and subcutaneous tissue, she passed swabs and then each instrument in turn. She took a deep breath and began to relax into the work, completely in her element within this close space beneath

53

the hospital.

But as Dunbar cut through the peritoneum into the abdominal cavity, there was a massive rush of bright red blood and she knew instantly that there was very little chance that Mr Fisher would survive. In fact, even as she used suction to clear out the blood and Dunbar cursed out loud as he strove to secure a ligature around a bleeding point, Dr Langley raised his head. 'So sorry, Dunbar, we've lost him.'

Jo took a deep breath and absorbed the sadness.

Dunbar tutted violently and threw his final blood-soaked swab into the bowl on the floor. 'Damn it.'

As was their custom in this particular theatre, they stood in silence for a few moments as Dr Langley said a few words to pay respect. The anaesthetist had been a medic during the last war, receiving medals for bravery when he'd continued to treat the wounded under heavy fire. It seemed appropriate that he was the person to mark the passing of yet another casualty of war. And knowing that Mr Fisher would go straight off to an overcrowded mortuary, where there was always so much confusion, and that it might take ages for his family — if he had any — to find him, this seemed exactly the right thing to do before they cleaned up and moved on to their next case.

Jo began to prepare the instruments as soon as they had poor Mr Fisher loaded onto a trolley and wheeled out of the door. It was another of Amy's soldiers next on the handwritten list that was pinned to the wall and Jo exchanged a sober glance with her as she came through the door with Private Robert Croasdale on a trolley. The young man was sobbing his heart out, lying flat on his back with both lower arms encased in so much bandaging it looked like he was wearing boxing gloves. A kindly porter patted him on the shoulder, muttering something, trying to get the young man to calm down, but he was beside himself with grief. Amy motioned for Jo to step outside so they could have a private word.

'I don't know if they've given you any detail of Robert's case but he's been regularly back to theatre over the past few weeks for surgery on his hands. He caught a blast from a grenade during training that made a real mess. We've been hoping to salvage something for him, even a finger and thumb on one side, but both hands are infected now and there are some areas of gangrene. He will lose both hands.'

'That's such a shame, after all those weeks of trying, the poor man.' Jo exhaled the breath she hadn't realised she'd been holding as Amy shared Private Croasdale's case.

'I know. And he's a farmer's son from Yorkshire, tough as old boot. He's absolutely heartbroken, wailing and crying all morning, repeating, "What am I going to do now, how can I be a farmer?"'

Jo felt her stomach clench; she'd grown up in a farming family and she knew it wasn't just a job, it was a way of life. She could still hear him sobbing through the door. She took a deep breath. 'Thanks for the information, Amy, we'll do our absolute best for him.'

As she came back in through the door, Dunbar was at the sink again, scrubbing his hands, and Dr Langley was preparing the anaesthetic. Dunbar twisted around and called loudly over his shoulder, 'Now young man, you need to calm down.'

Robert sobbed even louder.

Jo gave the surgeon a look and he turned back to

his sink without a word. 'Robert,' she said, speaking quietly, standing close to the patient but not crowding him, and indicating to the porter that she needed a few moments before they transferred him to the table. 'I'm so sorry that you have to go through all of this. I can't imagine how difficult it is for you. But you need to know that we'll do all that we can for you and even though we can't save your hands, we will save your life.'

Robert paused from his sobbing for a second and twisted his head ever so slightly in her direction. 'You are a healthy young man and I know you can't see it right now but there's still life to be lived.'

He took a long shuddering breath and then wiped a clumsy bandaged hand across his face.

'Can you do this, Robert?' she asked steadily.

He rubbed his hand over his eyes again and again until the loops of the bandage began to unravel. She stood by not saying a word, her stomach knotted with anguish. When he lowered his arm back to his side, he'd stopped sobbing, but silent tears now seeped down his cheeks.

'Can I wipe your eyes and nose, Robert?' she asked gently. He nodded and she used a gauze swab as a handkerchief. 'Are you ready?'

He looked at her again, more fiercely, his chin wobbling as he spoke at last. 'Yes,' he said. 'Yes. I'm ready.'

6

Mac ran to the maternity ward. It'd taken her ages to find her black stockings, they'd somehow got trapped beneath the rag rug that Jo had brought back the last time she'd gone home on leave. No idea how they'd got there, but at least she had them. She made a mental note to make sure she secured another pair; she still hadn't replaced the spares that she'd lost weeks ago.

'Late again,' called the maternity ward sister, Millicent Codey, as she walked briskly in the opposite direction. 'Sorry, Sister,' called Mac, but she wasn't too worried about getting into trouble with Milly, as the sister was known throughout the hospital. She might have a stern appearance when required, especially with some of the medical students and junior doctors, but Milly was the best when it came to her nurses. And her warm smile and rosy face had welcomed thousands of babies into the world and inspired hundreds of Stage Registered Nurses, including Mac, to take the short additional course in midwifery.

As she approached the door of Maternity, she heard the unmistakeable sound of a woman in labour, but it wasn't coming from inside the ward, it was down the corridor behind her. She turned on her heel to see a woman with long dark hair and wearing a simple brown smock that covered the magnificent curve of a full term pregnancy, leaning against the wall, gasping and breathing her way through a strong contraction. It looked like she was well on her way towards delivery.

'Hello,' Mac said. 'I'm Nurse MacDonald and I work on the maternity ward. Are you booked in with us? What's your name?'

'Mrs Sofia Gazzi,' she replied, breathlessly, her voice strongly accented. 'Please call me Sofia. And yes, I am booked.'

Another contraction came, even stronger.

Mac stood by, one hand on the woman's back and the other resting on top of her bump so that she could feel the strength of the contraction. As the pain rose to a crescendo, the uterus beneath her hand became rock hard and the contraction lasted for a good length of time. She could tell by a small but perceptible change in Sofia's breathing that she was getting close to the second stage of labour — the birth itself.

'Is this your first?' she asked, making sure to keep her voice calm as she eased the woman away from the wall and started to walk her slowly towards the door of the ward. Where was a wheelchair when you needed one, usually there was one sitting right there?

'Third baby,' gasped the woman, hit by another strong pain.

'Alright, you're doing really well,' Mac reassured as the woman gripped both her hands incredibly tightly. 'Are you completely alone?'

'Yes, my husband is Italian prisoner, he's gone to internment camp. My mother-in-law has the two children.'

'I see,' she soothed, easing her in through the door. She'd heard about the Italian men who'd been rounded up and shipped out last year when Mussolini entered the war alongside Hitler. Some of them had been in Liverpool for years and even fought in the last war on the British side. It didn't seem right that they'd been treated in such a way.

Sofia screamed and began to make an unmistakeable guttural noise; Mac knew that she had to get her to the labour ward or she'd be delivering this one in the doorway.

'I think your baby's coming,' she said calmly, putting an arm around her to support her over the short distance to where there was, thankfully, a wheelchair. 'Coming through,' she shouted as she steamed down the ward pushing the wheelchair. 'Are there any delivery beds?'

'Bay two is free,' called Myfanwy Jones, who was marching briskly in the opposite direction towards a woman who sat at the side of her bed clutching her abdomen.

By the time Mac had helped Sofia out of the wheelchair and onto the bed, she was starting to deliver.

'You're doing so well,' she urged, 'I can see the head.'

Sofia was already pushing and the head was emerging rapidly. Mac grabbed a delivery pack from the shelf behind her and in moments she had an area prepared. As Sofia gave another push, she saw the baby's eyes, nose and mouth appear in glorious succession. She adored this moment — the best part of the job.

'Oh, what a bonny baby,' she encouraged, 'he or she has a full head of black hair.' She guided the shoulders out as Sofia gave another huge push and the child slipped out in a gush of amniotic fluid. A whole, beautiful human being, already starting to take a first breath.

'It's a girl,' she called excitedly to the mother. 'And as soon as I've cut the cord you can have a hold of her.'

Sofia spoke some words in Italian and then she started to cry. 'My husband has two sons, he wanted a daughter for so long, and now he is gone.'

'I'm so sorry,' she said, almost in tears herself, wrapping the baby girl, and moving up the side of the bed. 'I'm sorry that he had to go away. But he will see her when he comes back, after this war is over. Isn't she beautiful, do you have a name for her?'

'Lucia,' she said quietly, 'It means light. I found out about the baby after Giovanni went to the camp last year. I sent letter but don't know if he got it, he always said that if he had a daughter she would be Lucia.'

'Good choice. Lucia Gazzi. It has substance and beauty.'

'Thank you. What is your name?'

'Moira MacDonald but everybody calls me Mac.'

'Mac...' Sofia smiled. 'It sounds very strong.'

'Do you want to see if Lucia will suckle? It always helps with the delivery of the afterbirth.'

'Oh yes, of course,' murmured Sofia as she stroked her daughter's face and then she pulled up the front of her smock and prepared to feed her baby for the very first time.

Mac moved purposefully to the bottom of the bed.

'Now, if you could just give me a few more big pushes and we'll get this sorted. That's it. Well done, Sofia, well done.'

In very little time, she had the satisfaction of leaving them both clean and comfortable in bed. A new mother transfixed by her baby's face was always a joyous sight and Sofia and Lucia were an image of love and contentment. When Mac emerged from the delivery room, Myfanwy and Sister Codey looked up from their paperwork and gave her a round of applause. She bowed, dramatically, and then started to laugh.

Sister placed a hand on her arm. 'Why is it, Nurse MacDonald, that you are always the one to find a labouring woman in the corridor or outside the hospital — or even once wasn't it outside Lewis's Department Store? How many times has this happened to you?'

'I've lost count and I've no idea. No idea. But wait till you see this baby girl. This one is an absolute beauty. I'll give the mother a bit of time to finish feeding and then I'll get them washed and changed and have them back on the ward as soon as I can.'

'Before somebody else comes running through the door with a baby about to be born, looking for Nurse MacDonald!' Myfanwy said, tucking a stray lock of her dark fluffy hair behind her ear. 'I always seem to get the long and difficult labours. The ones where you think the baby will never come or you need to get the doctor for a forceps delivery.'

Mac shrugged her shoulders. 'Maybe there's somebody in charge, up there,' she said, glancing to the ceiling, 'who knows that I haven't the patience of a saint like you.'

'Oh, I wouldn't say that,' she replied, smiling sweetly. 'I got very cross with a gentleman on a bus the other day when he refused to get up and allow me to access the seat next to the window. I had to stand in the aisle, swaying around, with my gas mask swinging all over the place.'

'I'd have shifted him for you.' Mac squeezed Myfanwy's arm.

'Nurse MacDonald,' called Sister Codey from two beds down, 'your magic is still working it seems, come

61

down here to Mrs Murphy, I think she's going into labour.'

'See you at break,' called Myfanwy. 'And just to say, I'm desperate to know all there is to know about that extremely handsome airman whom I saw you with outside the Nurses' Home earlier today.'

There are no secrets around here, thought Mac, as she bustled down the ward to assess Mrs Murphy. But Myfanwy Jones was so sweet-natured that Mac knew that she'd probably tell her almost anything.

The maternity ward was settling, they had just one woman in slow labour and the rest of the patients were bedding down for the night. Mac checked that all of the blackout curtains were in place before she left the ward. With Lucia born at the beginning of her shift and then little Charlie Murphy in the early evening, she'd brought two brand new lives into the world today. There were always those who muttered about how it was a shame, bringing babies into a cruel world full of war. As if people had a choice, as if they could stop babies being born, just because there was a war on. From what she could see there seemed to be even more women getting pregnant these days, and thinking about what she'd been doing with Don before coming into work, she could understand why. There was terrible misery with the war; the worst of things to endure. But she knew beneath the surface some invisible energy survived, making sure that they all kept going. And just occasionally, it still felt like there was excitement to be had. As she walked back to the Nurses' Home through the gathering dark, all she could think about was seeing Don tomorrow night.

★ ★ ★

Jo lay sprawled on her bed, engrossed in her book. *Far from the Madding Crowd* was a very engaging read; the depiction of rural life reminded her of home and she couldn't help but admire Bathsheba Everdene running the farm, as tough as the men. Knowing that Mac would be home soon and no doubt causing distraction, she was rushing to finish her chapter.

She checked her pages — just one more to go.

Bang! The door flew open and Mac bounded in.

Jo shot upright in bed. 'For God's sake! One day you're going to give me a heart attack!' She scrabbled around to pick her book up off the floor.

'Just wanted to make sure you were on your mettle. Awake, alert and ready for action.' Mac was smiling as she stood over her bed. 'The sky is clear, the moon is out, and I think we're in for a second night of bombing. One of the porters was telling me that when the moonlight reflects off the water it makes it easy for the bombers to follow the course of the river. Like a silver pathway, straight to their target.'

'Really?' Jo said, feeling sad to hear that. In the days before the war, when she was near the river at night, she'd often wonder if, one day, she would have a man in her life and they would look out over the water together, hand in hand. But not now. Even the river had become a tool of war.

She sighed and started flicking through the pages of her book to find her place, slipping a neatly folded piece of paper in as a bookmark. When she looked up Mac was still there.

'Before you ask, even though it's a Friday night, I won't be going out. I'm so sure that the bombers are coming tonight, I'm not even going to change out of my uniform. And Don had to go back to the base anyway so…'

Jo felt relieved. She was too tired and she wouldn't have had the energy to fight it out with Mac again. She rested back on her pillow, trying to repress a smile.

'I don't know what you're smirking for, Brooks. We're almost certainly heading for another night in Casualty with half the city packed in the pews and bleeding on the floor.'

Mac leapt onto the bed and started to rough up her hair.

'Get off me, you beast,' Jo kicked, squirming free and pushing Mac onto the rag rug that sat neatly between their beds. Once she could see that Mac was done with her teasing, she slipped onto the rug beside her and they both sat, as they shared stories from their day. 'I like the sound of little Lucia Gazzi…' Jo smiled, pulling herself up from the floor at last. 'Now, given that you're so sure there's going to be another raid tonight, I might just get changed back into my own uniform.'

'Good idea,' said Mac as she rummaged under her bed for the custard creams. 'Just three left,' she said, handing one over.

'I'll go and make us some cocoa when I'm dressed,' she mumbled through a mouth full of sweet biscuit, and then seeing Mac making her way to the window. 'And no, you can't go opening the sash so you can have a smoke,' she said firmly. 'What if you let out a chink of light and the bombers see it and we all get blown to smithereens?' Mac put her head on one side and started to plead but Joe stood her ground. 'No!' she said firmly, snapping fast the studs that secured her starched collar, then reaching for a clean apron and starting to pin it into place. 'And don't look at me like that, Mac. We can't take any ris—'

The air raid siren sounded loud and clear. Shocked, Jo stuck her finger with the pin, dropping a few tiny spots of blood onto her uniform. 'Darn,' she said, grabbing her starched cap, as Mac scrabbled for her shoes. They ran out of their room as all the doors flew open along the corridor and the nurses streamed out.

They were assigned to Casualty again. Together they made rapid checks on supplies before the injured started to pour in. As they counted bandages and checked bottles of saline, explosions sounded so loud, so close, even Mac looked shaken. When an especially big one fell, they both screamed and clung together. Already it was worse than last night.

Sister Reynolds rustled past them in her super stiff starched uniform; she seemed to be counting equipment, before shouting to an orderly to clean up the worst of the fallen plaster in the waiting room and then to run to the stockroom and bring more saline for the intravenous drips. 'And of course we'll need plasma,' she muttered to herself as she passed by.

Dr Hedley, a veteran of the last war, where he'd taken charge of a field hospital, had gone to meet with Matron, checking the emergency plan. He swept back into the department in his white coat, his pale face haggard from so many sleepless nights.

The decks were cleared and the department was ready and waiting.

Jo looked over at her friend. 'Let them come,' Mac murmured under her breath. She too felt ready to get on with the work. She knew from the previous night that once they got stuck in, it would fall into place, and the waiting just made her more nervous. She went back to the shelves and counted more bandages, dressings and slings. She made sure the shiny metal receivers were ready and they had enough towels and flannels to clean the worst of the dust off their casualties.

She jumped when the door swung open, but it was just the Air Raid Warden, Fred Townley, clanking through, heavy-footed, with his steel helmet, gas mask and haversack. He was calling by to check that they were all set and then began chivvying Dr Hedley over a sliver of light from one of the windows on the third floor of the hospital. Sister Reynolds tutted with impatience, pulling her long-handled scissors in and out of her uniform pocket as Fred continued to rabbit on.

'I'll send someone up to check the blackout and fix it,' Dr Hedley muttered, irritated and impatient with the elderly warden who never stopped telling them about how he'd served in the last war and how better organised everything was. From what Jo had read of soldiers squatting in trenches and the atrocious loss of life in some of the battles, she wasn't sure about all of that. Of course, the warden was only doing his job, but he never seemed to be able to see the bigger picture. The whole hospital was shaking with bombs falling outside. Even she knew that it was too late to be concerned over a tiny sliver of light. The city was being pounded to dust.

They heard their first casualties before they saw them: a woman screaming and a man shouting. Jo and Mac were both ready and they moved together as the door flew open and the screaming woman ran in with a large piece of broken glass embedded in her upper back, blood oozing down her white cardigan. It made Jo shudder, the red and white reminding her of the bad luck from the flowers in the vase that morning. She repeated, in her head, a quick mantra handed down by her mother — *don't be daft, don't be daft* — as she took the woman's arm, speaking calmly to her and guiding her straight through to the treatment room.

Mac had run forward to help a middle-aged man who was dragging a bloodstained leg, his trousers ripped to shreds. 'I've got you, you're going to be fine,' Jo heard her saying as she brought him through to the treatment room too. Mac had such a good voice for managing patients in distress.

Jo soothed her casualty whilst Dr Hedley scrutinised the wound and then reached for a metal receiver containing the instruments used to remove fragments of glass, metal or any other foreign bodies that resulted from a bomb blast. She exchanged a concerned glance with Mac. She knew that she was thinking the same — the air attack was all the more ferocious tonight, with explosion after explosion. It was louder and more vicious, the ground beneath their feet was shaking.

She felt a knot in her chest as she clung to her patient's hand. Dr Hedley was about to remove the glass. It was embedded superficially, but still, she needed to be prepared for heavy bleeding. As another explosion sounded, she squeezed the woman's hand and Dr Hedley grasped the jagged glass and pulled it cleanly out of the skin. Straightaway, she pressed a thick wad of gauze over the gush of bright red blood. Not too firmly, in case there were still some shards left in, but enough to contain the bleeding.

'All done. We just need to get your blouse and cardigan off,' she said gently, 'so that doctor can inspect the wound and we can get it stitched up.'

The woman looked at her with desperation. 'I was running home, I wanted to check that my kids were safe.'

'It's alright, as soon as we have you fixed up, you can go down to the basement shelter here, and when the 'all clear' comes you can go on your way.'

'But I don't know if they're safe,' she cried out, 'I left them with a neighbour.'

'They'll have gone to the shelter,' Jo said confidently. 'They'll be safe and sound.' She prayed that was the case.

Once the first patients were treated, Jo started to feel that the night might be lighter on casualties after all. But she knew that was because so far they'd only seen those people wounded in the immediate vicinity of the hospital. The rest would have been forced to take shelter, pinned down by a hellish onslaught. She couldn't even imagine what it must be like out there in the midst of the attack. For some reason, despite her concerns about the proximity of the hospital to the target area, she often felt safe and protected inside the hallowed space of Mill Road. As if doing the work they did somehow guaranteed their safety.

When the attack seemed to ease off a little, a stream of ambulance crew began running in with stretchers and more of the walking wounded. Bessie's crew was first through the door with two children, one at either end of the stretcher. A little girl of about three or four with big dark eyes and tufts of fluffy brown hair sticking out from under a soot-stained bandage, and an older boy lying at the other end, worryingly still. The girl was trying to sit up and she had a well-worn cloth dolly with one button eye missing tucked beneath her arm. She was reaching out to the boy who looked about seven. His face was black with soot and he lay motionless. Jo could see his chest moving up and down but his breathing was shallow. She felt his neck for a carotid pulse but felt just a flicker.

'It's alright,' she soothed as the little girl started to sob. But she knew that it wasn't. She needed to get the boy straight to the emergency ward that had been set aside for those with life-threatening wounds. She was sure he had a catastrophic injury and he would need urgent surgery if he was to stand a chance of survival.

'This is Polly,' said Bessie, speaking quickly. 'She has a cut on her head that might need a few stitches. And at the other end of the stretcher we have her brother, Frederick, who was found in the basement of their house. We couldn't find anybody else in the house who needed to come to hospital; we're not sure where Mummy and Daddy are.' The look that Bessie gave was easy to read — Jo would confirm with her later, but she was certain already that there were no other survivors in the family home.

'Right, Polly!' Jo smiled. 'Frederick has to go on the stretcher to see a special doctor. And I want you to come with me so that we can have a look at your sore head and see if we can fix dolly as well.'

She didn't have time to wait for the little girl to make up her own mind — she could see the boy's breathing changing. She scooped Polly up off the stretcher and held her fast, clinging to her as she screamed, 'I want Fred, I want Fred!' as the ambulance crew ran down the corridor towards the lift.

Polly was kicking and fighting hard against Jo and she needed to hold on with all her might. Her heart was breaking for the girl — she could have cried with her. But instead, she spoke gently over the wailing and screaming, 'It will be alright, it will be alright.'

Like her brother, the girl was covered in a fair amount of soot, and the smell of smoke and the acrid powder from the bomb clung to her clothes and hair. Jo sat down on one of the wooden benches. She felt the girl pulling at her uniform — her white apron now smeared with soot — nipping and pinching and trying to scratch. Jo held fast — she wasn't going to let her go. She might have run anywhere, even back out onto the street where the bombs were still falling.

'Shhhh, shhhh …' At last, she felt some release of tension in the girl's body. The poor little mite was exhausted. Jo started rocking her, in the way she remembered seeing her mother rocking her older brother when he was sick with diphtheria. She could still feel the tiny girl's heart pounding and her breath was broken by sobs, but there was, at last, some more relaxation in her body.

Polly was on the brink of sleep and when she reached up a small hand to stroke Jo's face, she did it gently. 'Mama,' she murmured as, mercifully, she slipped into a deep sleep. Jo adjusted her position so that she could put an arm all the way around her. She could feel the pressure of the girl's head resting against her chest, where her heart beat a steady rhythm.

'Poor little soul,' murmured Sister Reynolds, appearing in front of her. 'I've just had word that her brother died as they got him to the operating table.'

Jo could feel the child's rhythmic breathing against her body as a hard lump formed in her chest.

'Are you alright, Nurse Brooks?'

She could only nod in reply. Tears welled in her eyes but she clung to her task; she needed to stay calm, she

70

needed not to disturb Polly. What would lie in store for this little one now, barely more than a baby and the only surviving member of her family?

'I've had a large cot brought up,' Sister continued. 'We'll let her sleep as long as she needs and then we'll treat her wounds. I don't want her waking up in the basement, it's so dank and depressing now they've moved the children's ward down there. I know it's for safety but there's never any proper light. And we can keep a better eye on her up here. She's called Polly, isn't she?'

'Yes,' said Jo, glancing over to the cast iron bars of the high-sided cot that a porter was just wheeling into place. 'But we don't know her surname yet. It was Bessie's ambulance that brought her in.'

'I'll make enquiries,' said Sister matter-of-factly. 'Now, let me take her, I'll settle her in the cot. You get yourself a clean apron and bring in another walking wounded from the waiting room.'

They continued to work through into the early hours, and every time Jo went by the high-sided cot in the corner of the treatment area, she glanced at the sleeping child.

Whilst she was checking a bandage on the head of a young woman with curled hair who'd been hit by falling debris whilst making her way out of a pub, she saw Fred Townley shuffle in, covered in dust and looking exhausted, his Air Raid Precautions armband ripped and hanging loose, and his steel helmet dinted.

'You alright there, Fred?' she asked, walking straight over to him.

'What a night it's been. What a night. And I've just been hit by a lump of concrete.' He stood to show her the damage to his helmet and then he shook his head,

71

looking shocked.

'Come on, Fred, sit yourself down,' she urged, guiding him towards one of the wooden benches.

He slumped down without even a whimper of remonstrance. Very unlike their air raid warden. Usually, no matter what time of night, he would walk in, actively casting his eyes around for any contravention of regulations. But as he sat there, staring into space, she thought he looked like a broken man. 'I'll get you a cup of tea,' she said, 'We've got a couple of Women's Voluntary Service ladies still brewing up.'

He didn't answer and she was about to pursue it with him when the sound of a child wailing miserably stopped her short. She knew immediately that it was Polly. The girl began screaming, 'Mummy, Mummy. I want my mummy!' She felt a sliver of pain go through her as she raced back into the treatment area to find the child clinging to the side of the cot.

'There, there,' she tried to say, but the little girl cried out, 'Go away. Horrible, Go away!' Jo tried to reach out a gentle hand to her, but Polly screamed even louder and threw herself back, cowering away at the far side of the cot. 'I want my Mummy!'

Jo, almost in tears, tried to soothe her. 'Mummy isn't here right now.'

Polly threw herself down on the mattress, kicking her legs and began screaming even louder, 'I want Fred, I want Fred!'

Desperate to help, Jo took up the well-worn dolly that had now been discarded and tried to tempt her with it. 'Polly, Polly, hello Polly.' The child grabbed the dolly, crushing it tight to her body with one arm, ceasing from her howling for a split second to scowl at Jo. 'I want Fred,' she insisted, 'I want Fred!'

72

'My name's Fred,' said a gentle voice.

Jo turned to see the air raid warden, a genuine smile lighting up his exhausted and bewildered face.

'You're not my Fred,' spat the girl, but at least she'd stopped screaming.

'Maybe not, but I bet I know a song that your Mummy sings to you.' The girl was shaking her head forcefully. 'Oh yes I do,' Fred insisted.

Sister Reynolds walked by with a raised eyebrow.

'Are you ready?' he said brightly.

The girl just stared at him, her big dark eyes almost unblinking.

He started singing anyway, crooning along in the most tuneless, broken voice that Jo had ever heard. But the words were clear. 'Polly put the kettle on, Polly put the kettle on, Polly put the kettle on, we'll all have tea.' Fred took a gasping breath like a fish out of water. 'Sukey take it off again, Sukey take it off again, Sukey take it off again, they've all gone away.'

Polly lay still.

'Do you want me to sing it again?'

She nodded her head as she lay on the bed.

Fred sang the song over and over, holding onto the side of the cot.

Mac murmured wryly as she passed by that they'd better get an oxygen mask ready, just in case he collapsed. But Polly was sitting up now at the far side of the cot and she was clutching dolly in her arms and rocking her from side to side. When, at last, Fred was wheezing too much and simply couldn't sing any more, the child spoke, 'Please sing, Grandad. More. More.'

Jo felt her heart tighten with pride as 'Grandad Fred', his legs sagging with exhaustion and his voice breaking, gave one more rendition. When he was finished, the little girl came to the side of the cot and placed her small hand gently against his dusty cheek.

Jo could see tears in Fred's eyes.

'Where's Mummy?'

'Mummy's coming soon,' he said.

Jo took a deep breath, it didn't feel right that Polly didn't know the truth, but they needed her to stay calm. She saw the girl nod her head and then she sat down with her cloth dolly tucked beneath one arm, staring out through the bars of the cot.

Fred limped back towards the wooden bench where he'd left his steel helmet and gas mask.

'Stay a while, Fred, have a bit of a breather,' she overhead Sister Reynolds say, but the air raid warden shook his head, replaced his helmet and wandered back out through the door.

Polly didn't need any stitches and she was soon on her way down to the children's ward with a porter who Jo checked knew the words to 'Polly Put the Kettle On'. She watched as the man carried the little girl away, her wide-eyed face peering forlornly over his shoulder. She heard her start to cry as they turned the corner towards the steps that led down to the basement, then faintly, she could hear the porter starting to sing.

'Poor little lass,' offered one of the WVS women as she walked by with some empty cups. 'What a terrible thing to lose your whole family in one night and she doesn't even know about it yet. But at three, it might be easier than if she was older.'

Jo didn't know about that, surely the loss of her family would scar her forever. And she knew how busy they were on the children's ward, how little time they would have to explain to her what had happened. Jo would go and see Polly if she had a moment, but she knew that because her injury was light, they would soon move her to a children's home. Before the war, she might have been adopted, but given the scale of what was happening, there would be far too many children and not enough families.

When Jo and Mac walked out of the hospital in the early hours of the morning, it felt to Jo as if the world had shifted on its axis. The air around them was acrid, a mix of powdered mortar and smoke from the fires which still burnt brightly.

'Let's just walk a little way, I think we need to see,' said Mac.

A huge fire burnt at the bottom of a street where rows of houses had been obliterated. Rescue workers were crunching through glass and clouds of dust, frantically removing chunks of debris, looking for survivors. And down the side of the road, bodies waited for collection, covered by sacks or blankets or in one case a torn curtain. Jo saw an old woman clawing with her hands at a pile of rubble that she had no chance of moving. A fireman came to her with a shovel and started to help.

Suddenly, from the other side of the street there was a shout. They'd found someone alive. Jo gripped Mac's arm tighter. She wondered if they should try to help. But they had nothing left to give.

'Come on,' Mac said firmly, leading her away.

They walked back silently, side by side. This second night had certainly been the heaviest so far. How could the city withstand even one more attack like this? But even as Jo held on to Mac's arm, she saw firemen, policemen, civil defence, and ordinary citizens shovelling rubble, dousing fires with hoses, sweeping away debris. And then there was another shout, 'We've got a live one here.'

Jo felt an ache in her chest and had to fight to hold back the tears; these people were risking everything to save others and to reclaim their city. And she knew in that moment that the spirit of Liverpool was very much alive; the people were fighting back.

7

'No, no,' groaned Mac, as Jo shook her a bit too vigorously.

'Come on, sleepy head. You're on an early, remember.'

'Oh God, I've only just got into bed. I'm sooo tired.'

'Don't you dare roll over, I've got your clean uniform here, you have to get up. The ward needs you.'

'No...' She yawned, rolling over. 'I've given my all. I'm done.'

'Come on,' insisted Jo, 'I know it's hard, but I had to get up for an early yesterday. If I can do it so can you. And you don't want to be hauled up in front of Deputy Matron to explain why you weren't on duty, do you?'

'Aaargh,' cried Mac, sitting up violently, her curly hair sticking out at all angles. Jo couldn't help but laugh.

'Come on, I'll soon have you ready.'

'How can you be so bright and breezy at this time in the morning? It's not normal. It feels like the middle of the night.'

'Nonsense,' said Jo. 'It's six a.m.'

Mac was still bleary eyed as she walked with Amy Goodwin to the hospital. 'Wasn't it terrible last night? Where were you?' she asked, desperately trying to keep up with Amy's rapid stride.

'Well, Deputy Matron always sends me up to the military ward with the young soldiers. She thinks I've got some kind of magic touch with them. But it's awful for the shell-shocked ones during a raid. They go through terrible traumas. Billy Wilcox and Owen Evans were under their beds last night shaking and crying.'

'Poor things,' said Mac. 'People don't realise that the injuries aren't just physical — though those are bad enough. Jo told me about your young man who had to have his hands amputated.'

'Oh, yes. Robert Croasdale. He cried for days before the operation but now he just lies there with this empty look in his eyes. It's so sad.'

As soon as she was in through the door of Maternity, Mac went straight to Sofia Gazzi's bed. She was sitting up with her long dark hair loose around her shoulders and her brown eyes glowing with warmth; she was breathtakingly beautiful. Mac could only imagine the heartbreak that her husband must have felt as they led him away. 'Good morning, Sofia, how are you?'

'I am very well,' she said. 'The milk seems to be coming already and the nurses, they let me have Lucia out of nursery during the night to feed.'

'Oh, that's good. It's important to get the feeding established as soon as possible. But of course, you know that already.' Mac picked up the observation chart from the bottom of the bed. After losing more than one lovely new mother to childbed fever she was always on the lookout for a raised temperature that might indicate an infection brewing. But all seemed well with Sofia's readings. So far, so good.

'I'll call by the nursery later on to have a look at Lucia. We do another check on the first day— She's fine though, no need to worry,' she added, seeing the flash of anxiety in Sofia's eyes.

Mac saw Myfanwy adjusting her starched cap as she waited outside Sister's office, ready to receive the report. She walked over and linked arms with her. Myfanwy, lovely as always, turned immediately to give her a smile, but Mac saw dark smudges beneath her friend's eyes.

'You look tired, Myf. Where did you end up last night?'

'Oh, on here. It would have been alright, but we had two women who were labouring, and others who weren't able to make it down to the shelter in the basement. So we were pulling beds away from the windows and trying to make it as safe as possible for the women. It was terrifying hearing the whole thing going on outside. When I lifted a tiny corner of the blackout, I could see it all from up here. I wished I hadn't looked, Mac; I think when we're in here working we don't realise, but it is brutal. And we had one mum crying because someone had taken her baby from the nursery and not left him up here with her and the babies that were up here were screaming. And the building shook so hard one time I swear it swayed from side to side.'

'Oh, Myf, isn't it awful. And it feels inevitable doesn't it, that they'll be coming back for another round tonight?'

Myfanwy nodded and gave a sigh. 'I don't know if I can stand it. Not another night. But then if we have women who need to give birth — what else can we do? It takes so many staff to evacuate the patients. And I couldn't live with myself if I didn't come running when the siren went.'

'Oh, me too. I feel the same. It just wouldn't be right. But I must confess, I will be sorely tempted to stay away tonight. Guess who I'm seeing?'

Myfanwy giggled. 'Would that be Don, the airman?'

'Yes, indeed. And even if it's just for ten minutes, I don't care. I'm going out.'

'Well from what I saw of him—'

'Come on, nurses,' called Sister Codey, beckoning for them to gather in her office. 'We have work to do.'

Thankfully, they had a slow day on Maternity. Mac wondered if it was because the city was in shock, still getting its breath back. But she'd always thought that stress increased the likelihood of a woman going into labour. Anyway, she couldn't complain, at least it gave her some time to recover from the double shifts she'd been working over the last two days. And a more leisurely day meant she could spend some time with the babies. She loved going into the nursery; you could smell that concentrated newborn smell as soon as you came through the door and it always delighted her to see them all lined up in their cots next to each other. Big bouncing babies, small skinny ones, some completely bald, others with brown or black hair and one, with a shocking crop of bright blond. The sleeping ones were like little cherubs. Some of those lying awake snuffled and blinked their eyes or tried to escape from their swaddling. Others screamed blue murder. And if you were in here on your own with more than two bawlers, it was impossible. You could soothe one in each arm but beyond that, you were struggling. She loved it though, she even loved the bawlers. She sometimes wondered what she'd been like as a baby; with no family to pass the stories down, she had nothing to go on. But she was fairly sure that she would, most definitely, have been a bawler.

It was easy to spot Lucia with her black hair tufting up from her head. She was sleeping peacefully in her cot. Mac took a few moments just to gaze at her, leaning over to breathe in the smell of her as she lay swaddled firmly in her hospital blanket. She wasn't biased just because she'd delivered her, but she did think she was the most beautiful baby in the nursery. Her other delivery, little Charlie Murphy, who lay two cots away and sounded a bit snuffly, was a close second with his impressive wisp of sandy hair, though his face was a bit squashed up. No, it was definitely Lucia.

Carefully, she rolled the sleeping baby onto her back and unwrapped her from the blanket, feeling the warmth of her small body as she loosened the ties of the hospital issue cotton nightie. 'There you go, young lady,' she murmured, exposing her tummy to check that the suture on her umbilical cord was secure and there were no signs of infection. Then she checked her hips and turned over her small body so that she could check her back. 'All's fine, my beauty.' Mac counted the fingers and toes once more and then gently opened Lucia's rosebud mouth to glance inside. Still Lucia didn't wake. The final check was the labelling. After a number of incidents of mistaken identity causing terrible trouble, the hospital now had a policy of making sure that each child not only had a label on the cot but also a name band tied around the wrist with name, date of birth and weight. All was in order for Lucia Gazzi, born 2 May 1941, weight: 7 pounds 4 ounces.

At the end of Mac's shift, Myfanwy was still cleaning up after a delivery, so Mac walked back alone. It was rare for any of the nurses to get off on time and certainly Amy would be running late with all the commotion that had been reported from her ward today. After the events of last night, one of her young men had attempted to commit suicide. He'd smashed a bottle and hacked at his wrist with the broken glass. There were a lot of apparently bright and breezy young men on that ward who seemed to bear their injuries lightly, but all the nurses felt that they were only touching the surface of things. It would have been nice to have more time to encourage the men to talk about their experiences, but it simply wasn't possible.

She sighed, then forced herself think about little Lucia and Charlie again and it made her feel better. She glanced up at the clear blue sky — it was glorious, but it didn't bode well for the city. Unless the Germans had run out of bombs, it looked very likely that they'd be back for a third night of bombing. 'Give us a break,' she said out loud, turning her face to the sky, 'it's a Saturday night.' She had to see Don, even if it was for a couple of hours, an hour, even half an hour would do.

She tried to have a nap on her bed but that didn't work; the thought of Don's deep brown eyes kept sending tingles through her body. So she went for a bath, and then she did her hair and before getting herself dressed, she did a full tidy and clean of the room, just to give Jo a nice surprise when she came off her late shift. Most of the mess was on Mac's side, as usual, so she gathered up her discarded clothing, pushed a bundle of shoes that wouldn't fit in her wardrobe and a pile of magazines under the bed, and set out her undies for drying on the cast iron radiator. And then, she pulled the rag rug up from the floor and gave it a good shake before replacing it between the beds, running her hand over the dark red, brown and orange fabrics that Jo had combined so skilfully to add a touch of colour to their room. It was so tempting to lie on the rug and try and have a nap now but she daren't. What if she fell asleep for hours, leaving the love of her life waiting forlornly at the bar?

Come on, she said to herself, walking over to Jo's wardrobe to take one of the blue-patterned cups off the shelf, *get yourself a drink of tea and then go down to the common room and put a record on the gramophone.* She always livened up with a bit of Glenn Miller or Irving Berlin. She sang as she walked along the corridor towards the kitchen, 'Blue skies, smiling at me, nothing but blue skies, do I see ...'

Later, after she'd played and replayed 'Blue Skies' and 'Moonlight Serenade', she was buzzing with excitement. Drifting back to her room, she went straight to the mirror to apply her red lipstick. She loved the heavy feel of it on her lips and the colour was sensational. She fluffed up her hair and arranged it in a cloud of curls around her face. Then, stuffing her gas mask into her red leather bag and slipping on her high heels, she was ready to go.

Slinking along the corridor in her midnight blue dress with three-quarter length sleeves and her one good pair of silk stockings, she felt her legs slide provocatively against the fabric of her dress each time she took a step. It sent tingles through her body and she couldn't help but feel like a film star. And she couldn't lie to herself, she knew that all eyes would turn to meet her as soon as she walked into the pub.

Even through the dim light and the clouds of cigarette smoke, she could see his broad uniformed shoulders as he leant at the bar, his dark hair sticking up at one side where he'd pulled off his cap. A low wolf whistle from another man made all heads turn and he twisted around on his bar stool. His face when he saw her — she knew that she would never ever forget that moment. If she was shot or blown up in this war, she would use her dying breath to recall that split second when he turned to look at her. She stood, just in through the door, feeling the power of it. It made her ache in the pit of her stomach.

She took her time to cross the distance between them, maintaining eye contact all the way. He got up from his stool and walked, then ran, to pull her into his arms as the pub exploded in loud cheers. The feel of his body through his uniform was almost unbearable; she wanted to take him by the hand and lead him straight out to their house with the crooked door. But that would be rushing things. She had to make the most of this.

He put his arm around her and led her to a high-backed bench against the wall, down by the side of the bar. 'You look incredible, Rita,' he whispered in her ear.

'Well, who knows when I'll get another night out? Thought I'd make a bit of effort.'

He was shaking his head. 'But you don't even need to make any effort. In fact, yesterday morning—'

'Alright, no need to go into the detail. I think I know what you're saying.'

'I'll just get my pint off the bar, can I get you a drink?'

'Port and lemon please. I daren't have more than a couple, I've a feeling I might be needing to run back to the hospital in a few hours' time.'

She crossed her legs, feeling the slide of the silk beneath her dress. This was going to be a good test, she thought, as she watched him walk away from her. They'd been caught up in the moment each time they'd met so far. Now they were going to have to talk to each other properly.

'Cheers,' she smiled, lifting her glass and chinking it against his pint. 'Here's to us and the war effort.'

'Cheers!' He grinned and took a good mouthful of beer.

She reached out a hand and wiped the froth off his top lip, taking the opportunity to scrutinise his face in more detail. 'You have a tiny mole beneath your left eye.'

'Yes, I do. And my Italian mother always used to say that the place a mole grows is significant. For example, the one beneath my eye...' He smiled, pointing to the spot. 'It means that I cry a lot or that I can be emotional. And this tiny one here, just above my top lip, means I like kissing.'

'Well I think I know about the kissing already, but tell me more about the crying?'

'Well, as a kid, I craved attention. I've got two older sisters and they were always picking me up and fussing over me. And I often cried to my Ma and clung to her skirts, that kind of thing. So maybe there is something in it... Just wondering, have you got any distinctive moles?'

'Well, I do have one next to my belly button. What does that mean?'

'Mmm, not sure, but I really wouldn't mind taking a closer look later on. Just to make a proper assessment...'

'We'll see about that, aircrew,' she said. 'I'll have you know that I'm on more of a fact-finding mission tonight. Trying to decide if you're a suitable match for a respectable state-registered nurse like myself. So I might be asking lots of questions...'

'Ask away. I've nothing to hide.'

'So, question one, where are your family? Where do they live?'

'Well, we did all live in Liverpool, but Ma died six months before the war, from cancer.'

She saw the light dim in his eyes for a few seconds and she reached out a hand to give his arm a squeeze. 'I'm sorry, that's a bugger.'

'Yeh... and I know lots of people say this kind of thing, but she really was the best ma in the world. I don't think I'll ever stop missing her. But that's life, isn't it; it's all a part of life. And currently we're all living in the midst of loss after loss...'

She nodded. 'And your sisters?' she asked, withdrawing her hand and taking another big sip of her drink.

'They're in London. Both of them are adventurous types, they wanted to see something beyond Liverpool, so they moved there before the war. And now, Laura, the eldest, is working for the Ambulance and Lucille has volunteered for the Police. They're currently having a hell of a time dodging the bombs just like we are here.'

'So, none of your family still live here in Liverpool?'

'My dad used to, but he couldn't cope after Ma died, so he went back to Galway, to his sisters, and he'll stay there now. He wanted us all to join him once war was declared, to go and live in a neutral country. But none of us could do that, not even after Italy joined the other side; we wanted to stay here and fight.'

Mac thought it was good that he had the reassurance that his Dad was safe, but she couldn't help but feel a little disappointed. She'd been hoping that he had a home in Liverpool — if they were anything like Don, his family were bound to be lively. It was the kind of household that she'd always craved.

She could see a wry smile on his face. 'Maybe, if this war goes on and on, we'll all be wishing we'd left the country. So, what about you, Mac? You've never talked about any family, but you look to me with your red hair and your pale complexion that you might have some Irish blood in you. We might be half cousins or something.'

She took a sip from her drink, before putting her glass back down with a decisive clunk. 'I haven't talked about my family for good reason... I have none.'

'Oh,' he breathed. His eyes were wide, waiting for more information.

'I grew up in a children's home, not far from here. It's abandoned now; all the children were evacuated permanently at the start of war. I keep wishing that the Germans would drop a bomb right on it, blow it to smithereens.'

'So it wasn't the best place to grow up?'

'No, it wasn't, but I got out of there. I went straight to work in Ogden's Tobacco Factory and one day a mate of mine, she had an accident, got her hand trapped in a machine. So I had to give some first aid and I took her up to the hospital and it was strange, as soon as I walked through the door and I smelt the disinfectant and saw all those women in uniform doing really important work, I knew it was for me. So I asked the Casualty nurse about training and then as soon as I was old enough, I applied. It took me three goes to get in, they didn't seem overly impressed by my credentials, but once they saw that I was very determined, I think they got a bit worried that I might set up camp outside the hospital door, so they let me in.'

'You are quite something, aren't you?'

'I don't know about that, it's just I had nothing else, apart from my mates in the factory and my room in a grotty boarding house. I wanted to make something of myself, I suppose.'

'I can see that, and I like what you've made. I truly do.'

She leant over and kissed him on the lips, breathing in the smell of him, feeling the sensation all the way through her body. As she drew back, she whispered, 'Sorry, it's just that I saw you had a kissing mole, so I thought—'

He pulled her against his body, neither of them caring who was in the pub or what was happening around them.

She drew back at last.

'I think we might need to find a room,' he gasped. 'I'm just wondering if the house with a crooked door is vacant. I hope they haven't got around to bulldozing it just yet.'

Mac laughed.

He pulled his pack of Woodbines out and offered one.

'No thanks,' she said opening her bag to find her Dunhills, 'I don't really smoke those.'

'Oh sorry! Should I have brought a cigarette holder, is that your style?' he joked.

'Very funny. You just want to look all manly with your Woodbines. It's part of the image.'

'And what image might that be?'

'The aviator thing,' she chipped, playfully. 'You'll be growing a moustache next.'

'What are you talking about, woman? I'm training to be a radio-operator and a gunner, not a pilot.'

'And you couldn't grow a moustache, anyway, could you?' she teased. 'Not with your kissing mole, you wouldn't want to hide that.'

They laughed, and then Mac noticed a tall, uniformed figure standing by their table.

Don looked up. 'Zach!' he cried, jumping up from his seat. 'Good to see you. I'm thinking you weren't able to get transport to Tadcaster then? And you remember Mac, from the night before last, at the hospital?'

'Why, sure. How could a man forget Rita Hayworth?' he said, leaning in to kiss her hand. 'I am so sorry if we made trouble for you and your friend.'

'Oh, that's alright. The place was chaotic anyway. It's good to see you again, Zach.'

Don leant in and said quietly in Zach's ear. 'Mac thinks that all pilots have moustaches.'

'I do not,' she laughed. 'But that's the image isn't it?'

He smiled. 'I don't know, I've only done my flight training in Canada so far and there were plenty of mooses but no moostaches.'

Mac and Don cracked up laughing.

'I only came to find you, Don, to tell you that finally, I have a lift tomorrow morning, in a truck going to my base. So, maybe I'll be able to let you know about the moustaches...'

'This might just be the most important question of the war.' Don laughed, then lifted his glass and spoke quietly, 'Good luck to you, Zach. Maybe we'll meet again on some airfield, who knows. Now let me get you a Scotch.'

'Oh, well, honestly, I don't want to interrupt you two. I mean I know your time together is limited...'

'The more the merrier is what I say,' Don said, jumping up to go to the bar.

'Come and sit next to me, Zach,' said Mac with a glint in her eye and a smile at Don. 'It'll be nice to chat to a real pilot.'

'OK, if you're sure?'

'Sit,' said Mac, firmly.

'Fancy a smoke?' smiled Zach, pulling a pack of Camel cigarettes out of his top pocket.

'Yes, please,' she grinned, her eyes gleaming with mischief when she saw Don heading back towards them. 'I can never resist a decent cigarette... Zach, have you ever heard of Woodbines?' she said, loud enough for Don to hear. She saw him shaking his head and laughing.

When Don was settled back in his seat, they all said cheers and then Mac spoke more quietly to Zach, 'Are you sorry that you volunteered for this, now that you've experienced what's actually going on over here?'

'Well, I must admit it was a hell of a shock when the bombs started to fall on that first night. I ran for my life, into here, and that's how I met Don. But I haven't had any doubts, not yet anyway. Once I heard the stories of your guys at the Battle of Britain, that was it, I already had some flying hours and I knew I had to join up. And, let's face it, we'll end up in this anyway, it's only a question of time.'

'We're comrades in arms,' smiled Don, raising his glass for another cheers.

They chatted for a long time, and the conversation was easy, moving from the war to Hollywood films and favourite records. Zach was also a fan of Irving Berlin.

'Looks like we were made for each other,' Mac teased, linking his arm playfully.

'Oi! You promised to marry *me*, remember?'

'I did no such—'

At that moment the whole pub fell silent in a split second as the air raid siren started to wail.

'That's my cue,' Mac said, instantly up on her feet, hugging Don and giving him a kiss on the cheek and then quickly shaking Zach's hand. 'Got to go!'

Mac was already weaving her way through the customers hurriedly finishing their drinks and preparing to leave.

'Wait,' shouted Don, catching up to her up and grabbing her arm. 'We'll escort you, don't be going on your own.'

'That's OK, it's only around the corner.'

'No, we're coming,' he insisted.

Don ran beside her all the way with Zach following behind, as they dodged along the darkened street, through all the people streaming towards the air raid shelters.

'This is me!' she shouted, as soon as she saw the shape of the Nurses' Home looming into view.

She reached up and kissed Don hard on the lips. He clung to her for a moment, holding his breath. 'I know this might sound like I'm rushing, but I just need to tell you that I think I love you, Mac,' he murmured.

She pulled back from him, smiling, 'Don't get carried away, aircrew. You're only saying that 'cos there's a war on. Now, I need to go and you two need to find an air shelter, promise me you won't go back to the pub. Go, go! Bye!'

She glanced over her shoulder as she ran towards the door of the Nurses' Home. She could see the shape of the two of them standing side by side, still staring after her, just where she'd left them.

As the heavy door slammed behind her, she gasped, for there on the bottom step was her apparition, the little girl with tousled hair, and this time she was crying. 'I'm sorry, my darling, I just don't have time for you right now,' Mac said, sprinting past and away up the stairs.

Near the top she crossed paths with Jo, moving lithely as always, closely followed by Myfanwy, Ruth and Amy.

'I'll tell Matron you're coming,' Jo yelled.

Once in the room, Mac leant against the closed door for a few seconds to get her breath back. She could smell Jo's cocoa mingling with the remains of her perfume. 'There's no place like home,' she murmured as she kicked off her high heels, then taking one more deep breath, she lunged to her side of the room, ripping off her dress, dropping it down onto the floor like a shed skin. Scrambling into her uniform, she decided to keep her silk stockings on to save time. She'd got away with no stockings at all two nights ago, she thought, grinning to herself as she pinned her cap in place. Heading to the door, she grabbed the red lipstick and slipped it into her pocket. No time to take off her make-up so she might as well touch up what she had on. She turned quickly to have one last look at the room before throwing open the door and running full pelt down the corridor.

8

Panting, her cap askew, Mac slipped in beside Myfanwy Jones in the now familiar group of nurses assembled outside Casualty. Matron Jenkins paused to give her a stern glance. 'Glad you could join us, Nurse MacDonald,' she said, as she began to rattle off their allocations. 'Brooks and MacDonald — although you have done fine work in Casualty these last two nights, we need your expertise elsewhere. So, Nurse Lee to Casualty this time, Brooks to the basement theatre — we're still on catch up from last night — and Mac-Donald up to Maternity with Jones. The night staff need all the support they can get, there are at least two women in labour as we speak.'

Mac and Jo exchanged a look across the circle.

'And our Nurse Goodwin,' Deputy Matron always smiled at Amy no matter how busy they were, 'I want you, as always, to shine your considerable light on the ward full of young soldiers. Right, off you go nurses, and good luck!'

Mac grabbed Jo and gave her a quick hug. 'I'll miss you tonight, Brooks, stay safe will you?'

'And you, up there on Maty,' called Jo, already running towards the steps that led down to the basement.

A stream of mums carrying grizzling babies were making their way out of the ward towards the basement, as Mac and Myfanwy made their way against the flow. Mac saw Mrs Murphy, her eyes wide with panic, holding tight to Charlie. She tried to give her a reassuring smile, but the woman was staring straight

93

ahead, desperate to get down to the air raid shelter. She saw many other mums that she recognised but there was no sign of Sofia.

Once they were in through the door, she spotted her instantly, still in her bed. She wanted to go straight there and find out why she wasn't moving down to the shelter but Sister Codey was almost whirling on the spot as she stood agitated and shouting instructions in the middle of the ward.

'Nurse Jones, go down to the far end, we have a Mrs Rosy O'Donnell in slow labour, she needs someone with her. Nurse MacDonald, I need you to assist with pulling the beds away from the windows — those on strict bedrest can't evacuate to the basement — pull the beds as far away as you can, if a blast shatters the glass it will be terrible.'

Mac and Myfanwy ran down the ward together as the piercing sound of a crying baby echoed around the now almost empty ward. Bedding lay askew, a couple of empty cots were discarded in the middle of the ward and abandoned night drinks were untouched on tables.

'Good luck, hope she delivers soon,' she called as Myfanwy made her way to the labour bays. Seeing the first patient in her own designated area, she found Mrs Sullivan, a young woman, pregnant with her first baby, who'd been threatening to go into premature labour for weeks. She was crying her eyes out. 'Not again, not another night. I don't think I can stand it.'

'There, there,' Mac tried to soothe. 'We'll get through this. Now, hold tight, I'm just going to pull your bed away from the window.' She moved quickly, releasing the brake on the iron bed but the old wheels were stiff and she had to heave with all her might to drag it clear. Once she was satisfied that it was far enough away from the window, she reapplied the brake, taking a few seconds to put an arm around her patient's shoulders and give her a squeeze, before running down to the next bed. Mrs Branson, also an ante-natal on strict bed rest due to high blood pressure, had been in hospital for many weeks; she was lying quietly in bed saying a prayer with her eyes shut tight.

'Just moving your bed,' she shouted, but Mrs Branson didn't respond.

Sofia was next in line, sitting up in bed cradling Lucia. 'Why are you still here?' Mac asked, striving to keep her voice calm but really wanting her newly delivered mum and baby to be safe in the basement shelter with the rest.

'I've had heavy bleeding and I fainted this evening. So Sister has put me on bedrest. Strict. She says I might need iron.'

'Oh, I see.' Now it made sense. 'Well, I'm just going to move your bed well away from the window. Hold on tight to the baby!'

She heaved the bed and then she moved the iron-framed cot, squeezing it up tight to the bed, so Sofia could easily lean over and place Lucia back in once she was ready.

Two empty beds away, further down the line, a new admission was struggling to settle her baby, a red-haired boy who was bawling lustily. Mac picked up the chart at the bottom of the bed and glimpsed her name — Veronica Edwards. She looked desperately at Mac. 'He's only just been born less than two hours ago, I 'aven't even got a name for him yet. Sister said we have to stay in bed, we can't go to the shelter. Why?

Why can't we go?'

'Staying in bed is for your own good, Mrs Edwards. There's a high risk of haemorrhage so soon after delivery, particularly for women who've had a number of babies. It would be dangerous for you to be up and moving about. Try not to worry, we've just had two nights of bombardment and the hospital has withstood it all, no problem.'

'Well, that's cos it hasn't been 'it by a—'

Whump! The first explosion sounded. Close enough, but it didn't shake the walls.

Mrs Edwards screamed blue murder and the baby started bawling even louder. Mac heaved her bed away from the window as the porter who'd been moving the post-natal beds at the other side of the ward ran towards her. 'You see to the mother!' he shouted over the crack of another explosion. He dived down to apply the brake and then pushed the cot up against the bed, before running out through the door. Mac glanced to the far end of the ward. She hoped to God that Myfanwy's patient was progressing towards delivery.

Mac threw her arms around Veronica and her baby, cradling them both, as two more bombs fell in quick succession. She could hear the high-pitched scream of another baby — it could only be Lucia; she'd never heard her cry like that, not even when she was born. She wanted to go back up the ward to check on them, but right now Veronica was sobbing in her arms and needed all her attention.

In the quiet that followed, broken only by the sound of little Lucia gently wailing and Veronica and her baby both crying, it felt as if the whole ward was holding its breath. Waiting for the next one. Mac stood frozen, still cradling her patient. After a few minutes when no further explosion came, she breathed out and straightened up. Thankfully, baby Edwards had gone quiet now, falling asleep.

'He must be exhausted,' muttered Veronica, wiping her nose with the back of her hand. Her cheeks flushed to almost the same shade as her bright pink hand-knitted bed jacket.

'Let me put him in the cot for you,' Mac soothed. 'He needs to get some sleep. And then I'll make your pillows comfortable so you can lie down.'

'Will there be more bombs? Do you think there'll be more?'

'Yes, I'm afraid this is probably just the start of it. But I'll be up and down the ward and I'll come if you need me, Veronica, I promise.'

'Thank you, nurse,' she sobbed.

Mac clasped Veronica's hand, before turning to the other side of the ward, where further down, the two post-natal women were sat bolt upright in their beds, listening for the next explosion. Each woman was braced, holding tight to her baby's cot, keeping it pulled close to the side of the bed. Miraculously, both babies were still sleeping.

'We've been here the last two nights,' said the first woman, 'we know the score.'

Now that the ward patients were sorted, she decided to check if the nurses in the labour bays needed anything — she could still hear the groans of the labouring women at the far end of the ward. Stopping by Sofia's bed on the way, she smiled, seeing that Lucia was now quietly feeding. She couldn't resist going up close, just for a moment, to stroke the baby's head.

Sofia took her hand. 'We are in this together tonight,

Mac.'

'Yes, we are,' she replied tenderly, before running towards the far end of the ward just as the next bomb fell, louder and closer this time, making the building sway, just a little.

Mac poked her head into the first labour bay. Sister Codey was calmly soothing her patient as she gasped her way through a very strong contraction. When the pain eased, Sister looked up and motioned for her to step in — the single twitch at the corner of her mouth so slight that Mac might have thought she'd imagined it. 'Are all the bed-bound patients settled and secure away from windows, Nurse MacDonald?'

'Yes, Sister.'

'Right, you stay out there. The two night nurses have gone down to the shelter with the patients. We just have these few up here. Please do me a favour though, check the nursery to make sure that all the babies have been evacuated. I didn't get time to do it. I always worry that we'll leave one behind and the poor little thing will be left without its mother.'

Another explosion made the walls shake and some plaster fell from the ceiling as the patient was hit by another very strong contraction. 'You're doing well, Maureen, I think your baby is almost ready to be born,' Sister reassured. The woman in the bed seemed oblivious to the bombs falling; she was making enough of her own noise now and starting to push. 'That's it, Maureen, keep pushing!' shouted Sister as the walls shuddered around them.

'I'll just check on Nurse Jones, then I'll go straight to the nursery,' called Mac as she started to make a move. 'See you soon.'

Myfanwy was crouching by the bed, holding onto her

patient Rosy O'Donnell's hand and talking her through a strong contraction. Mac loved the sound of her voice — it could calm anyone, even during an air raid.

'How's she doing?' she asked quietly, as soon as Myfanwy straightened up and turned to her.

'It's slow. I wouldn't expect anything else, it's a Nurse Jones labour!'

'Yes, I see what you mean.' Mac said, wanting to grab hold of Myfanwy and hug her, hold onto her until the raid was over. Instead, she simply asked, 'Do you need anything?'

'I'd love a cup of tea,' Mrs O'Donnell groaned, rolling over onto her back. 'I just want this baby to come. Maybe a hot drink will do the trick.'

'I'll bring one straight back,' Mac assured her, reaching out to give Myfanwy's arm a squeeze. 'I just need to check the nursery first.'

The floor shook violently with another blast as she walked down the ward doing one last check, passing Sofia, serene as always, busy settling Lucia in her cot; and Veronica, grim-faced in bed, with her baby boy now thankfully settled. As the two post-natal women on the other side of the ward raised a hand to indicate that they were alright, she opened the door to the nursery. The room still smelt of newborn babies, but all of the cots stood empty. She'd never seen this room — her favourite in the whole hospital — without any babies and a feeling of sadness washed over her. She stood with tears welling; one cot was overturned and the others were a mess of sheets where the babies had been hastily removed. She stooped down to pick up a knitted bootee that had been lost, and slipped it into her pocket.

Remembering Mrs O'Donnell's tea request, she

stepped into the kitchen opposite. A number of items had fallen down off the shelves, but the urn full of hot sweet tea still stood ready and waiting as always. She took a cup and started to fill it, pausing briefly as another explosion rattled the pots and pans.

Just as she returned onto the ward, her feet crunching on grit and plaster, the floor shook again and tea slopped from the cup. She steadied up the saucer as she passed Veronica's bed, turning for a moment to muster a reassuring smile. Getting into her stride, she started to move down the ward.

Whoof! For a split second it felt as if all the air had been sucked out of the ward and Mac thought her eardrums had burst. The cup fell from her hand and she saw the tea seeping, as if in slow motion, into a pool on the wooden floor. She felt herself screaming and her lungs were burning. She was trying to run, knowing that she needed to reach Sofia and Sister and the patients. She saw Myfanwy running towards her, her mouth open in a silent scream. There was a loud splintering of wood and cracks were opening up in the walls at the far end of the ward. A huge chunk of ceiling collapsed and crashed onto the floor closely followed by an avalanche of debris. She was coughing on dust now and she could hear gut-wrenching screams and the piercing cry of a baby. A heavy sound like a big machine winding down started to churn in her head and she felt as if she was falling. Then everything went black.

★　★　★

In the basement theatre, Jo lay on the floor, all breath sucked out of her by the blast that had brought with it an incredible splintering and crashing. She tried to get up; she couldn't remember where she was. She called out for Mac, but she couldn't hear the sound of her own voice.

When she staggered up from the floor, coughing on dust and pushing gritty straggles of hair back from her face, she saw that she was in theatre. The light was dim but she could make out the operating table tipped at an unwieldy angle and their patient, a Chinese merchant seaman brought in from the docks yesterday with a large piece of shrapnel deeply embedded in his right thigh, lay skew-whiff but still anaesthetised with a theatre towel clipped around his incision. She sensed some movement and Angus Dunbar reared up from the debris at the foot of the table, shaking his head, his face covered in white dust and bleeding from a cut above one eye. He coughed and wiped his face, and then staggered towards the patient, placing a hand on the man's body to hold him steady whilst he pushed down on the broken operating table, trying to straighten it. Jo moved to help, shaking her head gently until some hearing came back. They soon had their patient back in a safe position.

'We've been hit,' gasped Dunbar, 'we've been bloody hit. Where's Langley? Where the hell is he?'

'I don't know,' she croaked; there was no sign of him. She shook her head again, trying to make things clearer. She could hear the sound of falling masonry, of water gushing in through the shattered ceiling. At the top end of the table, all she could see was a pile of broken stone and plaster that had completely blocked the door. She wondered if Langley had managed to escape, but knew it would have been impossible. With a tightness in her chest that made her breath rasp, she hauled herself around the table. All she could see was fallen debris and dust everywhere.

It was then that she spotted a tuft of white hair sticking up. Poor Dr Langley, completely buried, just the top of his head and his bloodied face showing. She moved closer. He wasn't breathing. Taking in the amount of debris on his chest, Jo realised that it would have been impossible for him to breathe. She tried to keep calm; it wouldn't help anyone if she fell apart. She straightened up and shouted over to Dunbar, a sob catching in her voice, 'He's dead. He must have been killed instantly.'

She saw Dunbar's face contort and he took a searing breath. 'Right, Jo,' he croaked, 'I need you to go and get help. See if you can crawl out through that window.' He pointed towards the broken remains behind her. 'It should lead you up to ground level. I'll stay here and stabilise the patient, ready for transfer. I'd only made the first incision so although he's going to have to keep his piece of shrapnel for a little while longer, he should come out of this perfectly fine.'

She nodded, taking a deep breath; at least their patient was safe. Her head was buzzing and her ears were still ringing, but she needed to be alert, she needed to think about what might be required. Seeing some swabs, a little dusty but still in a neat pile on the bottom of the trolley, she grabbed a handful and passed them to Dunbar, who was checking his patient's vital signs. He took them, still swaying unsteadily on his feet, and began applying them as a temporary dressing over the open wound.

Grabbing a towel from the trolley, Jo turned to the window and used it to remove the bigger shards of glass and pull out broken pieces of the wooden frame.

Leaning out a little way, through the dust she could see a glimmer of light above. With all the rubble lying in the passageway, she was far from sure that there was any way through, but she had no choice. She had to go.

'Can you make it?' called Dunbar.

'Yes,' she said, pulling her surgical mask back into position to help shield against the dust.

Carefully, she began to climb through the window. She was almost the other side when she felt a shard of glass rip through her stocking and cut into her leg. The searing pain made her gasp, sending a hard pulse through her body. It stung so much that it brought tears to her eyes; she was bleeding, but she had to press on. Coughing on dust, despite the mask, she felt her way through the dark passageway, crawling over rubble that ripped at her hands and knees. Finally, she came to a large stone lintel across her path, scrabbling over it, she was able to emerge at ground level. The light that had guided her way came from the many fires that burnt all around, their yellow flames licking through open space, up to the night sky. She pulled her mask away, gazing up to the stars for a moment, seeing the flicker of anti-aircraft guns and the spotlights continually tracing patterns across the sky. She felt lost, standing there, trying to make sense of everything.

Then something broke through, a voice, shouting hysterically — the ambulance station had been hit by an incendiary bomb. She looked to the back of the hospital to see a tower of yellow flame blazing towards the sky, and the outline of a burning vehicle. Then another explosion sounded and a broken wall crashed to the ground. She gasped and turned quickly; she needed to get inside the hospital and find help. Thinking she could walk down the side of the building and in through the front door, she started to stumble her way across.

A cold dread of realisation almost stopped her heart, and she had to clutch her chest to stop herself from falling to her knees. The walls of the hospital had gone. Unwieldy girders now hung down from what had been the upper floors. At least half of the building had been ripped wide apart.

'Help! Help me!' she screamed, swaying as she stood, both arms wrapped tight around her own body. Feeling an arm around her shoulders and a soothing voice in her ear she turned to find a fireman beside her, saying, 'Come on, nurse, we need to get you away from here.'

'No!' she shouted. In an instant she remembered what she had come for and she pointed down the side of the wrecked building.

'There are people trapped, a surgeon and his patient, down in the basement. I crawled out through a window. That way, down there.'

The fireman shouted for assistance and tightened his grip on her shoulders. 'Come with me, you've had a nasty shock. I need to get you to a treatment station. Come along—'

'No!' she repeated, wrenching free. 'No… I have to find my friend Mac and my colleagues. And see if there are any patients still—' Her chest heaved with a huge sob that stopped her from speaking, and the fireman tried once more to persuade her, but she staggered away, shaking her head. 'I'm a nurse, I have to help with the rescue.'

Making her way through chunks of stone and brick

and jagged pieces of metal, she saw a woman holding a baby, being helped away by another fireman. She stumbled towards her. The woman had blood in her hair and she was covered in dust, but she could make out a bright pink bed jacket.

'Did you come from the maternity ward?' she shouted, her voice hardly loud enough above the roar of the fire and falling masonry. The woman was crying hysterically, clinging to her baby, but she nodded vigorously. 'Is there anyone else alive up there?'

'It's all gone,' wailed the woman. 'The walls fell in. I couldn't see anyone, I just grabbed my baby and I ran, I just ran.'

9

Four fire engines pumped water onto the fires, damping them down, but Jo didn't have time to wait for the blaze to be out. She scrambled over chunks of masonry and splintered wood, pushing her way into what she could only imagine used to be the hospital entrance and, of course, the Casualty waiting area. No staff, no patients. She could see the splintered remains of one or two benches and some ragged streamers of bandage mixed in with other rubble, the only signs of what the area had once been. If she'd been here with Mac again tonight...

There was no time to feel the shock of it. She could hear shouts and someone screaming. She needed to help — and she needed to find Mac.

Almost growling with anger or sorrow, she didn't even know what it was, she pushed herself on, over more debris. Ahead, she saw two nurses covered in dust, their aprons torn and starched collars hanging loose, one at each end of a stretcher, carrying a patient who was sobbing loudly as he held onto his own drip bottle.

'Can you manage?' she shouted.

'Yes,' they shouted back, bravely striding through what used to be a corridor.

She saw two junior staff nurses without caps, hair hanging loose, frantically clawing at the ground, moving rubble with their hands. She stumbled over to them, almost tripping on a body covered in dust. She stooped down to check — no breathing, no pulse. Just

106

as she was reaching the nurses, she passed a second body. 'They're both dead,' one of the nurses shouted, then straightened up, her eyes wide and her breath coming quick. 'But there's someone alive under here, we heard them making a noise.'

Jo helped, clawing at pieces of stone and throwing them aside. At last, they uncovered the shape of a person, groaning loudly. 'Dr Hedley?' Jo called, as the casualty struggled up into a sitting position, coughing. As they helped him to stand, he screamed out in pain. 'His arm is broken,' Jo said, grabbing it and bracing it against his body.

'Aaargh, yes, fractured humerus I think,' he croaked, still coughing.

'I need to find something to make a sling for you,' Jo said, indicating for the nurses to continue supporting him.

She found her way towards what was left of the casualty treatment area. All the carefully stacked clean bandages and dressings were scattered wide and mixed with debris. She grabbed a handful and stuffed them in her pocket, but she couldn't find a triangular bandage. A bed sheet still covered one of the upturned examination couches. She grabbed it and pulled it free, knowing that she could make any number of slings and bandages with the fabric. As she walked, she pulled out the scissors that she always carried attached to her pocket on a chain and began to cut a square of fabric out of the sheet.

When she returned, Dr Hedley was rubbing his face with his free hand, still supported by one of the nurses. The other nurse was frantically checking the piles of rubble and tangled wreckage for more casualties. 'I've made a sling,' Jo called, dropping the remains of the sheet and quickly folding her cotton square into a triangle.

'There's more cloth there for makeshift bandages or slings. I can manage here, you help your friend,' she instructed the nurse who was still supporting Dr Hedley. He was hanging his head now and quietly sobbing.

'It's alright,' she reassured him, 'you're just in shock, that's all.'

He shook his head and when he spoke his voice was broken, 'Why did I agree to them using our hospital for casualties? We were too close to the target area… too close. We should have evacuated months ago.'

'You had no idea how things might turn out, no one could have imagined that the Germans would hit a hospital.' But inside she knew, she knew that she had indeed imagined it and she'd often worried about it happening.

She took hold of his broken arm, bending it at the elbow. 'Now, hold onto your arm, you know the drill. And I'll apply the sling.' She had the point of the cloth triangle at his elbow and reached up to pull the ends of the makeshift sling into a knot at the back of his neck. Feeling in her pocket for a safety pin, she secured the sling at the elbow. She felt him heave a sigh, and she patted his good arm. 'As you know, this is going to be sore for a while, and you should get properly checked over. The ambulances will be here by now.'

But he was shaking his head. 'No,' he said, meeting her eyes with a steely gaze, 'I'm not going anywhere yet. I have work to do.'

'You can't work like this, Dr Hedley.'

He pressed his lips into a firm line. She knew that

she had no choice but to let him go. As he staggered away, Jo heard a shout from one of the nurses. They'd found Sister Reynolds, who stood coughing on dust with blood pouring from a gash above her eye. 'Where are my nurses?' she was calling and when she didn't get an answer she began shouting, her voice slip-sliding into uncharacteristic panic.

Jo stepped forward. 'Sister Reynolds, we've been hit by a bomb. The nurses are helping the injured.' She could see a wild look of disbelief in Sister's eyes. 'You have a wound above your eye, let me put a dressing on...' She indicated for one of the nurses to hold onto her as she pulled one of the dressings from her pocket and applied firm pressure.

'Thank you,' Sister gasped, and then she gave a loud sob. 'It happened so fast, I couldn't get to the patients... Are any of them—?'

'We haven't been able to find them yet,' Jo replied, keeping her voice as steady as she could.

Sister shook her head. Tears were making tracks down her dust-covered face. Jo could never have imagined that she would ever see Sister crying.

One of the nurses handed Jo a bandage and she applied it to keep the dressing in position. Sister reached up a hand to wipe her eyes and then she took a deep breath. 'I can't feel any damage other than this cut above my eye. So let me go, nurses, let me go. I can help you.'

They released their hold and she swayed a little but then she dusted herself off, smoothing down her starched apron and pulling back her shoulders. 'Right, let's do what we can.'

As she lurched, unsteady with her first step, one of the nurses tried to take hold of her again. 'Don't fuss me,' she called, straightening up immediately. 'Now, let's work as a team, there must be others still lying buried. Nurse Ruth Lee was making her way out of the treatment room to the waiting area, let's see if we can work out where she might be.'

'I need to find someone else first,' Jo called, starting to move away. As much as she wanted to help Sister, she had to go for Mac.

The staircase to the upper floors of the hospital still stood, a testament to endurance with everything in front lying in ruins. The brass bannister shone, reflecting the light of the fires. Jo paused for a moment at the bottom and looked up, she could hear the crashing of timbers above and the ground shook as bombs continued to fall nearby. But she knew that she had to go up there. If she was to going to stand any chance of finding Mac, she had to.

She had barely taken three steps when she heard what sounded like the crunching of gravel and raised voices on the steps up ahead of her. She waited; whoever it was, was close, and she might need to help them. A group of young soldiers came down the stairs, an amputee on crutches, and two with bandaged heads who were cradling an injured patient between their bodies. 'Have you seen Nurse Goodwin?' Jo called. 'Is she safe?'

'She's injured, but she's coming out,' one of them called, as they moved past her, heading out of the building. Her mind raced; what kind of injury did Amy have? She would go to her ward first before she went up to Maternity. She wondered fleetingly why the young soldiers hadn't gone to the shelter, but then she remembered Amy telling her that they point-blank refused to move. Many of them had seen active service under heavy fire at Dunkirk, and they didn't see the point.

As she started to ascend, another soldier came by with his arm around a shell-shocked man who was crying and shaking violently. The soldier gave her a nod and said, 'You need to watch your step up there, nurse.' Before she could reply or think about pushing ahead, another shape emerged from the gloom: a broad-shouldered man with bandaged arms, carrying the tiny figure of a nurse in a crumpled uniform.

'Amy?' she gasped, seeing her friend, one lens of her round glasses smashed, cradled in the arms of Robert Croasdale. 'Are you alright? Are you injured?'

Amy tried to smile. 'Just a badly sprained ankle, I think. When the blast hit, I was thrown across the ward. Robert saw me, and I don't know how he did it, but he scrambled out of his bed and pulled me clear of a beam that was about to fall.'

'Well done, Robert.' Jo could see a glint of pride on his face. 'I'm going up to Maternity to see if I can find Mac — she was up there with Myfanwy.'

Amy nodded grimly and reached out a hand to her. 'They were higher up than us, I don't know how things will be up there.'

Jo gave her hand a squeeze. 'I'll see you soon, Amy, and hopefully I'll have Mac and Myfanwy with me as well. Now you need to get going.'

Robert gave a grimace of pain as he shifted Amy's weight in his arms but once he had her settled, he was steady as a rock. Jo had never seen or heard of a rescue quite like that one. She gazed after them for a moment, tears welling in her eyes. But she needed to press on.

Up she went, to the next level. There was more

debris on the stairs now and the edge of one section of the staircase had collapsed. She knew that she had to trust in the soundness of the surviving wall as she clung onto the brass bannister to keep herself steady. She could hear the horrible throbbing drone of bombers and the enormous whump of the bombs that continued to fall beyond the shattered walls of the hospital. She had to believe that once a building had been bombed, it couldn't be hit again.

She forced herself on, up another level, and found herself, at last, by the blown out remains of the door to Maternity. She could hear voices below on the other floors — fire and ambulance crews calling for survivors. The remains of the door hung in splinters, she ducked around it and then managed to stumble her way past a couple of upended wheelchairs and some twisted debris. Fighting her way through, as she fully entered the ward, she clapped a hand across her mouth in shock. Some beds nearest the door remained intact; one even still made up with sheets. The long wooden ward table lay upturned at an angle and one or two cots were mangled and tipped over, discarded on the floor. But what lay beyond took her breath away. The rest of the room was gone, the walls and ceiling collapsed into a gaping hole with floorboards ripped up around it, partly filled with broken stone and plaster and the twisted metal remains of beds.

Jo sobbed into her dusty hands. No one could have survived at the far end of the ward. No one. Even so, she inched towards it, past the beds. She saw broken cups and a knitted teddy bear amongst the debris as she picked her way across, carefully, one hand still clamped across her mouth. She didn't want to get too close; she didn't want to look down and see what might be there. But it was the only way she could search for Mac. She crept closer to the edge, feeling the creaking of the unstable building all around her. She paused for a second and stood to take a deep breath, her hands shaking. She breathed in and out slowly and started to count backwards from ten. It didn't help; she couldn't get beyond nine. Looking around, she tried to focus on the detail of her surroundings that were only lit by the flickering fire, the searchlights above and the light of the traitorous moon. She shuddered when she saw a crushed and discarded nurse's cap.

'Mac! Where are you?' she cried out in desperation. 'Mac!'

She heard a sound in reply, like the mewing of a cat. 'Mac?' she called once more and there it was again, answering, barely sounding human. Then it grew louder without any further prompting and she realised with a lurch of her heart exactly what the sound was. It was the cry of a baby, piercing now and rising in intensity.

'A baby, it's a baby!' she shouted to someone, no one, then fell quiet when, with a shuddering shift of the floor beneath her, she remembered the precariousness of her position. She strained her ears, still buzzing from the blast. She had to locate where the cry was coming from. She held her breath and tipped her head to one side, waiting for the next pitiful wail. She had it. The cry was coming from underneath a thick portion of collapsed ceiling that sat terrifyingly close to the gaping chasm in the floor.

Jo gritted her teeth, her whole body straining towards rescuing the baby. There was no room for recklessness; she knew that she would have to weigh up every single move if she was going to succeed.

The chunk of plaster rested flat above something she had to assume, given that the baby was clearly alive, could only be one of the cast iron cots. Fallen brick and chunks of stone rested on top of the plaster. She began to remove each piece carefully with both hands, drawing on all her strength for the bigger shards of stone. She kept working, digging deeper as the baby continued to cry. By the time she lifted the final piece of debris, the baby's cry was weakening. She needed to move fast. The piece of ceiling was big; she knew that she had no choice but to push and slide it away, down into the crater. It was risky; if she pushed too hard and the cot wasn't wedged on something, she could push the whole thing over. But this was her only chance.

She braced herself against the plaster and pushed, using all the strength she could summon in her arms and legs. It hardly budged. 'Grrrr!' she shouted in sheer frustration. 'Think, Jo, think!'

She leant over to check the other side of the fallen ceiling and moved some debris that could have been holding it back. Once more, she braced herself, 'One, two, three, pushhh!' The plaster started to give. She was fired up now, her heart thumping in her chest and her breath coming quick. Gritting her teeth and tasting blood in her mouth, with a final effort the chunk of ceiling fell away with a deadening crunch.

At first all Jo could see was grey dust, then she saw movement and a tiny hand poked out through a layer of grit. She could see the baby's head and in seconds she had the child scooped up and she could feel its tiny body warm against her own. The baby coughed, choking on the dust. Jo crouched down, pressing an ear to the tiny chest, but all she could hear was the sound of her own pulse, throbbing with fear. Wiping dust from the baby's face, she peered closer. She could see white skin, maybe the blink of an eye, and a full head of dark hair. Then the baby began to whimper and she felt it squirm against her; she knew, at last, that it was properly alive. Jo could feel her body shaking as she pulled up her theatre gown and used it to wrap the baby, cradling it in the crook of her arm, as a surge of emotion welled up from the pit of her stomach. With tears pouring down her cheeks she stood rocking and soothing the baby, knowing that there was very little chance that the child's mother had survived.

With her heart still pounding, Jo picked her way carefully through the broken ward towards the door. She squeezed through the narrow gap, protecting the baby against her body, retracing her steps back down the stairs as she heard the sounds of a rescue on a lower floor.

As soon as she made it down the last few steps, a nurse with dusty white hair and a bloodstained apron was by her side, helping her. She didn't realise until the nurse spoke that it was Sister Marks. Jo almost fell into her arms.

'Nurse Brooks, thank God you're safe,' cried Sister, her voice thick with emotion. 'And you have a baby? Where have you found this little one?'

'Up on Maternity, I was looking for my friend, Mac. I heard the baby crying and found it trapped in a cot.' Her chest felt tight and she had to fight to stop herself from sobbing out loud. 'But I couldn't find anyone apart from this little one alive up there.'

Sister Marks nodded and took her arm. 'Right, Nurse Brooks, do you want to give the baby to me? I'll take her to the clinic around the corner, that's where the casualties are gathering.'

Jo glanced down at the tiny bundle in her arms, reluctant now to part with it. She felt a strange ownership as the newborn gently squirmed against her body. But the baby needed to be checked over and fed — and Jo needed to continue her search for Mac. 'Yes, you can take it,' she said, 'but if there's a name band, can we just have a look. I don't even know if it's a boy or a girl.'

Sister Marks produced a torch and shone it onto the baby's arm; there was a name tag and she read the inscription out loud. 'Lucia Gazzi... born second of May nineteen forty-one, weight seven pounds four ounces.'

Mac had told Jo all about the beautiful baby girl whom she'd delivered only yesterday. 'Little Lucia,' she murmured, leaning down to look closely at her one more time before giving her a gentle kiss goodbye and handing her over. 'Promise me, Sister Marks, you'll let me know where they send her, so I know that she's safe.'

'I will,' Sister nodded. 'I will... But why don't you come with us, we need to get you checked over...'

She was shaking her head. 'I'm fine, I'm absolutely fine. I need to help with the rescue...'

'Nurse Brooks,' Sister said firmly — Jo steeled herself for a battle, but when she looked up Sister Marks was smiling. 'Take this torch, it might help you find your friend.'

As Jo stumbled away, Lucia started to cry. It made her pulse quicken again; she needed to find Mac, she needed to tell her that the baby was safe. Spurred on, her mind felt clearer and she was able to think through what she needed to do next — if Mac was alive she wasn't on the maternity floor, but it was possible that she might have fallen through to the floor below. If that was the case, then she might be lying seriously injured.

10

Jo knew that she would have to head up the stairs again. But as she approached, she saw a teenage boy carrying a small girl with a bandaged head. The child was Polly and she was clinging to her cloth dolly. She held back just for a moment, wanting to make sure that everything was alright, grabbing the boy's arm before he shot by. 'Where are you taking her?'

'Don't worry, Miss,' he said, slightly out of breath. 'They've managed to open up the basement shelter so me and my mates, he indicated other lads helping patients or carrying children, we live nearby and we're helping to get 'em out. I found this little girl in a big iron cot.'

'I see. Take good care of her. She's called Polly and her family were killed in an air raid. She's an orphan.'

The boy looked at Polly's face and then he pulled her in more closely. 'That's alright, Miss,' he said, 'I'll ask the ambulance woman to have a look at 'er, then I'll take her home to my mam. We only live across the street. She'll look after 'er for now.'

'Thank you,' she said, patting his arm. As the boy set off, Jo saw Polly put both arms around his neck and snuggle in close.

In the next moment another bomb fell close and Jo saw the ruined walls shake. She felt adrenaline pulse once, hard, throughout her body. And instead of cowering in terror, she ran up the stairs without any hesitation, moving nimbly, knowing where to take care — and at each level making a mental note of what floor she was on so she could be absolutely sure that she found the ward immediately below Maternity. There was no door at all here and she could see that the far end of the ward had also collapsed into a large crater; a blackout on one window was still intact but hanging ripped and askew and there were shards of glass everywhere. Bed tables, broken pottery and upturned beds obstructed her progress as she pushed her way through.

'Mac!' she screamed, 'Mac!' But all she could hear in return were the sounds of the rescue still going on below and the bombs that continued to fall on the city.

She clicked on the torch, flashing it slowly over the room, not knowing what she was looking for. 'Mac... Mac!'

The torch flickered. 'Damn! Don't you dare die on me now!' She banged the torch against her thigh and the beam came back. Panning slowly over the debris once more, something snagged her sharp eye. She angled the beam of light back again, checking if she was right. 'Yes,' she cried out, seeing a snip of royal blue — a staff nurse's uniform. She ran forward and got on her knees, frantically clawing at the debris. As she dug, she could see a large lump of stone lying across the casualty's chest — and straight away Jo knew that she wasn't breathing. 'Mac,' she sobbed. 'No...'

Then she noticed dark hair and felt a flood of relief, before quickly realising that this was another nurse who had died, one of her colleagues, some poor soul going about her work, trying to help others, just as Jo was. She looked closer, and a sob heaved up from the pit of her stomach. It was Myfanwy, poor Myfanwy.

Jo cried angry tears as she pushed the stone off her friend's chest. She pushed the soft hair away from her face. Then she reached for Myfanwy's hand, saying a silent prayer. 'I'm so sorry,' she murmured, putting an arm beneath her, 'I'm so sorry that this has happened to you.'

Jo began to move her friend's body over a little, so that she would be found when the rescue team eventually came up with stretchers. Once she had her clear, she leant down to give her a kiss on the cheek. She felt as if she could have lain down there beside Myfanwy and howled with grief, but instead, she grabbed the torch and forced herself to stand.

Her hand was shaking as she shone the light across the room. Then, she saw it: another tiny glimpse of royal blue.

'I'm coming!' she shouted, as she scrambled over to the spot, holding the torch steady so as not to lose the flash of blue. She quickly removed the plaster, uncovering two legs in ripped silk stockings ; the legs were still warm, and the casualty's chest was rising and falling. She had to move fast. Holding back sobs, she kept working until she could see the casualty's head — her starched cap was missing, her face and hair were covered in dust. 'Mac,' she sobbed, 'Mac!' Her heart lurched; the hair was dark, but then she quickly realised it was sticky blood.

'Mac!' she repeated over and over as she frantically tried to rouse her — but there was no response. Mac was unconscious, but still breathing; when Jo lifted her wrist to check the radial pulse, it was strong. She methodically felt over her arms, ribs and legs for any obvious fracture; all seemed well, which was remarkable given that she must have fallen from the ward above. Thank goodness the section of floor she had landed on had held strong — if it hadn't, there would have been no chance of Mac surviving. And if she'd been hit, as Myfanwy had, by a heavy piece of rubble…

There was no time to think — there was every chance that the floor would still collapse beneath them. She needed to stabilise Mac's condition and then call for help; they both needed to get out of here. The sudden image of her mother, receiving a call on the black telephone in the parlour, getting news that her only child was dead, was enough to stimulate Jo to act quickly. She pulled out a dressing and a bandage from her pocket. It was hard to see by torchlight, particularly amidst all Mac's hair, but she could make out a cluster of wounds that extended from the scalp onto her forehead — she could tell already that her friend would have a nasty scar. But right now, the most pressing concern was internal injury — could the trauma have caused a bleed on the brain? Had there been any other irreparable damage? Despite the anxiety that tightened her chest, she knew that she needed to function properly, to be alert and ready to take action. Positioning the dressing pad over the wound, she secured the bandage as fast as she could.

'I need to go and get help,' she said, as she removed her theatre gown and folded it into a makeshift pillow so that she could rest Mac's head more gently on the ground. As she straightened up again, she heard the 'all clear'. It sounded hollow, meaningless now that her world had already been blown apart.

At the top of the stairs she screamed so loudly that she thought her lungs might burst. 'Help! I need help! We have a live one up here. We have a live one!'

As soon as she heard a response from two floors below, she went back to Mac and Myfanwy. Moments later, Bessie fought her way into the space, leading the stretcher team.

'Over here!' Jo shone her torch to guide them.

'Nurse Brooks, is that you?' said Bessie. 'And is this our Nurse MacDonald?'

'Yes,' Jo said firmly, forcing back tears as she gave Bessie the relevant information. When she pointed to the lifeless form of Myfanwy just a few strides away, she let herself cry openly.

Jo insisted on waiting with Myfanwy while Bessie and the ambulance crew took Mac to safety, despite the danger to herself. It seemed like the only thing she could do for her now. She knelt beside her, holding her hand, whispering another prayer. Myfanwy was the sweetest, kindest person she had ever known, she would do anything for anybody... That this could happen to someone as gentle and generous as her, it was inexplicable.

When Jo finally descended the stairs behind the crew bearing the shrouded stretcher that carried Myfanwy's body, she started to feel the first wave of exhaustion hit her. She didn't want to leave Myfanwy here, waiting with the rest of the fatalities to go to an overcrowded mortuary somewhere in Liverpool, but she had no choice, she needed to make sure that Mac was safe. She placed a hand on her lifeless body to say goodbye before they placed her in line with the other deceased.

Emerging from the ruin of the hospital to where the ambulances were waiting, she could see Bessie beside Mac's stretcher, about to be evacuated, and felt a surge of relief that her friend was alive. She looked across to the Nurses' Home, yearning to retreat to the safety of her room, to go back in there and peel off her clothing. She peered through the smoke and her breath caught, the home had gone as well; what remained of it was collapsed in on itself, no more than a pile of rubble. She glanced down at her ruined uniform; all she had was the clothes she stood up in. Raising a hand to her head she realised that her theatre cap was long gone and her hair had partially unravelled down her back. Now, she just felt completely numb, beyond sorrow, beyond anything at all except the knowledge that at least she had found Mac.

A deep, unmistakeable voice broke through, calling her name. It was Dunbar, still in his dusty, now heavily bloodstained theatre gown, a cloth mask hanging around his neck, his hair white with dust.

She realised she couldn't speak. He came straight to her and put an arm around her shoulders. 'This has been a hell of a night for all of us. You look like you've been fighting the enemy single handed, Nurse Brooks.' She raised a hand instinctively, trying to fend off being given any sort of special recognition.

'We've all been fighting,' she croaked, her voice quiet against the crack of the fires and the low rumble of collapsing masonry. Her chest felt tight and she cleared her throat.

'What about Langley?'

'I stayed back, so that I could help dig him out of the rubble, and I carried him...'

Jo felt his arm around her shoulders grow tense. She stepped away from him and patted his arm as he stood with his head bowed. 'I'm glad you did that.'

He looked up with an exhausted smile. 'Well, don't tell anyone — confirmed atheist that I am — but I

123

even said one of those special little prayers that he was so fond of.'

'That was absolutely the right thing to do. And, I, well… I said one of those prayers as well, for my friend, Myfanwy Jones. I found her on the maternity ward. I think she must have been killed instantly…'

'Sorry to hear that Brooks — but what were you doing up there? It was only supposed to be rescue teams.'

'I was looking for my friend, Mac, and… I found her…' She pointed to the stretcher. 'She's unconscious; she has a head injury, but she's breathing.'

He moved over to the stretcher. 'Ah, yes, Nurse MacDonald,' he said, lifting the bottom of the bandage so he could take a peek at the wound. 'That's going to be a challenge to suture, and we'll have to check that there's no depressed fracture, but I think I can make a reasonable job of it.'

'So you can do it?'

'Well, we'll have to wait till we get to Broadgreen hospital, that's where they've been taking all of our stretcher cases. But yes, I'll make sure that I do.'

Jo approached Bessie, who was standing propped against the ambulance, her head bowed. Bessie tried to smile, but her face was rigid and tears were welling in her eyes. 'I should have been dead tonight,' she croaked. 'It should have been me…'

With a jolt, Jo remembered what she'd seen of the ambulance station. She put an arm around Bessie's shoulders. 'Did you lose a friend?'

Bessie nodded, wiping her tears away with the flat of her hand, 'I lost more than one; most of the drivers in there were killed… I'd swapped, you see, I'd swapped with Lillian Askew, she was due to go back

124

out but she looked awful, she was exhausted, so I told her to get a cup of tea and I'd go instead...'

'Oh, Bessie, I'm so sorry, but you couldn't have known.'

Jo felt Bessie take a ragged breath and then she nodded, pulling her uniform straight. 'We've all suffered losses tonight,' she said wearily, pushing her tin hat firmly into place, 'but we need to keep going, don't we, so let's get our Nurse MacDonald to Broadgreen.'

As Bessie took the bottom of Mac's stretcher, Jo looked up and saw Dr Hedley being loaded into the back of another ambulance. He was groaning in pain and holding onto his arm, still bound with her bedsheet sling.

'He wouldn't listen, he carried on treating patients with one arm,' Bessie called. 'The man deserves a bloody medal.'

Dunbar helped Bessie slide Mac's stretcher into the back of the ambulance. Then, he stood aside for Jo to clamber into one of the seats, jumping in next to her before Bessie slammed the doors shut. Reaching inside his trouser pocket, he pulled out two broken biscuits and a small hip flask. 'You'll be right as rain after one of these and a tot of rum,' he said with a smile. Jo was willing to try anything, so she took two halves of biscuit and ate them quickly, before washing them down with a big swig from the hip flask. She coughed a little, then took another gulp, before wiping her mouth with the back of her hand and passing the flask back to Dunbar.

The ambulance lurched as they started to move, so she quickly grabbed hold of Mac's arm to steady her. She felt a breeze on her face as the vehicle picked up speed.

125

'Sorry about the ventilation but we took a hit from a flying brick that smashed out the windscreen,' Bessie called back to them.

'That's the least of our worries, Mrs Wright,' Dunbar replied, tapping a cigarette out of his pack. Jo shook her head when he offered her one, but she did accept another tot from the hip flask and was glad of the warm glow in the pit of her stomach.

'Bloody idiots,' Bessie swore loudly as she swerved to avoid two men in RAF uniform who were running down the middle of the street. Jo gasped as the ambulance lurched; the men had leapt out of the way, but only just in time. She had every confidence in Bessie, however, as she sat at the wheel surrounded by broken glass, steadily guiding them around potholes and through falling debris, as they bumped their way safely across the ruined city.

11

It had taken a while after the 'all clear' sounded for Don and Zach to make it back up to street level from their subterranean air raid shelter.

'Well, that's the last time I do that. I'll be back at the bar next time.' Don coughed, dusting the grit from his hair. 'And that man singing and those children crying didn't help either.'

Zach was shaking his head. 'It was a hell of an experience, trapped down there... I sure could do with a drink right now.'

'Well, there's a pub across the road, if we can get through these people... Let's get a pint to wet our whistle.'

As they surged towards the door of the pub with a mass of eager civilians, Don jostled shoulders with a half-drunk man who was slurring incomprehensibly one moment and shouting the next, 'Have you heard about the hoshpital?'

Don grabbed him by the arm. 'What hospital?'

'The hoshpital thas been hit.'

'Which hospital?' he yelled, gripping the man by the lapels.

'Steady on, mate,' hiccupped the man. 'It might be the Liverpool Royal.'

'What do you mean might be?'

The man was shaking his head now. Don, exasperated, shouted at the top of his voice. 'Which hospital has been hit?'

'Mill Road,' said one and then another voice called,

'Liverpool Royal.'

Don could feel his heart hammering against his ribs. He felt like he could explode with frustration.

'I've just spoken to a woman who said that it was definitely Mill Road,' Zach murmured quietly at his elbow. 'It took a direct hit.'

Don cried out, slumping as if he'd been punched in the gut. 'What if Mac's dead, Zach, what if she's dead?'

'You can't think like that. Come on, we have to move, we need to go and find her. Which way is Mill Road from here?'

They ran down the street, dodging past civilians still pouring out of shelters, Don leading the way with Zach following close behind.

They could see the fires still burning and hear falling masonry as they reached the wreck of the hospital. Don and Zach raced along the middle of a street blasted with holes and lined by bombed-out buildings. As they ran, neither of them saw the ambulance with the windscreen smashed out until the last minute. The vehicle swerved to avoid them and the ambulance woman hunched over the wheel swore loudly as she passed by.

Don paused for a split second and then ran again, straight up to a fireman who was still playing water onto the fire. 'Where are the nurses, have any been killed?' he shouted, wanting to shake the man when he took a few moments to understand what was being said. When the reply came, his heart jumped a beat.

'Some nurses and doctors killed, some injured.'

'Where are the survivors?'

'Walking wounded in the clinic around the corner. The last of the ambulances have just gone. If you're

128

looking for somebody, start with the clinic. It's that way, in the out-patients department. Bomb didn't touch it.'

Don nodded and Zach was by his side as they ran together in the direction that the fireman had indicated.

The clinic room was packed full of people with an assortment of bandages and only lit by one emergency lamp hanging from the ceiling. There were groans of pain and someone was sobbing. Don saw five or six women sitting on a bench, covered in dust, with shards of glass splinters in their hair, one of them nursing a baby. He went over and began asking them about the nurses. They all stared back blank-eyed, then the woman with the baby shook her head. Frantic, he turned to the rest of the room and shouted, 'Has anyone seen a nurse with red hair? Any nurses?' Most people just stared at him but then a boy with his arm firmly around the shoulders of a much younger child spoke up. 'The nurses were here and a doctor as well, but they've all gone to the hospital to help with the stretcher cases. We're just waiting for transport.'

'Which hospital? Where have they gone?' Don begged.

'Broadgreen.'

Don gasped. 'That's miles away, how are we going to get there?'

Zach grabbed his arm and said firmly, 'We're going to walk, and if someone gives us a lift, great, but if not we will get there, I promise you.'

12

Dawn had not yet broken as the ambulance came to a halt outside Broadgreen hospital. Jo, hit by exhaustion, had slumped forward to rest her head on the stretcher as they swayed their way through the streets. She came to with a jolt, immediately checking to make sure that Mac was safe. Dunbar uttered a low growl and then yawned loudly, unsettling the ambulance as he shifted his bulk, anxious to be out through the back doors.

Bessie wrenched open the doors to reveal a strange scene lit by muted yellow light — yet another fire burning vigorously.

'Looks like they've hit a gas main,' Dunbar called over his shoulder as he clambered down.

'And the lights have failed in the hospital,' muttered Bessie. 'A public shelter was hit just down the road — it put everything out. I had a narrow miss; it happened just before I arrived with the first load of casualties. All the poor souls in there were killed, not one survivor.'

Jo drew in a breath, feeling the dulled sadness of it all.

'Right, let's move,' called Dunbar, single-handedly pulling the stretcher out of the ambulance, with Jo grabbing the foot, determined to keep pace with him. As they approached the building, she could see silhouetted shapes of nurses and porters against a moonlit backdrop, ferrying patients and stretchers backwards and forwards across the hospital grounds.

Emergency lighting rigged up inside the hospital cast an eerie glow as they moved in through the door to an area littered with casualties. Staff were crouched over stretchers, setting up drips and blood transfusions by torchlight. A hollow-eyed surgeon met them head on — he seemed to know Dunbar. Jo stood with the stretcher, her eyes fixed on Mac, as the doctors exchanged information and the surgeon indicated that they should take her to a corner where two chairs stood ready to receive a stretcher.

As they picked their way through, Jo could see that one or two of the casualties lay very still, close to death; others were moaning in pain. One, struggling to breathe, was urgently attended by a nurse, desperately trying to apply an oxygen mask.

Dunbar glanced back and gave her a grim smile before sliding the stretcher into place. 'You stay with her and I'll go and get some supplies and a decent torch so we can have a better look at that wound.'

Left alone with Mac's face a pale, helpless moon in the semi-darkness, Jo felt the anxiety that had been lodged in her chest start to grow until it felt like a tight knot. She knelt down beside the stretcher, checking Mac's breathing, and began desperately whispering words of comfort — saying them to soothe herself more than anything.

Seeing the bright beam of light from Dunbar's new torch as he wove his way back through the casualties helped her to steady up. They had no table to accommodate the instruments or dressings, so Dunbar placed them unceremoniously on the bottom of the stretcher. 'I managed to get some fine suture thread,' he murmured as Jo started to unravel the bandage.

'That's good,' she replied, her voice flat as she

removed the bandage, revealing the blood-soaked dressing pad. She threw the bandage beneath the stretcher; there was nowhere else to put it. Then, ever so carefully, taking just the corner of the dressing, she pulled it away to reveal the ragged star-shaped wound on Mac's forehead. Tears stung her eyes, seeing the raw edges of the wound on Mac's beautiful face. She swallowed hard as Dunbar leant in to have a closer look.

Then he checked Mac's eyes, opening them gently with his fingers and shining the torch in. 'Pupils equal and reacting to light, so that's a good sign...' Handing the torch over, he took up a pair of forceps and started to lift pieces of broken skin, examining the wound, making it bleed afresh. Jo's stomach tightened.

'She's going to have significant scarring. She must have taken a direct hit from a piece of flying debris,' he said. 'I'll do the best job I can, but apart from making the sutures small and using this fine thread, there isn't much else I can do to stop your friend from having what you might call, a distinguishing mark, for the rest of her life.'

'I understand,' Jo replied, her voice quiet against the background noise of the waiting area.

'But the good news is there's no sign of a depressed fracture, so that's a relief. But obviously we don't know what might have happened deeper in the brain...' She looked at Dunbar, who was staring at her with concern. 'You alright, Brooks?'

'Yes,' she replied, making sure her voice sounded firm.

Dunbar pressed a double thickness of swabs against the wound, absorbing the blood so that he could have a better look. 'Right you are, my beauty,' he breathed, removing the swabs, 'at least it looks like the skin edges will come together.'

Jo held the torch steady as Dunbar took up the needle and suture thread. She daren't speak, not wanting to cause any distraction as he steadily put in each stitch — his large hands incredibly adept for such delicate work — leaving a network of tiny black sutures holding each broken area of skin together.

As he finished and straightened up from the stretcher, Mac gave a groan and started to move her head from side to side. Jo's breath caught, 'Mac, can you hear me?' she called gently. She was sure Mac was trying to open her eyes. She took up some clean swabs and pressed them firmly against the wound to absorb any excess blood and then she reached to the bottom of the stretcher for a clean dressing and a bandage.

'Might be best if she sleeps some more but it's a good sign that she's starting to wake up.' Dunbar sighed, for the first time beginning to sound weary. 'I need to go and find my colleague, see it there's anything I can do to help. It looks like they still have patients waiting to be seen.'

Jo reached out a hand to him. 'You should get some rest.' He replied with a grunt as he moved away, checking patients as he went.

As she applied the final loop of bandage around Mac's head, a crisp voice spoke to her from the other side of the stretcher. 'Do you need any help?'

Jo looked up to see a dark-haired nurse in a blood-stained apron. Her thin face was set in a sombre expression.

'I'm OK.' Jo tried to smile.

'If you've finished here, come with me and I'll get

133

you a cup of tea, find you a place to rest.'

'No, no,' she was already shaking her head, 'I have to stay with my patient.'

The nurse cleared her throat. 'I do understand, but Sister has given strict instruction for all the staff from Mill Road to be given food and drink and somewhere to rest. We know what you've all been through tonight.'

Jo straightened up, glancing down to her uniform, seeing her own apron torn, covered in dust and blood. She put a hand to her starched collar and found it was hanging loose. 'I'm fine, honestly...' But then she looked down at Mac, lying so pale and fragile on the stretcher, and her whole body began to shake, tears streaming down her face.

'There, there.' The nurse moved to her side. 'Were you in the hospital when the bomb hit?'

She nodded and continued to sob.

'You're still in shock... You need to come with me.'

'No, I can't leave her, I can't. She's my best friend. I have to stay with her.'

The nurse glanced around the room.

'Well if Sister comes, don't tell her that someone has already spoken to you. I'll go and get you a cup of tea, a sandwich, and a blanket. You can make space for yourself down on the floor, beside the stretcher. No one will see you there.'

'Thank you, thank you so much,' Jo croaked, overwhelmed with relief. 'What is your name?'

'Nurse Barker. Are you sure that you'll be alright? If you do want to get some rest, I can call by regularly and check on your friend.'

Jo took a ragged breath and wiped a trembling hand around her face. 'I will be fine... I'll be too anxious if

I leave her...'

As soon as Nurse Barker left, Jo slumped to her knees, her legs too weak to hold her. As she lowered herself against the wall, she felt a sharp pain in her lower leg. Looking down, she saw her stocking ripped and stuck with dried blood. Until then she hadn't even felt the injury from the broken glass, but now it was stinging and the pain made her feel like sobbing out loud. She tried to rest back, but her body was stiff and aching. Gratefully, she saw Nurse Barker approaching with food and drink and a blanket to put around her shoulders.

Wrapped in the prickly hospital blanket, she wolfed down a corned beef sandwich, amazed at how ravenous she was, then she savoured the best cup of hospital tea that she'd ever tasted. She remembered putting the cup down on the floor, kneeling up to check Mac one more time and then resting back against the wall with the blanket pulled close around her.

The next moment, or so it seemed, she could hear a man's voice breaking through her sleep, frantic and shouting, 'Mac! Mac!'

Jo shot up, her heart hammering, her mouth dry, not knowing where she was. Jo recognised the airman leaning over Mac's stretcher, it was Don, Mac's new man.

He looked up at Jo, his eyes wild. Behind him was a taller man in air force uniform. Jo thought she recognised him, but her mind was foggy, still trying to catch up with what had happened.

She pulled herself up at the side of the stretcher. 'She's going to be alright,' she managed to croak. 'She has a head injury but she's been showing signs of coming round.'

Don looked directly at her, but he didn't seem to be able to take in what she was saying. 'What happened to her? What's the bandage for?'

'She was on the maternity ward when the bomb hit and she fell through to the floor below. She has a head wound and she's unconscious, but she has been showing some signs of waking up.'

'Oh, Mac…' The man sobbed, clumsily wiping his eyes with the flat of his hand. His quiet friend stepped closer to take his arm. 'She's going to be just fine,' he murmured, and Jo realised that she had seen him before — he was the American with the lovely blue eyes.

Don seemed to calm down. He started to kiss Mac and was in danger of dislodging the bandage that Jo had so carefully applied. She moved swiftly around to his side of the stretcher.

'Look,' she said firmly. 'You should really go and get some rest yourself. I think they're serving tea and sandwiches somewhere in the hospital…'

'No,' he was saying, shaking his head, 'I need to stay here with her… Where will she be going? Will she stay here in the hospital?'

Jo reached out a hand to try and steady him. 'We will stay here at least for a while, but then when she's well enough, I'll probably take her home to the farm with me.' Jo hadn't thought ahead until this moment, but as she spoke she realised that this was the best possible plan.

'What farm, where is it?'

'It's called Bracken Farm and it's up north, towards Lancaster. Mac's visited us there a number of times, she loves it. I think it would be a good place for her to recover.'

He nodded distractedly. 'But they can't leave her here, on this stretcher, like this.'

'I'll make sure we find her a bed, but she'll have to stay in the hospital, until she recovers.'

He glanced at her, his eyes bright, almost fevered. He nodded and then he gave a huge sigh and his shoulders drooped. 'I know you will,' he murmured, and then looking up at her, calmer now, he said, 'You must be Jo, she told me about you.'

She nodded.

'Well that's fair enough, I know you'll do the best for her.' His voice was quiet now. 'I can't argue with that and you're a nurse, you know what you're doing.'

'Why don't you go with your friend and get yourselves a cup of tea and something to eat?'

He shook his head, 'No, no... there are so many people here in much more need than we are. And we need to get going, I'm due back at the base and Zach's got to catch a lift to Tadcaster this morning. Yes, we need to get going...'

He leant down to give Mac a gentle kiss on the cheek and then rooted in his pocket for a piece of paper. 'This is my number at the base. Call and ask for me, as soon as you have any news. Call me. I've put my name there... Don Costello.'

'Don Costello,' Jo repeated, folding the paper into a square and placing it in her pocket.'

'I will ring you, I promise.'

The American gave her a warm smile and then he put an arm around Don and led him away. Jo felt relief as she saw them retreating; she was just too exhausted to deal with more upset, more pain.

★ ★ ★

Mac was sure that she could hear someone calling her name. A man, it was a man. He sounded upset but she didn't recognise the voice. She couldn't wake up anyway, she was far too tired and she needed to be at work first thing, so whoever it was would have to wait. She just needed to sleep. Then she was disturbed again, this time a baby was crying. Screaming and crying. It was getting louder, why couldn't someone go and soothe the child — she needed to sleep. But still the baby screeched and she was beginning to feel frustrated. *Oh for God's sake, I'll have to get up and see to it myself.* She forced herself to open her eyes; she was so sleepy, she felt like she'd been drugged. The baby wasn't crying any more, thank goodness for that — she might at least be able to get some more sleep. But someone was shaking her. 'Mac, Mac, wake up...' A voice she recognised... Jo. Such a pest, what was she doing interrupting her sleep?

'Mac!' The voice was more urgent, louder.

She opened her eyes, 'What?' she spat, irritated now.

Jo was laughing, and then saying, 'She's awake, she's awake,' as if it was some kind of miracle.

'What?' Mac growled, her throat scratchy and her mouth dry. She realised that she couldn't see properly and there was something wrapped around her head. She reached up a hand to pull it off. It felt tight.

'No, don't pull at the bandage.'

'The what? What's going on?'

Then she could see Jo's face. Her friend was leaning over her bed — and she was crying.

'I'm not that late for work, am I?'

Jo was laughing and crying now. 'No, you're not late, you don't need to go to work, Mac. You've been

138

injured … the hospital was bombed last night.'

Mac shook her head from side to side. No, that couldn't be right.

She tried to sit up, but Jo told her to lie down. She reached up a hand to her head, feeling something that was like a bandage… What was going on?

Then she saw Jo's face again, more clearly this time. Her hair was in straggles; she was smudged with dust and blood. Mac drew in a sharp breath that rasped her throat. She felt a pain go through her chest and then, without warning, came the sensation of something hitting her body, taking her breath. She gasped for air, trying to sit up; it felt like her breath was stuck hard in her chest.

'You've been in a bomb blast and you have a head injury. You need to lie still …' Jo's voice sounded tinny, distanced, but Mac could tell that she was anxious. Then she felt Jo take her hand. The warmth of her skin and the firm pressure against her own made her start to calm down, and then she began to cry. Jo stroked her hand, soothing her, telling her everything was going to be alright. In the end she drifted back into a place where there was no pain, no worry. She was so tired, all she wanted to do was sleep and sleep and never wake up.

13

Now, in the morning light, Jo could see the true state of the room they were in. Some of the stretchers had been cleared, probably because their occupants had died, she thought to herself grimly. And she could see Nurse Barker coming towards her, neatly sidestepping casualties as she went. 'We've set up some washbowls in the room around the corner for you nurses, and before you say anything, you've no choice this time — we all need to keep body and soul together.' Jo took a breath. 'There are also some clean uniforms if you want them, and some food and cups of tea. And you should probably think about calling your family to let them know that you're safe — news of the hit on Mill Road has spread very quickly. There's a telephone in Sister's office.'

Jo glanced down at Mac on the stretcher: her breathing was steady, her pulse was strong. There was no reason why she couldn't leave her, but her chest felt tight with anxiety just thinking about it. 'I can keep an eye on your friend,' Nurse Barker said quietly. Jo knew that she would be giving exactly the same instruction if their roles were reversed. It was the right thing to do. She'd seen Mac wake up and she'd spoken a few words. And just thinking about the washbowl made her more aware of the dried sweat on her body. Her scalp began to itch with all the dust in her hair. She needed to strip off her blood-stained uniform and dispose of it.

As soon as she walked into the room set aside for

the nurses, she recognised a small, hunched figure on a bench. 'Amy, are you alright?'

Amy straightened up and tried to smile. She couldn't speak for a moment and her voice was shaky when it came. 'What a night, hey. I'm just trying to take stock of who's here and who isn't… I've not seen Mac, did you…?'

'Mac's safe. She has a head injury but she's starting to wake up. I think she's going to be OK.'

'Oh, thank God.' Amy grabbed Jo's hand and gave it a squeeze.

'Have you seen Ruth or Myfanwy?'

'I don't know anything about Ruth but…' She knew there was no easy way of saying it, so it came straight out, and even as she was telling it she felt distanced from the words, as if she was repeating something quite ordinary. 'I found Myfanwy with Mac; they'd both fallen through from the maternity ward to the floor below. She was just lying there, with a heavy chunk of plaster on her chest … she was dead.'

Amy shook her head, tears welling. 'Isn't this terrible,' she sobbed, removing her broken glasses so she could wipe her eyes. 'And so many patients killed as well.'

Jo put an arm around her shoulders and held onto her until she'd stopped crying. 'Come on,' she said, glancing over to the long wooden table set with washbowls. 'Let's wash off some of this muck and then we can get a cup of tea.'

Amy stood but immediately shouted out in pain and sat straight back down again. 'I can't walk, I think my ankle might be broken,' she said, staring down at the bandage on her leg. 'I don't think I'd still be alive if it hadn't been for Robert. He was so brave, he must

141

have been in agony but he carried me all the way to the ambulance. Fancy being rescued by one of your own patients...'

'I know, it was incredible. Is Robert OK?' Jo asked gently.

'Yes, he's gone to the male ward with all of his soldier mates — they are such brave lads.' Amy's voice broke as she started crying again.

'They are...' Jo headed to the table to bring a washbowl back for Amy.

There were other nurses standing either side of the table washing their hands and faces. She recognised the two who she'd helped to rescue, Dr Hedley and Sister Reynolds. They glanced in her direction and nodded an acknowledgement, their faces pale and exhausted.

All of the nurses were stripping off their uniforms and changing into fresh clothes. After carefully removing her fob watch and the contents of her pockets and placing them neatly on the table, Jo followed suit, leaving her Mill Road uniform discarded in a heap on the floor. She started to feel better as soon as her arms were exposed to the air and she could see the clean white of her petticoat. She took up a flannel and dipped it in the warm water, taking her time to squeeze it out, before slowly wiping her face. Then, she washed her arms and her hands, over and over, needing to clean away the dust from the night before, squeezing and wiping, squeezing and wiping until her skin was reddened. Still on the bench, Amy had washed and now sat with a damp flannel pressed to her face, her broken metal-rimmed glasses sitting forlornly beside her.

Moving to a stack of uniforms to find her size, Jo

soon felt the benefit of clean fabric against her skin. She did feel better, but all she truly needed was to go back to the Nurses' Home and lie in the cast iron bath and wash her hair with fresh shampoo and rinse and rinse and rinse everything away. She couldn't believe that it was all gone — the rooms, the bath, the little kitchen with a gas burner. All gone in an instant.

She walked back to the table to collect her scant belongings, taking up the fob watch first and pinning it into place, then her scissors, notepad and pencil, and the piece of paper that Don had given her, pushing each of them carefully into their allotted pockets.

She was anxious now to get back to Mac and she realised how much she needed to visit the WC, then make a telephone call. 'I need to get going,' she said quietly to Amy. 'I'll come back and see you later. I'm going to speak to someone about getting you an X-ray on that ankle.'

Amy removed the flannel. 'That's a good idea, typical nurse, I told them when they offered that it was fine, it was just a sprain.'

Jo gave her hand a squeeze, 'Don't worry, I'll sort it, and I'll see you later.'

'See you later,' Amy said, tears welling in her eyes again.

Jo kissed the top of her head.

Alone in the bathroom, Jo was shocked when she straightened up from the sink and caught her reflection in the mirror. Her face shone clean, but her hair was dishevelled and thick with dust. She took the clip that held it in the semblance of a knot and shook it loose; her hair felt coarse and sticky in her hands as she tried to tidy it back and fix it in her usual style. Suddenly angry, she yanked at it with both hands, wanting to feel the pain. And then she knew what she needed to do. She pulled out her scissors and without a moment's hesitation started to cut away the length of it, chunks of hair falling into the sink, startlingly black against the cracked enamel as she hacked all the way round. Then, still not satisfied, she cut again, making it shorter this time, closer to her head. Breathlessly, she held her own level gaze in the mirror. *That will do*, she thought, *that will do nicely*. Scraping together her hair on the floor without one single sentimental tear, she chucked it in the bin, turning away from the mirror without another glance.

She could feel the curious glances in her direction from the nurses waiting in the long queue for the telephone as she walked by. But she didn't care what they thought about her new hair — already she felt lighter without it and it was nothing compared to what Mac would have to deal with. Anxious to get back, she decided to skip phoning home and not to wait in the queue, so she picked up a hot cup of tea and made her way back towards the waiting area. If Nurse Barker asked, she'd tell her she'd eaten a sandwich — though seeing the thick doorstops of bread wedged with corned beef, she just couldn't face it.

Dunbar was by Mac's stretcher peering at her dressing and he looked up as she approached. His eyes widened when he saw her new look. He started to smile and was about to speak, but the door swung open with another ambulance crew and he moved quickly to inspect the casualty. Jo put her cup down and went to see if she could help, but Nurse Barker was already at the stretcher.

The ambulance crew breathlessly reported the details of the case. 'This is Ruth Lee, a nurse from Mill

144

Road. She was buried in the rubble for eight hours, we were lucky to find her alive. She has a compound fracture of her right humerus but no other injuries apparent... we've given her an injection of morphia.' Ruth. Jo could hear her own heartbeat, it made her head buzz, but she was beyond feeling shock. Instead she stood there watching, with dull certainty, what was passing before her eyes.

Dunbar gave her a concerned glance as he walked by with the stretcher and she held up a hand to indicate that she was alright. In the next moment, Nurse Barker, striding ahead, called back over her shoulder, 'I'll see if there's a theatre free.' Dunbar looked back at Jo with a grim smile — everything was under control. The best thing she could do was return to Mac. The buzzing in her head was starting to fade but then she thought of Myfanwy... Ruth wouldn't know about her yet, she would still be oblivious. There was so much grief to come.

Mac began groaning quietly on the stretcher and reached out with one arm. Jo took her hand, speaking quietly until she settled back into a drowsy state. She was about to make the most of the quiet moment to have her cup of tea, when Matron Jenkins strode into the hospital. Jo swallowed hard; even in the current situation she couldn't help but wonder if she'd done something wrong and would get a telling off.

'Nurse Brooks?' Matron frowned. 'You look different... What the heck have you done to your hair?'

'Well... I... It was...'

Deputy Matron's rigid smile unnerved Jo further. 'Well, never mind that, I'm here trying to round up my troops... Ah, I see you have our Nurse MacDonald. I heard that you'd rescued her. Have you laid eyes on anyone else?'

'Yes, I've seen Nurse Goodwin and they've just brought Nurse Lee in on a stretcher, she has a compound fracture of the humerus, and there are others from Mill Road through there,' said Jo, pointing in the direction of the room where the nurses were getting changed.

'Good, good. That's reassuring.' Matron cleared her throat and her voice was ragged when she spoke again, 'As you will no doubt be aware, we lost a fair number of nurses...'

Jo nodded, not sure if she should reach out a hand to Matron as she stood with her shoulders held square and tears running down her cheeks. 'I know, Myfanwy Jones was one of them, I saw her...' Jo said quietly.

Matron took a handkerchief from her sleeve and wiped her eyes. She looked up. 'Yes, sad news, sad news.' Then, clearing her throat again, she asked, 'And how is our Nurse Mac doing?'

Thrown out by the uncharacteristically gentle tone of Matron's voice, Jo was momentarily stuck for words. 'She... she has a head injury that's been sutured and I'm monitoring her condition.'

'Good, good... I did hear that you also rescued a baby, is that correct?'

'Yes.' As Jo said it, she almost surprised herself, but she had. She had saved a baby. 'Yes, the baby was called Lucia Gazzi.'

'Well you'll be pleased to know that the child's grandmother turned up at the hospital and she took the baby home to the family — two other children, two brothers I believe.'

'Oh, that's such good news.' Tears sprung to her eyes. The baby had lost her mother, but she had been found by her family.

'Yes, at least we managed to save one baby from up there. There... there were others...' Jo could see Matron was starting to break down at this — it was a huge tragedy. 'The other mothers, the ones who were in the shelter, they're heartbroken...' She stopped, unable to continue.

Jo reached out a hand and held onto Matron's arm until she could get back her composure. 'Well, I have to say, that we are so proud of all you nurses, getting on and bringing out as many patients and injured staff as you could... You were all heroes out there tonight.'

Jo was starting to shake her head, she was going to say that they'd only done what they needed to do; it was in the blood, an instinct that all nurses had. But something about Matron's dignified posture and heartfelt words made her stop short and instead, she simply said, 'Thank you.'

Matron Jenkins gave a small smile, and then she was off, stalking across the room, inspecting the remaining casualties as she went and taking Nurse Barker to task over something.

Jo, still reeling from the heartfelt exchange with Matron, reached out and grasped Mac's hand for support.

'Ow! That's a bit tight,' Mac muttered. 'What are you doing? Where am I?'

'Mac, we're at Broadgreen hospital, we've been evacuated.'

'Mmmm, somebody was muttering something about that earlier.' Mac tried to sit up on the stretcher, in danger of upsetting the whole thing. 'What's this? What's happened?' she grumbled, grabbing at the bandage.

147

'A bomb fell on the hospital, you were hit by debris and you have a head injury. Dunbar stitched it up for you.'

To Jo's horror, Mac swung her legs over the side of the stretcher. There was nothing she could do to stop her, so she helped her to stand and supported her when she wobbled. Pushing the stretcher to the floor, Jo freed up a chair and lowered Mac, still complaining, onto the seat.

'Bloody hell, Brooks, I seem to be feeling a bit dizzy.'

'You probably need to lie down again. You're concussed, you've been out for the count.'

'Yes, but there are patients here... I need to be working, I need to help.'

'They're all being looked after, they're just waiting for beds. There's nothing you need to do right now.'

'Well, shouldn't we just go home?'

Jo cleared her throat. 'That's another thing... the Nurses' Home took a direct hit as well, it's all gone.'

'Everything?'

'Everything, except what we stand up in.'

Mac rooted in her pocket and pulled out her lipstick. 'Well, at least I've got this! I must have put it in my pocket, I don't really remember...' Then, as she put the lipstick back, she brought out something else: a baby's bootee. She held it in the flat of her hand, staring at it, trying to make sense of it. Her eyes started to fill with tears.

'I've just heard that little Lucia Gazzi is safe, she's gone home with her grandmother.' Jo said gently.

'Who's that? Who?' Mac murmured.

Jo felt the nub of anxiety lodged in her chest begin to grow; clearly Mac's memory was affected. And now she could see her friend's shoulders drooping.

She looked exhausted. Jo gently took the bootee from Mac's hand and pushed it in her own pocket.

'I heard a man's voice, was there a man here?' Mac mumbled.

'Yes, it was Don.'

'Don? Who the heck is Don? I don't remember anyone called Don.'

Jo's concern grew. She knew that some memory could be lost after a blow to the head and sometimes it came back, but not always. If Mac had forgotten Lucia and Don, maybe there were other things that she wouldn't be able to recall.

She'd promised to ring the base to tell Don how she was, but it would have to wait for now. She needed to be sure of what she was going to tell him.

'I think I do need to lie down,' Mac drawled, lurching to the side.

'I've got you,' Jo soothed, 'I've got you.'

As she knelt to settle Mac back onto the stretcher, Jo could feel herself wilting with exhaustion. She knew that she would have to get some proper rest soon but first, importantly, she needed to ring the farm and let her parents know that she was safe. Once Nurse Barker was back in their vicinity, Jo gestured for her to keep an eye on Mac and made her way to the phone.

There was just one nurse in the office now on a call — Jo could see her through the window, crying freely and dabbing at her eyes with a white handkerchief. But despite there being no queue for the phone, Jo couldn't stand still; it suddenly felt overwhelmingly hard to wait. What if her mother had already heard the news; it would cause so much worry and pain. She just needed to speak to her mother, now, and instead of any concern for the nurse she felt twitchy, jangled.

Aware that she was out of kilter, she started tapping her foot to stop herself from impatiently banging on the door.

Relieved to hear the click of the receiver going down, Jo began opening the door before the nurse had even started to move. She gave her a nod and a small smile as she slipped past, anxious to get hold of the phone. Her breathing was ragged as she stood at the desk with the heavy receiver in her hand. For one split second, she couldn't remember what number to ask for, but as soon as the operator answered, she had it, and she was able to be put through. As she listened to the ring tone, pressing the receiver tight to her ear, she imagined the black telephone with the heavy cord sitting in the middle of the parlour table. She could see her mother wiping her hands on her apron, shushing a cat out of the way, coming through from the kitchen to answer…

'Hello, Bracken Farm, Jean Brooks speaking.' It caught Jo by surprise. And the sound of her mother's voice was all it took for her to instantly dissolve into tears. She could barely speak. 'Jo, is that you? Jo?' Hearing a note of panic in her mother's voice, she tried to control herself enough to be able to summon a broken voice and tell her all that had happened.

She could hear her mother's steady breathing as she listened carefully. Then her calm voice said matter-of-factly, 'You need to come home, Jo. Come back to the farm and bring Mac with you.'

14

As Jean Brooks steered the Austin down increasingly narrow lanes, Jo sat in the back with Mac, her chest tight and tears still in her eyes from the hug that her mother had given her and the sob that she'd felt her hold back. Now, looking out through the car window, seeing the green hedges full of white hawthorn blossom and her favourite red campions edging the road, almost brushing the car as they bobbed along, she was starting to breathe more easily. May was always a good time to come home.

Jo glanced across at Mac, resting her bandaged head against the car window, seemingly uninterested in her surroundings. She had nursed patients with head injuries before and she knew that memory loss could be temporary but, as yet, Mac wasn't showing any sign of a reliable recovery. Jo would have liked to have had her seen by a specialist, but with the extreme demand at the hospital there'd been no chance of it. At least Dunbar had been very attentive, making sure to see them twice a day until the immediate danger of a bleed on the brain had passed. He hadn't pulled his punches when it came to warning Jo that it could be a lengthy process, that as the brain recovered, patients could drift in and out, and there was absolutely no way of knowing whether Mac would ever be her old self again. Although Jo already knew that, it had been hard to hear it spoken out loud.

In the moments when Mac had come back enough to smile and make a joke, Jo had been elated. But over the twenty-four hours they were waiting to travel, she hadn't really seen much of her old friend.

She'd rung Don at the base to tell him; he'd been momentarily speechless, clearly distraught, when she'd broken the news that Mac had no recollection of him whatsoever. In the crackly silence of the telephone line, she'd felt his anguish. He'd thanked her and told her to call him again, saying he wanted to know how Mac was doing and that he would come and visit her at Bracken Farm. Jo could only foresee more pain for the poor man. Though he seemed a bit cocky — a good-looking and full of himself type — he appeared to be genuinely kind and he was head over heels for Mac.

As Jean waited to turn right at the familiar gravelled crossroads, Jo heard the scrunch of the tyres on the road and she knew that they would soon be home. She couldn't wait to see the farmhouse. Feeling a warm ache in her chest, she took Mac's hand and gave it a squeeze. She turned her head slowly and gave a wan smile.

'Not far now,' Jo said, trying to make her voice light. 'It's ages since you came to the farm, isn't it?'

Mac blinked and then withdrew her hand, thrusting it into the pocket of the ill-fitting brown coat that she'd acquired from the Red Cross pile of second-hand clothes for those who'd been bombed-out. Jo saw her turn wordlessly to rest her head against the window.

Jo held back a sigh, desperately hoping that the activity of the farm and the fresh air would do Mac good, bring her back to life. But it felt like her friend still had a long way to go.

'Here they all are, coming out of school.' Jean

glanced back over her shoulder, laughing at the happy sound of children's voices. Seeing them streaming out of the same village school that she'd attended — linking arms, giggling, running along the lane — Jo was reminded of those wonderful summer days when she'd run home from school, cutting through the fields, as free as a bird. And even though the children now all carried gas masks, it didn't seem to dim their exuberance. Just seeing them made her feel that she was breathing in a little joy.

'Ooh, there's Leonard, our new evacuee, he's from Salford,' Jean called. 'I'll just pull up and see if he wants a lift.'

'Len!' she shouted, winding down the car window. 'Hop in, we'll give you a lift.'

Jo saw a thin lad with mucky knees and untidy blond hair heading towards the car. Jean leant across to open the door, then turned and said, almost apologetically, 'We've put him in Michael's room.'

Jo felt a stab of pain; to her it would always be her brother's room, and it unsettled her to think that another boy had just moved in. Seeing him shamble awkwardly to the car, and the look of pleasure on her mother's face, for a few fleeting moments she felt uncomfortable. The first lot of evacuees that they'd had last year had been from London — two small girls, and somehow that hadn't bothered her. And they'd soon gone home like many others in the first wave, reclaimed by parents who had been expecting a blitz that didn't come immediately.

'Hello, Len.' Jo made herself smile at him as he twisted around to shake her hand. 'And this is my friend, Mac,' she said, by way of explanation, when Mac didn't react to his arrival with any kind of greeting.

153

The boy flushed bright pink and quickly turned back to face front, leaning slightly forward in his seat as if urging the small car along, anxious to be on his way. Picking up on his eagerness, Jean revved the engine and made the car hum along, bumping cheerfully over the rough road.

'Len's been a really good help with the milking and rounding up the sheep — he's just about got used to our country ways.'

The boy nodded and turned to give a crooked smile.

'I must admit,' Jean chuckled, 'I've never seen anybody so excited to see a sheep or a cow in my life — hey, Len?'

He was smiling at her mother now. 'Well, we don't have many cows in Salford.'

They were soon driving up the lane — bordered tightly by dry stone walls — that led directly to the farm. As they climbed the last stretch, it always felt like the world was opening up, and Jo craned her neck to catch the first glimpse of the farmhouse, set back in splendour at the foot of the fell, flanked by trees at either side.

'You look a right pair!' Jean laughed as Jo helped Mac out of the back of the car. 'Are those the best clothes that the Red Cross could provide?'

'I'm afraid so,' Jo called, above the noise of their farm dog, Gyp. She felt Mac clinging to her as Gyp continued to bark an excited greeting, frantically wagging his tail as he jumped up and down, rattling the heavy chain that tethered him to his kennel. 'Good boy,' she called, wanting desperately to go over and give him a scratch behind the ears, but Mac was on the verge of tears now, she needed to get her inside the house. Jean was at Mac's other side, helping her cross the cobbled yard as Len slipped past them and went to hold the back door open. 'Mind your head,' Jean called, as she did to everyone when they came through into the low-beamed entrance hall. 'Now let's help you off with your coat... Len, go and put the kettle on will you, love?'

Once Jo was sure that Mac was settled in a comfortable chair by the cast iron stove, she crouched down for a moment to stroke the tabby cat with a ripped ear who always lay sprawled there, already starting to feel her body begin to relax. The cat raised his head to give her a quizzical look. 'Alright, I'm just saying hello, you can go back to sleep now.' When she straightened up, she saw Mac still hunched in the chair, taking little notice. Whenever Mac had visited in the past, she'd filled the room with her chatter; straight away she'd help to make the tea and butter the scones.

Jo sighed. She caught her mother's eye and they exchanged a mournful look, then Jean nodded. Jo intuitively knew from that one gesture that her mother was telling her to give Mac time and she would be back to her old self. At this stage, Jo was far from sure that would be the case, it felt like it would take some sort of miracle. But at least they were back now, not crammed into a hospital ward waiting for transfer.

Looking around the kitchen, Jo realised how much she'd missed home. She always did, but after the hospital had been hit all she'd wanted was to be back here. Walking to the kitchen table, she placed a hand on its solid form, feeling the smooth wood, almost white from years of being scrubbed clean. It was only a table, but it held so many happy memories of family meals. It was a symbol of all that was important, something that helped hold them together as a family even after Michael's death.

Jo opened the pantry door and glanced in. A batch of scones was cooling on a rack, the smell filling the room, and some freshly churned butter stood to the side. The shelves were full of last season's pickles and home-made jams and a bowl full of eggs stood on the table.

Next, she wandered through into the beamed sitting room, with its familiar brocade chairs and small settee in front of the fire, the radiogram tucked in the corner, ready and waiting for the news or one of the light entertainment programmes that they listened to of an evening. Glancing over to the oak sideboard she saw the green pottery swan with a glued wing — the one that Michael had knocked off when they'd been playing tig inside the house. She could almost catch the echo of him. It made her chest ache, thinking about that day, seeing his face as he stood right here, just hours before he showed the first sign of getting sick.

She went through into the parlour with its stone-flagged floor and the black telephone sitting importantly in the middle of the polished wooden table. Jo felt her skin prickle; it was always cold in here, even when the old range that nestled in the wall was lit. There was a dampness to this room, a feeling of the past life of the farm. Jo had always had a sense of it, even as a child, especially when she'd open up the cupboard beneath the stairs, dark and dank and still stacked with boxes of ancient bric-a-brac and old books — pieces of history from previous generations of the Brooks family, all jumbled up together.

The door at the bottom of the oak stairs was firmly closed, separating the busy life of the farm from the upper floor that sat serenely above. Jo knew that her room with its flowered wallpaper and beamed ceiling would be neat and clean, ready and waiting.

Having gone full circle, she pushed open the door that led back to the entrance hall and found a cheeky hen that must have snuck in. 'Go on — shoo, shoo!' she cried, laughing as the hen flapped and clucked, making a real show of being evicted.

When she shut the door firmly behind it and turned back into the hall, she picked up the sound of quiet voices coming from the kitchen. She listened for a few moments before going in; it was good that her mum had got Mac talking.

In the kitchen, Jean placed a hand on Mac's shoulder. 'We're all fine here,' she told Jo confidently. 'You go and see your father, he's in the top field with the heifers. Get your boots on and go up there and join him.'

Henry Brooks looked up from his task and saluted her as she approached, his hair stuck out at all angles and the work jacket that he always wore was ripped at the elbow. He was tying up a gate. 'I need to keep that lot secure in there,' he said, gesturing to the heifers cavorting in the top field, kicking up their heels and racing around. 'They've all gone a bit daft since the weather got warmer.'

He raised his eyebrows when he saw her new hair. Then he took a deep breath and she could see tears shining in his eyes. 'You had a near miss there, lass,' he said quietly, his body held tense. 'It must have been terrible.'

'It was,' she said. 'I was lucky to find Mac alive.' Her voice was small and quickly lost amidst the open fields and the wide blue sky.

157

He nodded and reached out to take her hand. 'Only time will tell,' he said steadily, 'and nature is a great healer, I see that every day.' They both stood looking out over the field, dotted with yellow buttercups. Then he took a large linen handkerchief out of his pocket and gave his nose a good blow. 'Right, well, we need to be getting these cows in for milking, don't we? Young Len will be coming up to help and then we'll be on our way.'

She linked his arm and he smiled at her, pushing his handkerchief firmly back into his pocket. He turned and scanned the field with the heifers in, his hand over his eyes, shielding from the sun. When he looked back, Jo followed his gaze and saw Len approaching. 'And there he is, coming to help with the cows.' She saw the tousle-haired lad walking towards them with a spring in his step. He'd slipped into his work boots and looked very much at home as he came over the rutted field. He was taller and skinnier than Michael, but with the sun in her eyes seeing him now, her heart skipped a beat. It could have been her brother.

'I know what you're thinking,' Henry murmured, giving her arm a squeeze. 'Your mother took to him straight away but I found it hard, having him here. That cold winter when Michael died from diphtheria, some part of me closed up, and I didn't even realise it...' He was pulling his hankie out of his pocket again. Jo waited whilst he wiped his face. 'But then this poor lad came, half-starved, full of nits, and he'd had a hell of beating from some bastard — bruises all over his back. And when your mother had him cleaned up and got him eating proper food, he started smiling a bit and showing interest, following me round the farm like a shadow, like you and your brother used to... I had no choice then, I had to let it be.'

Jo nodded and gave his arm a squeeze. 'Of course you did… and he seems like a nice lad.'

'Aye, he is that. And what fun we had when he first arrived. He'd never so much as seen a blade of grass, never mind sheep or cows, and he was scared to death of the hens. You should have seen his face the first time I brought him round the fields, his eyes were like saucers and he was running round like one of those young heifers in the field.'

'It's so good that you're able to offer him a different life, it's terrible in the cities.' Jo shivered as she remembered what she'd left behind, picturing the hospital as she'd last seen it. 'I can't even begin to describe…'

'We've seen some photos in the paper, big buildings left like piles of rubble. Thank the lord we didn't know about the hospital until you rang, it would have been terrible for your mother, waiting for news…'

'Well, I'm here now, and I'll be staying for as long as it takes for Mac to get better.'

Henry nodded. 'I'll see you at tea-time,' he called, raising an arm as he walked towards Len. She stood and watched the two of them together, heading off. Yes, it was a good thing that they had Len.

Jo slept on the floor that night beside Mac. She'd kept the curtains open so that she could see the stars in the sky, like she used to when she was a little girl, always wishing for something, always dreaming. Now, all she wanted was for Mac to get better and be herself again. And she knew that in a week it would be time for her to remove the bandage and take out the stitches. Nurse Barker had kindly supplied clean dressings and some suture scissors so that it could all be done at home. But the thought of seeing that raw wound marring Mac's forehead, a constant reminder that she would carry for the rest of her life, it made Jo not just sad, but angry. And what if she didn't recover her memory or her vigour, what then?

'We'll get her right,' Jean had said earlier, when Jo had come back downstairs after settling Mac in bed. But even though she had nursed plenty of head injuries before and knew it would take time, this was Mac. She wanted her to be better right now — even three days had seemed too long.

★ ★ ★

Mac woke gasping — it was black, she was falling. She sat up in bed, struggling to make sense of where she was. In the pale light coming through the window, she could see flowered wallpaper. She felt restless and irritated; she was sure that she should know this place...

Slipping her legs over the side of the bed, the cool of the wooden floor on the soles of her feet was pleasant. When she stood, the long nightgown that she was wearing fell softly around her legs. She looked down at it; it was bright white and came right up to her neck in a ruffle. Just for a second, she panicked. Could it be a shroud? Was she dead? *Steady on*, she thought, feeling at her arms through the fabric of the long, lace-trimmed sleeves. Her body was warm and she was breathing. She took an extra deep breath just to check.

And this room, it did seem familiar... She opened the door, and the brass thumb latch gave a satisfying click. Creaking her way down the wooden stairs, she opened the door at the bottom and then she was lost.

Just as she was about to go back up the stairs, she saw another door, she pushed it open to find some coats hanging and boots on the floor. And when she opened the back door cool morning air caught her and she breathed it in, filling her lungs — wherever this was, it smelt fresh. She walked out onto stone cobbles, her bare feet slipping on the dewy wetness. She could hear cows mooing and then a dog was barking fiercely. She stopped, not wanting to go further, needing to turn around. As she walked back towards the door it opened and a broad-shouldered woman in leather boots and a rough apron carrying a bucket appeared. The woman said, 'You're still in your nightie,' and then she started to laugh — a deep, throaty laugh — and in that moment something clicked inside Mac's head. It was Jean — it was Jo's mum.

'Where's Jo?' she said, aware now that she was out on the cold stones in her bare feet with a cool, morning breeze ruffling her thin cotton nightie.

'She'll still be tucked up asleep on the floor by the side of your bed, you must have come straight past her,' Jean said, putting down her bucket and leading her back inside. 'I've just lit the stove; let's get you a cup of tea. You look a real sight in your night attire with that bandage round your head... Come on, I'll make you some toast.'

As soon as she smelt the food in the kitchen, Mac's stomach rumbled; she was so hungry, she probably could have eaten the whole loaf. When Jo emerged, also in bare feet, her eyes round with concern, it was easy for Mac to smile and pat the chair next to her. 'Come on, Jojo, come and have some toast with me. Tell me what's been going on?'

She could see that Jo was starting to cry and it worried her. 'What's up?' she said, 'I'm sorry that I left you in bed, but the thing is, I think I must have been asleep for a long time, my head feels all fuzzy and I can't quite remember what's been going on.'

Jean leant over Jo's shoulder and poured a tot of brandy in her tea and Mac watched her take a big swig before she started to speak. 'Do you remember anything about the bomb falling on the hospital …?'

Mac felt the shock of it anew and the wound on her forehead started to throb.

As Jo started to gently tell her all that had happened, even though it felt like some story that she hadn't been a part of, she absorbed the horror of it — how could she have been the only nurse to survive on the ward, what about Myfanwy, Sister Codey, and all the mums and babies? The sadness of it twisted in her chest, left her sobbing. The next thing, she could feel Jo's arm around her shoulders, and the heaving of her chest — she was weeping as well.

The terrifying thing was, she still had no recollection of any of the events. And as Jo continued to tell her more — she mentioned a man that she'd been seeing, someone called Don. She told her that he looked like a young Clark Gable, but she didn't know anyone by that name, didn't know anyone by that description. There must have been some kind of mix up.

As she sat, shaking her head, denying all knowledge of this Don, she started to feel a pain behind her eyes, she thought that she probably needed to rest — but how could she rest when she should start pushing herself to recall these events? Having had glimpses of things that she should know, she felt lost, like there was a whole important part of her missing. As she tried to hold onto it, the image of Clark Gable drifted through her head and then became fainter. She could already feel it all slipping away, until it had gone too far to remember what had even been there.

15

Jo had been putting off ringing Don Costello again. She didn't want to have to tell him that Mac still didn't know who he was, but a promise was a promise. So, later that day when Mac was napping, Jo stood with the receiver gripped in her hand, listening for any sound from upstairs. Once she was sure that Mac was still sleeping, she fished the scrap of paper out of her pocket, reading the number over and over, trying to decide the exact words that she should use; then, she took a deep breath, and dialled.

A gruff voice answered and said he would go and find Don. As she waited, she could hear the sounds of the airbase — the clank of metal on metal, a cackle of laughter, the slow rumble of an engine in the background. She pictured the scene, trying to imagine the mechanics in their oily overalls and the men in uniform.

Lost in her thoughts she was almost shocked when an urgent voice crackled into life, 'Hello, Mac, is that you?'

She could hear a wolf whistle and teasing voices in the background. 'Hey Costello, is that your girlfriend?'

'Sorry, Don, this is Jo,' she said steadily.

'How is she? Is she OK?' He sounded frantic, shouting into the receiver; then his voice was muffled as he covered it with his hand and she could hear him telling his friends to shut the hell up.

'Yes, she seems to be recovering, it'll be another

week or so before we can take the stitches out, but she's been getting up and dressed and she's eating we —'

'Does she remember me now? Can I see her?'

'Well … the thing is Don… like I said, sometimes it can take a while for memory to come back fully and, well, she still can't recall who you are.'

'No, that can't be right. She must remember me, she must …'

'I've spoken to her today, I've told her about you again and she has no recollection.'

She heard his cry of anguish.

'I'm so sorry, but this might change, loss of memory is often temporary.'

'But how long will it be, are we talking days, weeks…?'

'There is no way of knowing. All I can do is keep ringing to tell you how she is. If there's any change, I promise, I will let you know straight away.'

'No, no, I'm not settling for that. I need to see her. If I don't get to see her, she'll never remember me.'

'I don't think that's a good idea — she must have been deeply traumatised by what happened to her. Seeing you too soon… it might set her back.'

There was a pause as he thought it through. 'No, I'm coming,' he said.

'But Don it's—'

The receiver had already clicked down and she stood for a few seconds listening to the buzzing of an empty line. Was he right? Would it help Mac to see him? But what if she was blocking memories not because of her head injury but to protect herself? Jo had seen enough shell shock since the war began, she knew how terrible it could be. It needed careful

165

management and, from what she'd heard and seen of Don, he might be the sort to blunder in and only cause more harm. Replacing the receiver, she tried to reassure herself with the fact that it would be very unlikely that an airman from Kirby would be able to make it all the way up here.

★ ★ ★

The days went by in an endless routine of getting up, helping Mac dress, keeping her occupied and, if she was well enough, making sure that she had a short walk in the garden. There was still no further improvement of Mac's memory and, for Jo, going through this day after day with someone she was so close to was harrowing. Her clinical experience sometimes went out of the window, leaving her feeling increasingly impatient and sometimes startled that Mac, who was always so sharp, still couldn't remember properly. Only yesterday, they'd been talking about how last Christmas Eve they'd had a party in the common room ... Mac could remember every tiny detail of that particular occasion and she'd told the story of Amy having one too many drinks and falling over whilst dancing the jitterbug and them all laughing so much they cried. It exasperated Jo that Mac's memory was so selective — sometimes she almost felt like shaking her, especially at times when she needed to talk through some of the things that had happened to try and get her own head straight. She did wonder if what Mac was now suffering from was more to do with the shock rather than the physical injury. If that was the case, then it wouldn't be easy for her coming out of

166

it. She'd heard Amy's stories about what happened to some of the soldiers.

Sometimes, Jo envied her. Especially at night, when she lay anxiously on her mattress on the floor, listening to Mac's breathing, and she felt jangled by even the smallest snuffle or murmur. Over and over in her dreams, she was there on the broken stairs, holding her breath, her heart pounding in her chest. And then, gasping, as once again she saw Myfanwy's dead face, and she was scrabbling in the debris looking for Mac, shouting for help, but her voice was tight, locked inside her chest. Sleep was her enemy now and when she glimpsed her reflection during the day, and the dark smudges beneath her eyes, she felt like a walking ghost.

She had also been troubled by the prospect of having to remove the stitches. When Mac had asked, she'd tried to give a full description of the wound, but she knew that she was painting an optimistic picture. Once or twice, when she'd been renewing the bandage, Mac had asked if she could just have a little peek, making it sound as if she wanted to catch a glimpse of some treat that lay in store. Each time, Jo had claimed — and Mac had agreed — that they didn't want to risk any infection by removing the dressing pad. But today was the day and Jo felt sick to the stomach, wishing that it was her head that had been broken.

As they stood in the kitchen, Jo waiting for the instruments boiling in a pan on the kitchen stove, Mac began unravelling the bandage. 'Come on Jojo, get the suture scissors, it's feeling all itchy under here and I can't wait to wash my hair.' She had the bandage off and just the pad remained, caught on a suture.

'You need to come into the light,' Jo instructed, trying to use her nurse's voice. But she could feel her chest tighten and as soon as she removed the pad and saw afresh the full extent of the wound, her hands began to shake.

She cleared her throat, and her voice when it came was unnaturally light. 'It's all clean and it's healed very well. I'd forgotten just how many stitches there are though, it's going to take me while to get them all out.'

'Take your time, I'm not going anywhere.' Mac smiled, resting back in the chair.

Jo's hands were still shaking as she removed the first couple of stitches, but once she caught the rhythm of the task, she managed to lose herself in it and focus. With a pair of forceps in one hand and suture scissors in the other, she worked her way steadily around the unusual shape. It was like a star. She placed each black stitch on a square of clean white cloth, bringing her closer to the moment where she knew that Mac would be running upstairs to their room and looking in the dressing table mirror.

'All done,' she said, leaning in to inspect the wound after the final suture was removed. The red lines of the scar were not yet softened by time, but stood raised and angry against Mac's pale forehead. The skin was tight and puckered in places, pulling her eyebrow up and a little out of line. There was still some dried blood in her hair.

Jo realised she was staring, holding her breath. She didn't know what to say.

'I'm thinking it's not good,' Mac said, meeting her eyes, on the level.

She opened her mouth to speak but Mac was already on her feet and running up the stairs. There was silence. Jo stood with the forceps in one hand and the scissors in the other. The clock on the parlour wall ticked — she'd never noticed how loud it was before.

Then, a miserable wail shattered all other sound.

Jo threw her instruments on the table and raced upstairs, her breath caught in her chest, making it feel tight. Mac was sitting on the bed, crumpled. She looked like she'd been hit hard in the stomach and had curled in on herself. She was sobbing, her breath rasping in her chest.

Jo pulled her into her arms. 'I'm so sorry, Mac, so sorry.'

Within a few seconds, she sensed her mother at the door, and they exchanged a tearful glance. 'I'll put the kettle on,' Jean murmured as she quietly withdrew. Jo held onto Mac, as the heedless sun continued to shine and shine through the bedroom window.

Eventually, Mac drew in a ragged breath and started to shiver. Jo pulled the blanket off her own bed and wrapped it around her, swaddling her like a baby. Then she murmured for her to lie down, telling her that she was exhausted, that she needed to sleep. Mac made no sound as Jo knelt by the bed with one hand resting gently on the blanket until she fell asleep.

Jean stood at the door again, speaking softly. 'When she wakes up, we'll get her washed and we'll do something with her hair.' Practical as always, she was already thinking about the next step. But Jo knew that it wasn't going to be as simple as that; there were so many things that Mac was going to have to deal with in the coming days and months.

★ ★ ★

169

Mac woke, boiling hot. She threw off the blanket she was wrapped in. What the heck? It was the middle of the day and the sun was streaming in through the window. She felt grubby, her skin crawled, and for one glorious moment she was lost and she couldn't remember why she'd been sleeping.

Then it hit her; she reached up a hand to feel the shape of the scar on her forehead. The skin was tender as she ran her fingers over its raised lumps and bumps, tracing it, trying to get to know it. But then she caught another glimpse of it in the dressing table mirror and seeing again how it puckered and pulled at her forehead, she wanted to take a knife and cut it away. She covered it with the flat of her hand and then glanced in the mirror again, her eyes filled with angry tears.

'Shit, shit!' she swore under her breath and she started to scrabble for her shoes under the bed with the other hand. Then, once she had them on, she clattered down the stairs, almost tripping and falling as she burst through the door and into the entrance hall. Her horrible brown coat was hanging there. She rummaged through both pockets. Where were her cigarettes? Had she brought them with her? She couldn't remember. Almost sobbing now with frustration, she looked up to find Jean Brooks standing in the doorway to the kitchen. She had a pack of Dunhills and a lighter in her hand. 'I thought you might be looking for these,' she said calmly. 'You left them the last time you were here. I've been keeping them for emergencies.'

'Thank you.' Mac pulled her hair across her forehead, then opened the back door. Out in the yard, she felt dizzy and she needed to lean against the wall of

170

the dairy. The sun was relentless; it didn't seem right that the weather was so bloody nice, not when she was feeling like this. She wanted it to thunder and pour with rain. Her hands were shaking as she took out a cigarette, but the simple act of placing it between her lips and flicking the lighter helped her to calm, even before she'd taken the first drag. Hearing the clanking of metal, she looked up to see Henry coming out of the dairy with a bucket of milk. He didn't pass any comment, just gave her a nod and a smile.

She looked down at the ill-fitting grey skirt that was the only thing that she had to wear. How could she even begin to feel like herself when she didn't even have any of her own clothes? The white blouse was better, but given the choice, she would never have gone for anything that had such a droopy lace collar. She felt like a sad portrait of a bombed-out victim. For some reason it made her want to laugh. *Oh Christ*, she thought, *I'm not only sad, I'm also unhinged.* She sighed out the smoke, starting to feel her body relax a little, and reached up a hand again to try and arrange her hair to cover the scar. Feeling the dried blood, she started to pick at it, throwing the fragments down onto the cobbles. She didn't know what she was going to make of this, not yet. She didn't have a plan, but she was damned if she was going to let it beat her.

The sound of a motorcycle in the distance snagged her attention, so she ground the cigarette out on the stone wall and walked down the yard, towards the gate, hoping to catch a glimpse. The motorbike was spluttering and slowing down and the farm dog had started to make a racket. *It must be coming here*, she thought, stopping in her tracks and instinctively stepping into a shadow.

Strange … It was a man in a blue uniform, complete with side cap — RAF. She couldn't recall any mention of a Brooks relative who was in the forces. He dismounted the motorcycle, wobbling a bit, and then parked it up in the yard. He then removed his cap and smoothed his dark hair. He was very good-looking. Immediately, her hand went back up to her forehead, covering the scar.

He started to walk towards her, smiling. 'Mac, Mac!'

He was running now, running at her. She panicked, looking around for someone to help. How did he know her name? Who was this?

She froze, her body locking up as her mind scrabbled desperately trying to tell her something. She was sure that there was an important thing that she should know. She could have screamed with frustration.

And then the man grabbed her, hugging her, his hands all over her. She screamed, pushing him away. 'Get off me!'

'Mac?' he cried, taking a step back, and then he was in tears. 'It's me. It's Don. Remember?'

A voice called from behind. It was Jo. 'Don? Don! You should have told me you were going to visit, we needed preparation for this!'

Preparation for what? Mac thought. *What the hell was she going on about?*

That name… Jo had asked her a few times if she could remember a Don, but she would definitely have remembered a man like him… She was dizzy now, starting to feel panicky. Something was dawning on her, a new horror descending.

She could hear Jo talking quickly and forcefully to the man, and it sounded like she was telling him off.

He stood there in tears, gasping for breath. The whole thing was horrible and she knew that she needed to get away, so she ran back up the yard and into the house, closing the heavy wooden door behind her and leaning against it, her chest heaving. She heard Jean's calm voice and then she felt the world tip sideways and everything went black.

When she woke, somehow, she was back in bed and Jo was sitting on a chair next to her. Her head was hurting and she seemed to have flashes of bright light coming and going, even with her eyes closed. She just wanted to blot things out, so she closed her eyes and forced herself to drift off again. That's when things started to get difficult. She was gasping, she couldn't breathe, she didn't know if she was asleep or awake. The room was dark but full of flashing light. She brushed at her face, certain that she could feel grit falling from the ceiling. And then there was a terrible screaming and the piercing cry of a baby. She could see Myfanwy running towards her, her mouth wide with terror. Mac tried to help — she shouted, but she couldn't hear the sound of her own voice. The walls were cracking open, beds were rearing up in the air, and still the sound of a baby screaming. Everything was collapsing in and she saw Myfanwy's terrified face once more. Then, all of the air was knocked out of her and she was falling, falling—

She woke screaming. She was fighting for her life — fighting someone off. Forcing her eyes open she saw in horror that it was Jo. The door clicked open and Jean was there as well.

Later, when she woke again, she had no idea how long she'd been in bed or what time of day it was, though there was no light now from the window and the curtains were closed. She could hear Jo saying, 'I told him not to come, I told him he should wait… I don't even know how he found us, he must have memorised the address.'

She heard Jean respond that he must be heartbroken and not thinking straight, and that he'd borrowed a motorcycle and come all this way…

The man who had come … Don. Maybe she did remember him? She couldn't be sure. The pressure inside her head was making it feel tight; she couldn't think straight. But she could hear the tone of Jo's voice and she sounded worried. In that moment, Mac knew that she needed to do something, show them that she was alive and kicking.

'Christ, I could do with a cup of tea,' she managed to croak.

Immediately Jo was there, fussing, as she always did. 'Thank goodness, I thought you were never going to wake up.'

She heard herself tell Jo not to worry and then she lay for a moment, needing to get her thoughts straight. She was going to have to put some real effort into this if she was going to make things any better — not just for herself but for Jo and Jean as well. She didn't know if she was ready for it or not — her head wasn't right and she felt like she had a tight ball burning behind her eyes — but this was important. She could spend the rest of her life feeling bad about being the lone survivor, but she had to make herself accept that it wasn't her fault, random things happened, especially in war. And there were so many people worse off than she was. She owed it to everyone to get herself up and moving and to try to make sense of things. The war was still raging, she needed to think about what she could do to help.

'I'm alright,' she said, forcing her arms to work so she could push herself into a sitting position. 'I've just been a bit mixed up that's all… and the last thing I want to do is cause you and your mum any worry. I need to try and get things straight in my head… I want you to tell me everything about that man who came, everything. I think it's possible I do know him after all. But first, Jojo, I need a cup of tea and a smoke.'

Jo was in tears now. 'I think you're going to be alright, I think you are. And you can have anything you want, anything at all.'

16

It was shady in the wood, the ground dappled by sunlight and covered with glorious bluebells bending their demure heads delicately on green stems. The earth smelt of damp and the promise of summer. Mac wanted to lie down amongst the flowers, spread out her hair and gaze up to the green leaves. She had never seen such intense green, and the combination of that with the blue of the flowers and the peaty brown of the soil took her breath away. She squeezed Jo's hand. 'Thank you for bringing me here... I know I'm not usually one for a walk in the country, but this place is like heaven.'

'I know.' Jo smiled. 'We came home at exactly the right time — the bluebells are just lovely, aren't they?'

Mac breathed in the smell, turning her face up to the branches and the blue sky above. 'Do you think places like this can actually help to heal people?'

'Well maybe not the body, but certainly the soul.'

Mac let go of her and walked on ahead, turning circles as she went. 'I'm healing, Jo, I'm alive and I'm healing...' She laughed. 'And one day I might even be able to look at myself in the mirror.'

'We'll have to work on that,' Jo replied, but she didn't want to really think about it now. She'd begun to reconcile herself to a life without her Rita Hayworth good looks and she knew that most people would say, 'Well, you had a lucky escape, you're still alive, that's all that matters.' She often heard those voices in her head and she knew that they were right, but she wasn't ready to completely let go of the anger or the frustration when she couldn't remember new things properly — or anything at all from the days around the bomb blast. Try as she might, she still couldn't recall a single thing about Don, though Jo had told her the story of how they'd met and when she'd last seen him — the night of the bomb. But she had no intimate memory of him. Anyway, it didn't matter, he was probably only interested in her looks, so that was the end of that. Since his visit, he'd tried to ring, to speak to her, but she didn't want to do that. What could she possibly say except, 'I'm sorry, I don't remember you.' The last time that he'd rung, Jo had said he was getting a bit frantic and shouting into the phone. She'd felt concern for him, like you would for any stranger. She'd half-wondered if she should speak to him to make him feel better, but it would be clear that she didn't remember him and she didn't want to make things worse.

Turning around on the path, she looked at Jo for directions.

'We'll go down by the river,' Jo pointed the way. 'There's an abandoned mill, we can sit for a while and then we'll start back.'

'OK,' she replied, eager to be walking on ahead, feeling at last that she had some strength in her body. She had more energy every day now and she hadn't said anything to Jo yet, but she'd started to yearn to go back to work — she missed her nursing so much. She didn't think that she could go back to Liverpool though, she wasn't even sure that she could work in a hospital, but last year she'd known a nurse who was going off to join the army — it all sounded so exciting, so real. Soon after, they'd been in the thick of it at Mill Road once the Blitz started, so she hadn't thought much more about it, but in the last few days it had been there in her head again... She might speak to Jo when they got back.

The sound of running water met her before she could even see the mill — it had a lively feel to it as it tumbled over the smooth stones of the river bed and then took a dip and flowed faster towards what had been the mill wheel. The remains of it still hung, broken, and by the look of the rotting wood, it had been many years since it turned. Mac gazed up to the crumbling stone walls, covered in moss. The roof had started to fall in and there was a gaping hole. It looked like it'd been bombed, and something about the shape of that hole made her catch her breath.

She gazed at the building. The sound of the river seemed louder now, a little threatening. It made her want to move, to get a different perspective. There was a rough path, cobbles long-covered by moss and overgrown with grass, but at this time of year it was passable. She continued to walk, glancing at the stone lintels and broken windows. At the other side of the building there was a large double doorway where the carts must have passed in and out. A patch of sunlight shone on a circle of white daisies on the ground. She was almost sure that she heard the distant echo of a child's laughter. Maybe it was the little girl with tousled hair; she remembered her from her life before her injury, but she hadn't seen her for a while now.

One of the mill doors still hung on its rusty hinges, lopsided, its blue paint peeling in flakes. Blue paint... crooked door... the sound of a man's laughter... She felt her heart begin to race and her body prickled with sensation. And the man was laughing again, and then

178

she saw herself pulling open a lopsided blue door. She gasped, she could see the man's face now — Don. He was smiling up at her, and then she was loosening his tie and kissing him. She was gasping for air now, not able to breathe and her head felt like it might explode.

Then, she heard Jo's voice. 'Whatever is it? Are you alright?'

Mac fell to her knees on the hard cobbles. 'I can remember,' she sobbed, 'I can remember.'

She took deep breaths; she knew that she needed to calm down. Jo was pulling her up from the ground with strong arms. At first she couldn't move, but with Jo's help they managed to get back to the lane and then it was easier from there. As they walked, her mind went over and over the scene that she had in her head. How could such a vivid memory have been lost for all these weeks? It terrified her to think what else she might have forgotten. The worst of it was, now that she had the memory, it wouldn't leave her, and others were coming through, tumbling in on top of each other. She was running, running and she was on the ward with the mums and babies... Beautiful Sofia Gazzi was sitting up in bed, smiling, with Lucia in her arms...

She heard Jean's concerned voice as Jo dragged her in through the door of the farmhouse. She knew she probably needed to lie down, but she was brewing with anger now for some reason she couldn't pinpoint. No, she'd spent far too long lying in bed already. She needed to be up — and most of all she needed a smoke. She turned back out to the yard again. Jean came with the pack of cigarettes and a lighter. Even though she had a buzzing noise in her head, she was adamant that she was safe to be left on her own outside, propped against the dairy wall.

She needed time to think about Don.

★ ★ ★

A few days later, the weather took a turn for the worse — showers of rain fell intermittently and there was a real nip in the air. Mac was out in the yard again, one hand shoved in her coat pocket, her eyes focused on the distance as cigarette smoke drifted across her face. She was waiting for the sound of a motorcycle and she'd told Jo that she needed to do this alone. Taking a final drag on her cigarette she dropped it and ground it out with the heel of her boot. Immediately, she slipped another one from the pack. She cupped her hands as she lit up, the wind causing her to pull the brown coat tighter around herself. The cold breeze ruffled her hair and she ran a hand over her face to brush it back, flinching when her fingers caught the still tender edge of the wound. Instinctively, she flattened the new fringe that she'd cut into her hair to cover the scar. Having a new style still felt strange, but she'd get used to it.

Shifting her weight from one foot to the other she took a deep drag. She'd been impatient for this to be over ever since she'd asked Jo to make the phone call, and not knowing exactly when he'd arrive, this was the third time that she'd found herself waiting in the yard, straining her ears to listen. Just as she was grinding the butt of the cigarette onto the cobbles — wondering if she should have worn her Fifth Avenue red lipstick and deciding immediately that she'd done the right thing, she didn't want to give him any encouragement —the dog started to yap excitedly. Hearing the faint purring of a motorcycle in the distance, her skin prickled with sensation. He was coming.

She stood out in full view this time, both hands in her pockets, holding the brown coat tight around the curves of her body. Watching him dismount and secure the motorcycle felt strange, like a rerun of the last visit. But this time she had no fear; she stood boldly in the middle of the yard, ready to say her piece.

She saw him remove his cap and smooth his hair before replacing it. He smiled instantly when he saw her waiting. His face was open, hopeful, as he walked up the yard but then as he got closer, she saw him narrow his eyes and his pace slowed.

He knows me better than I remember, she thought wryly, taking a step towards him, ready to deliver the speech that she'd prepared — to tell him what they'd had was just a brief fling, the kind that was so common in war, and now it was best if they just go their separate ways and so on.

He stopped and stood with his head bowed. She started to walk towards him, ready to get it over with. When he looked up, she was completely unprepared for the fire in his eyes; she felt it right there in the pit of her stomach, and the words that she'd been about to utter evaporated.

'I know what you're going to say,' he said, his gaze still burning into her. 'But just listen to me first. I'm going away tomorrow, I've finally got the go ahead for the gunner training. And as soon as I'm finished, I'll be posted and I don't know where I'll end up or what will happen to me... So I just need to tell you something—'

'No, no...' she said, holding up a hand, trying to stop him.

He looked her straight in the eye.

She was still shaking her head but he ploughed ahead. 'I know that we hardly know each other, but the connection that we made in those few days… it's something that I've never experienced in my whole life. I've dated plenty of women, I'm not ashamed to admit to that, but you, Mac, you have blown them all out of the water.'

She felt a heavy ache in the pit of her stomach, this wasn't going the way that she thought it would. She needed to try and take control of the situation — she wanted him to get a grip on reality.

She squared her shoulders and spoke up, trying to adopt a mildly outraged tone, 'We're in the middle of a war… what we had was just some fling. You'll move on soon enough and between missions you'll find other women, that's how it is in wartime.'

He was shaking his head, and there it was again, that look.

She took a step closer, till she was in reaching distance of him. 'Look at me, Don. Look at me.'

'I'm looking,' he said, his deep brown eyes still burning.

'I'm not the same carefree woman that you met only a few weeks ago, I'm changed.'

'You look the same to me,' he said reaching out, his hand skimming the sleeve of her coat.

'Take a look at this!' she demanded, pushing aside her fringe to reveal the full extent of her scar. She saw him look away as if in pain.

'I'm not your Rita Hayworth now!' she shouted, suddenly angry.

He glared back at her, holding her gaze. 'Yes you are,' he said, taking a step closer, his voice catching on a sob. 'You always will be.'

'Ha!' she spat, letting her fringe fall back into place. She shook her head, backing away. But he was still coming towards her and she could see the rapid rise and fall of his chest as he reached out and pulled her into his arms. It felt so good to feel the warmth of his body, to breathe in the smell of him. In that moment it was all that she wanted.

He held onto her and buried his face in her hair. 'I love you, Mac. I just love you.'

She couldn't stop herself from crying now. And all she wanted to do was kiss him; if only she could slip back into the days before the bomb, when they'd spent that morning together in the house with the blue door. She wanted, more than anything, to have that innocent time back, to be free, not knowing what the next day might bring. But she had a lump in her chest, like something stuck, and she knew that she could never be that woman again. And this man, he was young, he would be airborne soon — who knew what might happen to him. She knew that she couldn't take the risk, something was already broken inside of her and she couldn't cope with anything else, not yet.

She stepped back, holding him at arm's length. 'I'm sorry, I'm so sorry,' she repeated, a miserable mantra. 'But this is the wrong time, I just can't do it.'

He reached out for her once more, and she could see the tears in his eyes, but she steeled herself against weakening. She knew this was the best thing that she could do for both of them. She told herself that, and she made herself believe it.

But still he came towards her, even as she backed away, looking almost ready to fall to his knees. 'Mac...'

'No,' she said firmly, starting to feel angry now.

'You have to listen to what I'm saying. It's over.'

She turned her back on him, not able to bear the sadness of it all. She started to walk back to the house, but he ran after her, stepping in front to bar her way, taking her in his arms.

'No, I don't want you,' she screamed, pushing him away and running towards the door, desperate to be free of him and all these feelings that he thought he had.

Once she was at the door, she glanced back to where he still stood, alone in the yard. He was gazing after her, his arms down by his sides, the wind gently ruffling the lock of dark hair that fell on his forehead. She saw him sigh and start to turn away. She pushed her way in through the door and ran inside. She couldn't watch him go.

17

Mac was still awake as the early morning light came through the window and the cockerels around the farmyard began to crow, answering each other loudly and softly from a distance. She hadn't slept properly for three nights, not since Don had visited, and each morning she'd been subject to this noise from the farmyard. What is it with the male of any species, she thought to herself — most of them just want to make themselves heard. *Cock a doodle doo, cock a doodle doo.* She slipped out of bed, trying to catch a glimpse of one out of the window. She could see him there, a large cockerel on a pile of dung, stretching his glossy red-brown neck, flapping his wings, making a real show of himself. The hens were pecking around on the ground, getting on with their daily business, and there he was, taking his time, greeting the new day.

Jo was sleeping quietly, her cropped hair ruffled on the pillow. Mac knew that she'd have to speak to her today, her mind was alive with the army nurse plan that she'd been brewing. Now that her memory seemed to have been properly restored, it was time to make a move — and she was hoping that Jo would want to join her. She wasn't counting on it, knowing that Jo could never be persuaded to do anything that didn't feel exactly right. But she knew, just as surely as that blasted cockerel crowed every morning, that she couldn't rest until she'd properly joined the war effort — after what had happened at Mill Road, it felt like a calling even stronger than becoming a nurse.

She was going to be an army nurse, and the red scar that prickled on her forehead felt like a mark of initiation. She couldn't wait to speak to Jo about it, so she resolved to do it this afternoon — they'd already planned to go out for a picnic.

Later, as they chugged up the steep fell road in the car, Mac held her breath — she'd wanted to get on and tell Jo about her plan as soon as they were in the car, but seeing the amount of focus she had when she was driving, it wasn't a good idea. And this road was so steep, she wondered at one stage if she might need to get out and push. But the brave little Austin crowned the hill and they were soon rumbling over a cattle grid and bobbing along between gorse bushes, passing moorland sheep grazing at the side of the road. At one stage, they had to slow right down whilst a scraggy ewe sauntered in front of the car. Mac had never seen so many sheep.

And then Jo swung the steering wheel, turning off the road and into a lay-by, with a spectacular view looking out across Morecambe Bay. A true city girl, Mac had never thought she'd be one for 'a view', but this was breathtaking and the murmur of the wind as it buffeted the car made it even more exciting. It felt like they were on top of the world. She could see light glinting off the sea, and up in the sky, small aircraft were buzzing backwards and forwards across the bay — they seemed playful, almost picturesque.

Mac turned to Jo, aware that she was sitting very quietly and staring out of the window. She seemed miles away. Mac knew it was always best to leave her when she was like this, but listening to the tick of the car engine as it cooled, she couldn't do it, she had to say something.

'Are those Spitfires up there, over the bay?' She didn't think they were, but she couldn't think of anything else to say.

Jo spoke at last, 'No, I think they're Tiger Moths, the Air Force use them to train fighter pilots. Morecambe is a training base.'

'Is it?' she replied, genuinely surprised. They'd visited the seaside town before the war, and it had been a jolly place with people on holiday, ice cream, donkeys on the beach, and a funfair. She hadn't even thought a place like that would have been requisitioned for the war. 'Everything's changed hasn't it?' she added. 'Do you remember going on that big dipper? I screamed my head off and you nearly threw up.'

'Ha!' Jo said, letting go of the steering wheel and resting back in her seat. 'It seems like a lifetime ago doesn't it.'

'It does... but I tell you what, as soon as this is all over, we're going to the seaside again and we're going to have candyfloss and everything.'

She could sense Jo easing back in her seat. 'Well don't get it all stuck in your hair like last time,' she smiled, 'I had to cut it out with my scissors.'

'Oh yes, I'd forgotten about that, but don't you worry, by the time this war is over I'll be much more competent with candyfloss.'

'In fact, though,' said Jo, lowering her eyes, 'we might not have to wait that long, Mum was saying that the funfair and the beach have stayed open for all the Air Force personnel, and they have dances and everything.'

When Jo looked up, Mac could see that her face was pale and her eyes were wide. She seemed as if she was about to say something else, but no words came.

Mac wanted to tell her to spit it out but instead she said, 'How strange, I would have thought that if it was a training base there'd just be people in uniform marching up and down the promenade.'

Jo gave a tight smile. 'Oh, I think they do that as well, as part of their basic training, but it sounds like there's plenty of entertainment. And they have the Women's Air Force stationed there too, Mum knows someone who trained to operate a barrage balloon, of all things.'

'Crikey,' said Mac, interested. 'I just thought they tied them up and they did whatever they did all by themselves.'

'No, apparently you've got to position them and control them, to make sure that they're an effective deterrent to enemy aircraft.'

'Pity we didn't have one on the roof of Mill Road hey, Jojo?'

'It is,' she sighed, sounding a little distant again and then she took a deep breath and when she spoke, her voice was solemn, 'I need to tell you something. I've been thinking about it for a few days now...'

Mac waited. 'Go on.'

'It's just that, I don't think I'll be able to go back to Liverpool, not after what happened. I just can't stand the thought of being there, in another hospital, wondering when another bomb was going to fall — even the sound of the air raid siren — I don't think I could do it. And I keep thinking about Myfanwy, I can't get her out of my head. She was an only child like me and I can't even imagine what her parents must be going through. It could be me and you next, we might be the ones... So, I've been thinking I might apply to the military hospital in Morecambe.'

Mac hadn't even considered that Jo might be making her own plans. It took her by surprise. 'Really?' she said, gazing down to the bay, wondering what kind of hospital they could possibly have down there in what seemed, to her, like the middle of nowhere.

'Yes. It's in that new hotel, The Midland, we went in there, remember? It's that beautiful white building on the seafront.'

'Yes, of course,' Mac said, remembering it very well. She seemed to recall that they'd gone in for cocktails and it had a magnificent curved staircase that she'd imagined walking down in an evening gown and elbow-length gloves.

'Well, I don't know what you think, and I don't want to rush you, but I think we should both get back to doing what we've been trained for, what we're good at, and they're looking for more nurses right now. I know that Liverpool is your place and I'm not sure how you'd get on in Morecambe, but Mum and I thought it might be a good idea for us both to apply. What do you think?'

Mac was stunned. She took a breath before speaking. 'I'm really sorry, Jo, I don't think I can do that. It's just that, well, I've been thinking about what I need to do, and I want to be an army nurse.'

'The army?' Jo switched round, her face scrunched in horror.

'Yes,' she replied weakly.

'I was thinking about it at Mill Road even before the bomb, but with the Blitz going on, we were always so busy, and we were in the thick of it anyway. But now that things have changed, I don't feel like I can go back to Liverpool either and, well, having felt the blast of a bomb, and I know this probably sounds

189

strange, but it just seems the right thing for me to do.'

Jo's eyes were wide and she didn't seem to know what to say.

'It's not that I'm fearless, far from it, it's just that I've survived it once and I feel like I can do it again.'

Still Jo didn't answer.

At last, she simply said, 'But, we've always worked together…'

'Yes, we have,' Mac said, trying to control her trembling voice. And then Jo started to cry, and they turned towards each other and clung together like two small children. 'I didn't think anything would ever separate us, not even this bloody war.'

'Come on, let's get out and have a proper look at this view,' Mac said eventually, wiping her eyes with the flat of her hand. She pushed open the car door and jumped out. The breeze was cooler than expected and it caught her by surprise, lifting the hem of her skirt. She ran around to the other side, laughing as she met Jo opening her door, helping to pull her out of the driver's seat.

Slightly out of breath, she rested back against the car with Jo beside her. She felt so much better, feeling the breeze, hearing the steady trickle of the water that babbled in a constant stream off the fell. The land dropped away steeply to flat green fields, she could see every detail — brown cows in a field, a plume of smoke from a farmhouse chimney, and beyond, a strip of sand and then the white shining waters of the bay with the shadowed outlines of the Lakeland fells, more rugged, at the other side. She closed her eyes, letting the breeze blow her hair back from her face, breathing it in.

'What's that?' she said, hearing a noise, almost like

a child's rhythmical call. Jo smiled. 'Oh, my goodness, I've not heard that for years, you have to be here at a particular time to hear a cuckoo.' They were both listening intently, and Jo reached out to hold Mac's hand.

'Cu-ckoo, cu-ckoo,' the bird sang. Mac was thrilled, she loved the sound and at least it was a bird that she'd heard of. They held hands and listened for as long as the cuckoo continued to call.

All the while the small planes continued to buzz over the bay and Mac couldn't help but think of Don. By now, he'd be up in the sky somewhere, learning how to shoot down the enemy. And the reality was he'd be out on operations soon. Seeing the planes swooping and diving she was struck by how unprotected the men were up there — how easy it would be to die.

She felt a shiver go right through her. She needed to stop thinking about Don but that was easier said than done, he seemed to have got under her skin. 'Come on, let's get back in,' she called, running round to the other side and jumping back in as Jo slipped into the driver's seat. 'Now,' she said, twisting round to reach a box on the back seat, 'I think it's time we had some coffee and one of those delicious egg sandwiches that your mother packed up for us.' As she poured the hot coffee into two matching enamel cups, a strong smell of alcohol met her nostrils. 'Blimey, I think your mother must have laced this with brandy.' She took a sip. 'It's got a hell of a kick to it.'

'She always does that — and you know what, even if it burns a track right down to my stomach, there's nothing else in the world that I'd rather have right now.'

'Cheers to that!' Mac handed her the enamel mug. 'Here's to us, together in spirit, always.'

'Cheers,' said Jo, sounding forlorn.

Mac heard the sadness in her voice; she couldn't bear it if Jo was unhappy. 'We *will* always be together, Jo, you know we will. How can we not? We've not only lived and worked together for all these years, you saved my life. Not many people have a bond like that, do they?'

Jo's eyes were shining. 'I suppose not, that is a bit of a tall order isn't it?'

'We're friends for life, you and me, and as soon as this war's over we'll be back together again.'

Jo nodded, taking a sip from her coffee. 'Crikey, that is strong,' she gasped. 'It's as if she knew that we were going to have a bit of an emotional time on our afternoon out.'

'Your mother knows everything, I think she's tuned into every forecast. I bet she even knows when the war's going to end — ask her, she'll be able to give you a date and a time.'

Jo started to giggle.

Mac took another big bite of her sandwich and with her mouth still half full, she started to speak quickly, as if she'd just remembered something. 'And there's another thing, about me and the army... There is another reason for joining up...' She paused to swallow the remains of the bread. 'I've always wanted to drive a jeep.'

Jo spluttered out a laugh, coughing on her drink.

'Imagine me driving a jeep!' Mac laughed. 'I've never even been behind the wheel of a car.'

192

THREE YEARS LATER

18

Normandy, July 1944

Mac gripped the wheel as the jeep bounced over a rough, pockmarked road, her foot flat on the accelerator. Dust flew into her eyes and gritted her teeth, but she kept going; the sound of heavy fire across the enemy lines was strengthening and the sky was now black with allied planes. She glanced at the passenger seat, checking the supply of morphia that she'd been sent out for. What use would it be, if on the way back, the whole bloody lot bounced out of the jeep or smashed on the floor. They'd had a huge influx of casualties in the last two days, and this stock was crucial.

Hitting a boulder, one hand flew off the steering wheel, and she grabbed back control, hauling the battered vehicle back on track, her heart thumping against her ribs as she saw how close she'd been to hitting a splintered tree at the side of the road. She flattened the accelerator again.

Seeing at last the hospital tents in the distance, she slackened off a little. The jeep had rallied nicely, but she knew it was only just holding together. She'd checked the oil and topped it up before setting off, but the engine sounded ragged. She didn't want to break down now and have to make the rest of the way on foot.

Sister Lloyd was waiting at the door of the tent, her sharp eyes narrowed against the sun. 'Thanks, Nurse

MacDonald,' she said, grabbing the box that rattled with bottles of morphia, calling back over her shoulder as she dodged briskly between beds. 'I'm sorry I had to wake you, I know your night shift was hellish, but I couldn't think of anyone else who I could rely on to bring this back in double quick time.'

'I'm happy to help,' Mac smiled, following Sister through to the medicine store, checking patients as she went, noting that they'd admitted even more new casualties since she left her shift at 8 a.m. Men were crammed in on stretchers, and one poor soul was writhing in agony.

Sister was already inserting a needle through the rubber bung and drawing up morphia into a glass syringe. Once she'd checked the level, tapped the side, and depressed the plunger by a tiny amount to expel the air, she immediately fixed another needle and drew up another dose.

'Do you want me to help you give some of these injections?'

'No,' Sister said firmly, gesturing in Vera's direction. 'I'll ask Nurse Darlington to assist, I want you to go back to the dorm and get some more sleep.'

Mac nodded, knowing it made sense; working in these conditions was hard enough, and they had to make sure that no one went under — only last week a nurse had been sent home, her spirit completely broken by the relentless stream of soldiers mangled and broken by war.

Back in the dormitory tent the other night nurses — Lucy with her dark blonde hair mussed on the pillow and Edith, her neat black plait hanging over the side of the camp bed — were both still sleeping soundly. Lucy's discarded clothing lay like a pool on the bright green grass that formed the temporary floor of the tent. As Mac stripped off her battledress tunic, through the tent flap she could see a big gun that had been abandoned by the Germans — the hard metal seemed surreal next to a leafy hedge and some wildflowers. Especially so in quieter moments, when hedge sparrows and robins could be seen perching on the barrel.

The grass inside the tent was already showing patches of wear and some areas were turning brown; she knew this would continue to worsen until they were called to 'up sticks' and move. As the allied forces continued to push back the Germans, so they crept forward as well.

She peeled off her dusty shirt and khaki pants, unlaced and slipped off her heavy boots, and gave herself a quick wipe down with some cold water, which ran down her neck and between her breasts, making her skin tingle. Glancing in the small mirror that Vera had erected on one of the tent poles, Mac brushed back her hair with damp hands. The fringe that she'd cut in had grown out years ago, it had been irritating and she'd never got used to it. And it didn't matter now because she could look at herself in any mirror and even feel proud of the star-shaped scar on her forehead. At first, every time she'd caught a glimpse it had reminded her of the worst day of her life but now, well, it was a part of her and if people asked her how she'd got it, she'd tell them it was what you got for being a survivor.

It was hot in the tent with the sun beating down on the canvas, so she didn't bother with a nightie and slipped into the camp bed in just her vest and lace cami knickers. She hoped Matron wasn't due to make an inspection; all nurses were supposed to wear the regulation khaki underwear with baggy elasticated waist — 'passion killers' was what her friend Vera called them.

Despite the heat, the sound of allied planes overhead and the relentless racket from the camp, Mac did manage a couple of hours sleep. Feeling groggy when she woke, she reached for a cigarette and lay back on the bed smoking, one hand fiddling with the silver locket that she wore alongside her dog tags. She noticed a stack of unopened letters on a canvas stool next to Vera's empty bed. No doubt from her big family, all living in her native Newcastle. She loved to hear the never-ending stories of Vera's family life — all the spats and disasters, despite which it was clear there was so much love between them all. It was sad for Vera, though, she'd been working in a hospital during the Blitz, when Brian, her fiancé — home on leave from the army — was killed outright in a bomb blast. Vera had had to take time off work and when she'd eventually gone back to nursing she just couldn't settle. In one of the dreams she'd had about Brian, he'd told her that she should join the army, take over from where he'd left off. Mac had always wondered if she should have perhaps taken a bit more time to consider Brian's request. Anyway, Vera had dutifully fulfilled the request from beyond the grave, and that's how they'd first met, at basic training camp in Oxford — staying in lodgings inside one of the colleges.

What a time they'd had there, going out at night, dancing, making friends, and Oxford had felt so safe, well away from the Blitz. She'd become close to Vera, not as close as she was with Jo, but close enough for them to have a meaningful connection. And Vera's

198

letters from home were an endless source of entertainment. Mac didn't have much to offer in return
— Jo wrote sometimes, and her letters were quirky
and full of kind regards and details of her work, but
she didn't give much else away. And then there was
the occasional letter from Don, of course, who wrote
every now and then, having wangled the address out
of Jo and her mum. His letters were hard to read —
all he did was repeat that he couldn't forget her, he
would be seeing her again once the war was over —
and she never knew if the feeling in her chest when
she got one was anxiety or excitement. All she knew
was that it was far too precarious to have 'feelings'
for any man who was risking his life day after day in
the service of his country. Any thoughts of Don were
also inextricably linked to that time after the bomb at
Mill Road. It had taken her a full year to stop having
flashbacks whenever she heard a loud noise. She had
to keep all of it at bay, so that she could keep working — and it was the work that made her able to do
so. She was trapped. Anyway, it made sense to protect
herself; she knew that she had to be free from the
agony of worry about some airman who she knew, if
she was honest with herself, could well and truly have
been the love of her life.

She was expecting another letter soon and just the
thought of it bothered her so much it made the scar
on her forehead start to prickle. She pushed herself up
from the bed, shaking her body, stretching her aching
back, telling herself that she didn't care whether he
sent one or not. All she ever needed before another
night shift was a cigarette and the best tinned bacon
and beans that the army mess could provide.

Walking through the hospital tent that evening,

closely followed by Edith and Lucy, she was immediately on her mettle. The ward was full — iron-framed beds crammed together where men lay propped up on pillows, many of them still in their torn and battle-stained tunics, with tin hats or military caps on the orange boxes that served as lockers. Her eyes scanned the patients, checking their condition, aware of the white bedsheets that hid the atrocity of their injuries. One young soldier, a gunshot wound to the chest, was bloated and blue, struggling to breathe — she noted that he would need a change of oxygen cylinder soon. She'd got used to the daily sight of raw flesh and the glint of bone from the hideous wounds that these men bore, but that didn't mean that she was inured to it. She hated what bullets and bombs and incendiary devices could do to men. They were only a month or so on from the D-Day landings and already there were those who were saying that it was just a question of time before it was all over but sometimes it felt like even one more day was just too much.

Even now, another grim party of soldiers was waiting in the area reserved for new admissions, their white faces dirty and unshaven, their battledress torn and stained. Exhausted, they slept on stretchers or lay on the floor. Another group lay quietly side by side, far too still, exuding the smell of burnt flesh; each with a bottle of plasma strung up from the tent roof with a bandage — the fluid absorbing slowly through red rubber tubing. Identical in their despair, the group were indistinguishable from each other with their hair and eyebrows singed off and their arms and faces blackened by bits of metal and explosive under the skin.

Sister Lloyd, a strand of greying hair escaping from

the cloth turban that she always wore on duty, took a deep breath and gestured for them to gather round to take the report. Her voice was heavy with exhaustion as she rapidly went through the list of stable, critical and newly arrived patients. The new patients included the tragic group of burnt men; they were a tank crew, something that they often saw, four men together who'd been blown up and incinerated, all at the same time. The men lay side by side with their commander, Sergeant Greenlees. Mac absorbed the sadness of it all, she had to swallow hard to keep focused, not to get emotional. One of the men had suffered the worst of it, his right leg burnt so badly that it had been amputated already. The rest lay with severe burns, their lives in the balance. She knew they would have to watch these men very carefully; often the respiratory passages could become swollen and cause suffocation.

Report drew to a close and Mac exchanged a smile with Vera as she began to take instruments out of a steriliser, putting them into an enamel receiver, making last minute preparations before she went off duty. She looked so young and delicate in her oversized khaki trousers and army boots, but in the last few weeks Mac had come to know just how tough she was. The other day staff were frantically restocking the supplies that were kept on trestle tables in the middle of the ward — sterile dressings, rubber tubing, antiseptic, bandages and adhesive tape. This was essential work, emergencies such as haemorrhage could happen very quickly and supplies had to be close at hand. Mac always did her own checks mid-way through the night, and she made sure that they had plenty of morphia drawn up and ready to go.

Once the day staff had gone to their rest at the end of their shift, Mac took charge and handed out duties to the group. First on the list, as always, was identifying those most in need of pain relief. Every night, she promised to herself that if they had time, she would make sure that they went round with washbowls and flannels to try and clean some of the lingering grime off the men — but each night she was frustrated; they were always too busy, having to content themselves with an early morning wipe of face and hands at best. Then, she'd provide clean pyjamas — if they had enough supply — to the new admissions still wearing torn and bloodstained uniform. The other priority was of course fluids — she always checked that Jim, the night orderly, went round regularly offering drinks of tea or water. And if a soldier couldn't drink, then a saline drip needed to be set up, otherwise even the strongest of men would stand little chance of survival.

One young soldier, Peter Tyce, who'd been with them for over a week, was shouting out, plucking at his sheet and moving his head agitatedly from side to side. Mac went straight to him. 'Where am I?' he croaked. His mouth was dry and sticking together and his lips were cracked.

'You're in hospital, remember?' Mac replied, reaching for a spouted cup and trying to give him a sip of water. He was no more than a boy. His innocent blue eyes searched her face for a moment, looking surprised, and then he began muttering jumbled words. She lifted his head from the pillow, supporting it with her arm, and tried to give him a drink — but he fought against her, scrunching his face, the water dribbling down his chin. After she'd settled him gently back on the pillow, he opened his eyes and to Mac's distress, called out for his mother. She grasped his hand to calm him, while trying to work out why he was so unsettled. He wasn't able to articulate whether or not he was in pain, so she pulled back the sheet to check the abdominal dressing that covered a large wound — a vicious piece of shrapnel had ripped into his upper abdomen, tearing his liver in two and embedding itself dangerously close to the spine. After hours in surgery to dig out the shrapnel and stitch up the internal damage, he'd emerged with a blood transfusion and a red rubber drain to prevent an accumulation of fluid inside his abdomen. After surgery, Mac had received him back on the ward, her breath catching when she saw his bonny face creased with pain.

Now, she just needed to work out what was happening, see if there was anything that she could do to ease him. There was nothing leaking from the dressing and nothing else untoward that she could see. This was something else — and she was starting to worry. She pulled the sheet back up and peered at his face — the whites of his eyes had a tinge of yellow. Her heart sank. He was developing jaundice due to the liver damage, a very bad sign. She knew from past cases that this often heralded a rapid deterioration in condition. Poor young Peter would never see his mother again; he was almost certainly dying.

He looked at her again, frowning. 'It's alright, Peter, I think you might have a bit of extra pain from the surgery, that's all. I'll get you an injection.' This set formula of words was all that she could offer, what else could she say?

He reached out and grabbed her arm. 'Mam,' he called, 'where's Mam?'

Mac swallowed hard, 'Your Mam's at home waiting

for you, don't you worry. And she loves you very—'
She fought now to control her voice. Kneeling down
beside the bed, she took his hand and stroked his hair,
helping him to settle, all the time remembering what
a senior nurse had once said to her when she was a
probationer — 'care is love made visible'. As a young
nurse, she'd wondered about that — especially when
she'd been haring up and down a long ward, rushing
to catch up on innumerable tasks. But she'd soon had
experiences when she knew it to be true.

The man in the next bed, Captain Josef Barylak,
raised his head, his eyes full of sadness. As a member
of a Polish tank division who'd fought hard on the
beaches, he'd lost many men. Mac caught his eye, and
an unspoken understanding passed between them.

She cleared her throat. 'I'm just going to get that
injection for you, Peter, I'll only be a minute.'

She stayed with him after the injection, holding his
hand. *We are their family now*, she thought, wishing that
she could stay longer, as always. But already another
soldier was shouting and trying to clamber out of bed
and she still hadn't been able to have a proper look
at the tank commander and his crew. She adjusted
Peter's pillow so that it was in a more comfortable
position, brushed his hair back from his forehead,
and promised that she would come back and check
on him as soon as she could.

Edith was already with the tank crew, her face intent
as she checked pulse and temperature and made sure
that the huge dressings that covered the burns on each
man's lower body were intact. When Edith looked
up, they exchanged a glance — they both knew the
score for these poor men. All too often they'd had
whole tank crews hospitalised in this sorry state. Mac

204

scrubbed her hands clean and then went to inspect, lifting the corner of a dressing to make sure that the Vaseline gauze and 'magic dust' as they all called it — the penicillin and sulphonamide antibiotic powder — had been liberally applied. Seeing the extent of the burns on the three crew, she knew that despite the plasma and the brave attempts to treat the wounds that they bore, far too great an area of tissue was lost. It was unlikely that any of them would survive. The tank commander, however, had fared better — both his arms were burned, but beyond that, his chest and torso were intact. He stood a fighting chance. She tried not to think about the pain he would have to bear when he found out that all his crew had perished.

Another lap of the tent and she passed Corporal Vince Earnshaw's bed — all the nurses made the effort to do so, at least two or three times per night, as it was a rare moment to smile. When Vince had been admitted with a compound fracture of the tibia, there'd been an almighty row. Tucked inside this big fella's jacket was a small dog — a little terrier with a patch of brown over one eye — that he'd picked up as a stray. Vince had clung to the dog, swearing at anyone who tried to take little Ambrose off him. Sister Lloyd had ordered the nurses to remove the dog as it was simply not hygienic. So once Vince was in theatre, little Ambrose was given to one of the mechanics to keep in his equipment store. The poor little creature had howled and howled till nobody in camp could stand it any longer. And Vince had been in floods of tears when he came back from surgery, stranded in bed with his leg encased in plaster of Paris. So, the mechanic had brought the dog back — smudged with a bit of oil but still wagging his tail. Sister had stopped him at the door, ordering him to turn right around. He'd asked her to step outside and they'd had some heated words, Mac had been told. In the end, Sister had turned to see the mournful faces of two nurses at the door of the tent and she'd had no choice — the dog would have to stay, whether she liked it or not. So every day, Ambrose trotted around the camp, and every night he came back to Vince and lay snuggled on the bed beside the big man, sleeping soundly. 'Not under the covers,' Sister had insisted and all the night staff had confirmed that this would be done according to her instruction — making sure each morning to untuck the little dog before Sister came on duty.

Seeing faithful little Ambrose now, his nose and one ear poking out from under the sheet, made Mac smile.

Between 3 and 4 a.m., when it got so busy that the hours flew by, she felt a shiver go through her body. Since working regular nights, she'd got used to this time just before dawn when if a life hung in the balance, more often than not the patient would succumb. She went to check on Peter — she'd already called for their surgeon, Major Rossiter to have a look, just in case there was anything surgical that they could do, or, clutching at straws, any medicine that might help. He'd come from theatre — where they were still working their way through the new admissions — shuffling in his white rubber boots, his operating gown stained with blood. Standing there, grey and tired, he'd shaken his head and confirmed her suspicions. 'Just give him some more morphine, if he needs it,' he'd said wearily. 'I need to get back, we've got one already anaesthetised and Dr Grant will already be looking at the X-rays.'

Mac could see that Peter's breathing was shallow; he'd deteriorated even faster than she thought he would. She knelt by his bed, held his hand, and as the first pale light shone through the door of the tent, he quietly took his final breath. Once his face relaxed, he looked like a sleeping child. So many times she'd sat like this, as had all the nurses. She knew that she'd got used to it — you had to. But the dull ache of it settled inside her chest, like a weight. She would use it later to spur her on, but right now, it rested there. She had no idea how much more of this she could take, or what she would be like when the war was over, but this was the work that she'd come out here to do and unless she was shot or blown up, she would keep doing it.

'Goodbye, Peter,' she murmured, pulling the sheet carefully over his face, immediately aware that another patient was consumed with pain and shouting, 'Nurse, nurse!'

19

RAF Mildenhall, July 1944

Don patted his chest, a ritual gesture he made before every mission. He kissed the well-worn magazine cutting of Rita Hayworth, before slipping it into the breast pocket of his fur-collared flight jacket, right above his heart. What had been a routine on his first few flights, years ago, had quickly become superstition. All the men had their own rituals, and none would neglect them.

In those early days, when he was a wireless operator, he'd been blasé about his layers of clothing, but now that he was a full-time gunner, confined to a Perspex turret in below-freezing temperatures, he even wore silk stockings, fleecy long johns, a thick knitted jumper and extra socks beneath his electrically heated full-length suit and gloves. One thing that was key to his performance with the gun was avoiding distraction. If he was cold, he was more likely to make a mistake, and if he made a mistake, the whole lot of them could go down.

He'd chopped and changed through different crews; many of the men he'd flown with were already dead and gone. And the gunners were most at risk. It seemed such a long time since the beginning of the war, no one had imagined it would take so long. The old hands like him were getting weary, numbed by death after death, constantly seeing planes shot down and falling from the sky. He sometimes had flashbacks to the faces of those who had been lost, young men with their whole lives before them — happy, smiling faces.

They all lived one day at a time, acutely aware of the empty bunks that were a reminder of how many they'd lost on each mission. But he'd fallen lucky right now, he was with a good crew. As they waddled together in their layers of clothing and flight helmets towards the four-engine Lancaster bomber, he could see each of them saying their own prayers, thinking their own thoughts. Glancing up to the cockpit he saw the shadow of Flight Lieutenant Carl O'Brien, their skipper, already installed, ready and waiting for the signal to move. A quietly spoken Canadian, he'd easily made his mark with the men: always calm in a crisis, and despite his leisurely manner, he was sharp. They'd need every ounce of that tonight, they were on a mission to Stuttgart — the city would be heavily defended and the sky would be full of flares and anti-aircraft fire.

Time to board. He took a deep breath and crossed himself.

'Come on, Costello, get yourself up here.' Ray Lovell, another Canadian and an experienced flight engineer, was always lighthearted, even when things were tense — he kept them together, kept them going. You couldn't help but feel invincible with someone like Ray on board.

As Don scrambled onto the plane lugging his parachute, the wireless operator — a new lad from London — sprang up behind him. Young Tony reminded Don of how he'd been at the start of the war: bright and shining and eager to have a go. Hearing a shout and the noisy drawl of their rear gunner — a lanky Australian, only ever known as Ginger, who claimed to be the longest surviving gunner of the whole war — Don turned to smile. They all knew Ginger was full of bullshit, but he was damned good with a machine gun, so that was all that mattered. Ginger jumped aboard, patting Don on the arm as he passed, and calling out some playful abuse in a mock Scottish accent to their navigator — Gordon 'Scotty' McAllister — who was kitted out with his lucky tartan scarf and already huddled up in discussion with Johnny Diamond, their bomb aimer. 'Aye, piss off, you skanky Aussie. Get yourself in your box, where I can't see ye or hear ye.' Ginger guffawed with laughter and started singing, 'On the bonny, bonny banks of Loch Lomond...'

Fearless, as always, Ginger moved swiftly, sliding along and squeezing into the cramped rear turret, the most exposed position by far. Don always took his time, even after so many missions he still had to deal with that initial tightening of his chest as he stood in the metal belly of the plane. He glanced up to Scotty and Tony, their heads together at the table with all the maps and instruments, and beyond the glow of the instrument panel and the murmur of conversation from the cockpit. When Johnny Diamond raised a hand before heading forward to his position in the nose, where he'd have to lie flat staring at the landscape below, Don knew it was time to move. Scrambling up into the canvas triangle that would support him in his position as mid-gunner he manoeuvred his head and broad shoulders into the metal and Perspex dome that would serve as his only protection. He took a few moments to settle his breathing, plug in his oxygen, and check that his parachute harness was secure.

For a minute or two, all he could hear was the sound

of his own breathing, then the peace was shattered as Lancaster after Lancaster started up their engines. The metal crate of the bomber vibrated as they taxied out and then rattled and shook with increasing intensity as they raced to the end of the runway, O'Brien heaving them up into the air right at the last moment. Don could see other aircraft all around them, a stream of bombers stretching out across the night sky. Even after all his years in combat, this moment always made his heart beat a little faster.

He pulled down his goggles, switched on his electric gunsight and the intercom, so that he could communicate with the rest of the crew. And then he stared into the blackness, praying that the shadow of a fighter wouldn't appear. Trying to stay calm as the time slipped by as they headed East, towards their target, he found himself thinking about all sorts of things, but often it was Mac. There'd been other women since then, of course there had, but they'd been passing moments; not one of them had stuck, not like her. And always, right now, trying to distract himself, he played back in his mind the moment she'd stepped into the pub the night of the Mill Road bomb, when he'd turned and seen her standing there. He could return to that memory over and over and never get tired of it.

A searchlight panning the sky caught his breath and shut out all thought apart from what was happening right now, up ahead. Instantly he was on alert. Anti-aircraft flares were streaking the sky, followed by short bursts of tracer shells.

'Here we go, everybody set?' Skipper's steady voice crackled over the intercom.

'All set, Skip,' each one of them replied. Don's

hands were in position, gripping the gun. In the sky ahead were a mass of bursting shells and wild flashes. How the hell were they going to fly through that?

Still the bombers were sweeping towards their target — they had no choice, they had to go through with it. Don gasped — a German fighter plane was right there, less than a hundred yards away.

'Port side down, see it?' he called, trying to keep his voice calm.

'Got it!' Ginger almost growled.

'Hold steady, he might not have seen us,' Don advised. He held his breath as the fighter drifted by so close that he could see the turquoise gleam of the dials in his cockpit. Then, it was gone. 'Ahh, looks like we can let sleeping dogs lie...'

'Yep,' came Ginger's voice, sounding almost a little disappointed.

But in a matter of seconds, the fighter was back and he had definitely seen them now.

'Bandit back! Above rear on the port side.'

Skipper responded, 'Right, do you see him, Rear gunner? We'll try a corkscrew manoeuvre, let me know when you're ready?'

'Roger that.'

Don could hear Ginger breathing and then he shouted, 'Corkscrew starboard, go, go!' The engine screamed and the evasive drill commenced, sending the Lancaster spiralling down, trying to shake the fighter off its tail.

A moment of radio silence. Don could feel the sweat pouring down his face.

The fighter was back, there were two of them now.

'Two bandits, port and starboard, coming in five hundred yards.'

'Pilot to gunners, let them come in a bit nearer, then shoot the buggers down.'

Don let them come, as close as he dared, then he squeezed the handgrips of his gun, hard. The deafening rattle of ammunition shaking and vibrating his Perspex dome. In seconds he was coughing on smoke and the stench of cordite. He clung to the gun until he could see one of the fighter planes on fire and falling away. The sound of Ginger's gun continued and then his voice crackled into life, 'All sorted, skip.'

They continued to steer their course, flashes of red and grey smoke all around as shells burst and the Lancaster shuddered, rising and falling as she ploughed on.

At last they were over the target.

'Bomb doors open,' shouted Scotty. And then, 'Bombs gone.'

Don felt the plane lift, once the weight had gone. He could never hear them exploding but the smell of cordite was acrid in his small turret.

'Bomb doors closed, time to go home,' sang Scotty's voice.

Don gazed down to the streets and buildings of Stuttgart, seeing the red and yellow flashes of many explosions, all streaked with bright white photo flashes from the aircraft cameras. Many fires were burning. It always triggered the memory of those nights in Liverpool at the beginning of the war, running through the streets with debris falling around him and that American pilot — he couldn't even remember his name now. As he looked down, he could see the detail of a city, there would be people down there, crouched in air raid shelters, praying they didn't get hit. Earlier in the war, he'd had to steel himself against thinking

213

too deeply — he'd taken advice from the old hands about that — but now, mission after mission, he could feel it all creeping in, weighing him down. Of course he was glad that he was part of the resistance to an enemy that had caused such terrible destruction, of course he was, but there was no triumph in this, not any more. It felt sad to be dropping bombs on a place where people were just trying to survive, like everyone else in this world of war.

A Halifax bomber nearby lurched as if it had taken a punch and instantly burst into flames. It reared up, its nose in the air, and then it fell quickly. No one will get out of that, Don thought, matter-of-fact in his assessment, all the while forcing back his own fear by repeating in his head, 'It won't happen to us, it won't happen to us.' It was the only way that he could keep going. And he knew that some, like Ginger, truly believed it.

The darkness closed around them as O'Brien moved the Lancaster to a higher altitude where they would have more cover during their flight home. Don saw another bomber flying side by side, even as he watched it started to lurch, and then, without warning, it burst into flames. He felt a slow ache in his chest as he craned his neck, trying to see if the crew were bailing out, but there was nothing. In moments the nose of the plane dropped and he watched as it cut a path downwards, one wing shearing off, disintegrating as it went. He shuddered. 'It won't happen to us, it won't happen to us.'

Ginger's voice crackled over the intercom, 'Just so you know. If we get hit, I'm going to ride this baby down.'

'What the hell are you on about?' Don shouted,

horrified at his bullshit. 'If we can bail out, we will!'

'I'm coming with you, Costello,' Tony's voice sounded small, exhausted.

'We're on our way home,' Skipper's voice, steady as always, 'We're making good spee—'

His voice was cut short by a heavy rattle of exploding shells as a vicious sparking white tracer whipped the side of the plane. Terrifyingly, the Lancaster seemed to stop dead, and then it lurched sideways.

'Jesus Christ, Jesus Christ,' someone was shouting. Don could see both port engines ablaze. The engines screamed in agony as the nose went down, chunks of metal peeling off the tailfin.

'Pull the bugger out,' someone shouted, and then O'Brien's voice, 'Abandon aircraft, abandon aircraft.'

Don whipped off his gloves and uncoupled his oxygen, using all his strength to push himself down from the turret as rapidly as he could. The fuselage was full of smoke and flames, the aircraft cracking and lurching violently. He could just about make out Scotty and young Tony, shot through by shrapnel, neither of them moving. He could hear shouts from the cockpit as O'Brien and Ray fought to bring the plane level. But the deck was sloping badly now, soon it would be vertical. Don saw a parachute sliding down and he grabbed it, trying and failing to click it to his harness. Screaming in frustration, he tried again, but still it wouldn't connect. The Lancaster shuddered, it was starting to disintegrate. He propped himself against the hard metal of the fuselage, gasping for air, fighting with the harness again, and this time it clicked into place.

Stumbling now towards the rear, he saw the shape of someone. It was Ginger wearing his parachute;

he opened up the escape hatch, turned, gave Don a thumbs up, and then he jumped.

Don struggled to breathe through the smoke, and he could feel the intense heat of the fire and hear ammunition exploding. As he got closer to the escape hatch, he could see flames outside. Crawling on his hands and knees as the Lancaster continued to tilt, he hauled himself up to stand at the open door. As soon as he poked his head out, he felt a fierce wind grab him and he was whipped out. Hurtling through the air, he fought once more with the harness of the parachute and at last he felt the jolt as it opened. Then, he was drifting down, and could see their Lancaster curling rapidly away beneath him, streaming with flames. He'd only seen Ginger bail out and he knew that two of the crew were dead, probably killed outright. He just hoped that Ray, Johnny and O'Brien had bailed out, but he knew that they were probably still in there.

All he could see was the flash of explosions in the black night sky as he continued to float, with no idea where he was or how he would land. He realised that he was crying, though somehow, he also felt calmer now. He'd always thought that if this moment ever came, he'd think about his father, his sisters or his dead mother, but all he could see was Mac's face. She was leaning in to kiss him and he was breathing in the smell of her, and now he was floating away.

There was no pain when it came, the black earth reared up to meet him and, in the end, he sank into it with a grateful thud.

20

Normandy, August 1944

'Nurse MacDonald, wake up.' A quiet voice was calling her from a distance.

'Jo, you pest,' she muttered, 'Let me sleep …'

'Nurse MacDonald,' the voice insisted, and now someone was shaking her arm.

She sat up in bed, 'Sister Lloyd?' she croaked. 'Sorry... I thought I was back at Mill Road, sorry.'

'That's alright, and I'm sorry to wake you once more with the same request, but can you make a dash for us again, down the line, to get some supplies.'

Mac was rubbing her eyes and sitting up. 'Of course, yes, of course I can.'

'Excellent,' Sister whispered. 'One of the mechanics has already checked the jeep, so you're ready to go. Just make sure you get a cup of tea and a bite to eat first.'

Scrambling up from her camp bed, Mac felt almost fully awake already, excited, as always, by the prospect of another outing in the jeep. She washed her face, raked a comb through her hair, and had her uniform and army boots on in double quick time. Checking that a pack of cigarettes was in her top pocket, she turned to leave, but her eye caught a letter on the canvas stool next to her bed. It had to be from Don. She swept it up and slipped it into her pocket, knowing that she didn't have the time to read it now, but she would savour it later.

The items requested — another box of morphia and an additional supply of intravenous saline complete with rubber giving sets — were ready and waiting as soon she arrived. So, with a few wry comments from the orderly who managed supplies, asking what the heck they were doing to need so much stuff, she was on her way back, her foot flat on the accelerator. Bumping along the supply route, with dust flying and her hair blowing back from her face, she felt wide awake and loving every bit of wild freedom that driving the jeep gave her.

Hearing the unmistakeable drone of heavy aircraft, she glanced up — a group of allied bombers, probably on reconnaissance, were black against the sky. She'd got so used to the sound of planes overhead; she found it comforting. But in the next second there was a single loud explosion and the torturous spluttering of an aircraft engine. Glancing up, her heart lurched when she saw a plane on fire, veering wildly out of line. Either it had suffered a catastrophic fault or somehow, even though they weren't yet over enemy territory, a random German gun, still manned and looking to take down whatever it could, had come into play. Whatever the reason, the plane was now plummeting very fast. 'Oh Christ!' she shouted, anchoring on the brakes — it looked like it might land right on top of her. Stationary now, she could feel her breath coming quick as she watched two men parachute out as the plane, consumed with flames, continued its trajectory, hurtling towards the earth. She gritted her teeth, bracing herself, feeling the boom as the aircraft slammed into a rutted field. The ground shook violently, rocking her trusty jeep. Glancing up, she saw two parachutes drifting down at what seemed like a leisurely pace. One poor man was on fire, the other slumped in his harness. She readied herself.

Both of them landed in a cloud of dust on the road ahead. She cranked the jeep into gear and zoomed towards them, screeching to a halt and throwing herself out onto the road beside them. Going straight to the man who was on fire first, she grabbed the parachute into a bundle and used it to extinguish the flames. Straightaway she could see that he wasn't breathing; he had probably died before he even hit the ground. She ran back to the other one, who was groaning in pain. His foot was twisted out of line — one ankle was definitely broken, but of more concern was his ragged breathing and an ooze of bright red blood coming from his flight jacket. She unclipped his parachute and pulled him free, opening up his jacket and ripping apart his shirt. Yes, it was there, he had a penetrating wound to the chest, probably from shrapnel. Aware that enemy snipers might be lurking, she quickly glanced around, her mind clawing at a distant memory of a drill from basic training — there was a pistol in the glove box and she knew how to use it — that was the only thing she needed to know right now.

Blood was everywhere and sticky on her hands. Not wanting to waste any time running back to the jeep for the medical kit, she removed her tunic and ripped off her shirt, bundling it up and pressing it firmly to the wound. She saw him open his eyes and he tried to speak but blood was coming out of his mouth.

'Look at me,' she called, making eye contact with him, 'I need you to say calm.'

He opened his mouth again, his eyes were pleading, terrified.

She shook her head, 'Don't try to speak, I'm a

nurse, I can help you.'

She could hear his breath rasping and his chest sounded tight — she knew he had a collection of blood and air in the pleural cavity, compressing his lung, and if left unchecked it would extend and cause enough pressure to kill him. She needed to act quickly. She'd seen the doctors perform the procedure many times, but it was different knowing that she had to do it herself. And yet she had no choice; he was hardly breathing now.

'Press this, as hard as you can,' she shouted, placing his hand over the bundled shirt. She jumped up, ran to the jeep and grabbed the medical kit, pulling one of the rubber giving sets out of the pack. As she stood catching her breath, she wrenched off the large bore needle, used to connect it to the infusion bottle. Not ideal, but it would have to do; she had nothing else, and if she didn't have a go, he would die anyway.

When she ran back to his side, he'd passed out. She pulled away the remains of his shirt to reveal his chest; he was barely breathing. 'Come on, you can do this,' she growled, using the fingers of one hand to feel down his chest, finding the right space between the ribs, gauging the correct line. She had the needle in her other hand, she needed to use it. Taking a deep breath, she stabbed straight between the ribs. Holding her own breath and leaning in very close to listen, she almost collapsed with relief when she heard the hiss of escaping air. As it continued, so his breathing improved, and then he slowly opened his eyes. She tried to smile at him, telling him to lie still, that he was going to be alright, but she knew that if she didn't get him back to camp soon, she would probably lose him anyway.

She removed the needle cleanly, then she grabbed a swab from the medical kit and pressed it firmly over the puncture wound; with her other hand, she pushed aside her blood-soaked shirt and grabbed a large field dressing to cover the chest wound. Then, needing to apply as much pressure as possible to seal the wound, she grabbed a wide bandage. Using all of her strength, she rolled him side to side to apply the bandage all the way around his torso, pulling it tight. And then, quickly, she took another bandage to support his ankle; this was no substitute for a proper splint but at least it would provide some stability.

They had to get moving if he was going to stand any chance of making it.

'I need to get you into the jeep, so this might be painful,' she said.

He nodded, thankfully more responsive now, and then he grabbed her arm, gasping, 'What about the crew ... Did they ...?'

She shook her head and his body slumped. 'I'm sorry,' she said gently, 'but we really do need to get moving, your injuries need treating.'

He groaned in response then nodded his head.

She manoeuvred the jeep as close as she could, right beside him, and stashed the new medical supplies in the back. There were some ready-prepared morphine injections in the medical kit, and she stuck one in his leg, at least it might help him on the journey when it started to work.

'I want you to push up and move on the count of three,' she shouted, 'One, two, three.' He pushed with his good leg, screaming as he moved. She heaved with all her might, but he fell back to the ground. 'You can do this,' she shouted. 'On three again... One,

221

two threeee…' He yelled and screamed in pain, but this time he did manage to grab the side of the jeep. 'Hold fast,' she shouted, breathless now as she braced herself to fully support the weight of his body from behind. Miraculously, he managed to use his arms to pull himself up and scramble into the passenger seat. As she helped straighten him, telling him to lean back on the seat, his face was pale and contorted with pain. 'I know you're in agony, but I can't do anything else until we get to the hospital. It isn't too far now.' She grabbed her tunic from the dusty road and jumped into the driver's seat, checking the pistol in the glove box — just in case.

Crawling along at half her usual speed — anything faster would have killed him — she regularly glanced over at the airman to check his condition. The journey seemed to take forever, but finally she saw the hospital tents coming into view.

Sister Lloyd, Vera and an orderly ran straight out to help her, incredulous at the sight of the injured airman in the passenger seat of her jeep.

'I told you to go for supplies, not more casualties,' Sister said as she swiftly moved to check the man's pulse and breathing. 'Now, what's your name, young man?'

'Sergeant Bruce Logan, pilot,' he grimaced.

Mac stood to catch her breath. Her vest was coated in dust, her shirt still abandoned on the road, and only when she wiped the back of her hand around her face did she realise that her hands were covered in dried blood.

After she'd handed over the details of the pilot's injuries and he was safely in theatre, Sister Lloyd brought her a medicine pot full of brandy. 'Get that inside you. Nurse MacDonald, you've done an incredible job today.'

Mac knocked the brandy back and she could feel it hit the spot. Sister began to say something about taking the night off, but she shook her head. 'I'm OK, I want to help, I'll be perfectly fine by tonight.'

Sister Lloyd narrowed her eyes, prepared to argue the case, but then she started to shake her head and patted Mac's shoulder. 'You're a woman after my own heart, Nurse MacDonald. For better or worse, that certainly does seem to be the case. Go with her Nurse Darlington, make sure she's tucked up in bed.'

Mac was glad of Vera's support. After all the frantic activity, the exhaustion had suddenly hit her right between the eyes. The way she now felt, she thought that she might even need somebody to help her get undressed. Whilst Vera went for some warm water and a clean towel, Mac stripped off her khaki pants, giving them a shake to get rid of the worst of the dust. Hearing the rustle of paper, she remembered the letter in her pocket. She pulled it out and ripped it open, holding it in her bloodstained hands as she sat on the camp bed to read.

At first, it didn't make any sense. She grabbed the envelope to check that it was meant for her, and yes, there was her name and the Bracken Farm address crossed out and rerouted by Jean — but it wasn't Don's handwriting. As she read the words, the true horror of the few short lines, written in an unsteady hand, began to sink in.

Dear Mac,

I'm sorry to write this but I promised Don I would if anything happened to him. He gave me the forwarding address

223

years ago, just in case. He's been reported missing in action, presumed dead. His plane was shot down. Don was a good bloke and we will all miss him.

Yours faithfully,
Harry Steele (me and Don did our gunner training together but I'm ground crew now)

Her hand was shaking as she held the letter. She felt like she'd been winded, as if a blow had been dealt right to her core. She hadn't realised she was crying but tears were dripping onto the letter. Reading the words again just to make sure, she could hardly see through her tears.

She heard Vera's voice, and then she felt an arm around her shoulders and the letter gently being removed from her grasp. 'Mac, I'm sorry, so sorry.' Hearing the words, spoken with such feeling, Mac gasped, and a sob broke through, and then she was wailing, unable to control the noise that came out of her body. Edith and Lucy were awake now, and they gathered around, all trying to comfort her.

21

RAF Blakehill Farm, August 1944

Jo had got used to the early morning scramble when she was on a mission. Always up first, she washed, dressed, ran a brush through her spiky, short-cropped hair before waking up the others, making sure that none of them left behind any essential kit. She was on the bottom bunk, beneath a nurse who had immediately reminded her so much of Mac that it had been very easy to make friends. Miriam was tall, elegant, she had a lovely rolling accent and was always laughing and teasing Jo about her English ways. 'Back home in Trinidad, we wouldn't even be worrying about that so much, Jo,' was her stock phrase. Miriam's warm companionship was exactly what she needed; their missions were increasingly tense, and they were landing ever closer to danger as the allies pushed further into enemy territory.

This morning, Miriam wasn't assigned to a mission, so while she continued to sleep, Jo left the Nissen Hut with the other Flying Nightingales, who like her, would be heading for their aircrew breakfast and complimentary orange, before boarding their Dakotas. She was still flying with Alec MacNab, the taciturn pilot who she'd been paired with from the start. Her orderly, Chris, had told her to pay him no mind and explained that he was from a fishing boat family. MacNab was uncomfortable with having a woman on board because where he came from, women were never allowed on the boats as it was thought to be bad luck. She'd been flying with him for two months, but he was still clearly uncomfortable with her; surely, by now, he should be starting to get over it.

This morning MacNab called through a cheery, 'Good morning, Corporal Brooks,' when she clambered aboard in her prickly battledress tunic lugging panniers of medical supplies. Chris raised both eyebrows and gave her a wicked smile, before whispering, 'He'll be inviting you up to the cockpit for a wee drop of whisky from his flask, next.'

Jo punched his wiry arm. 'Don't be daft, he'd only try to lure me through there so he could scowl at me some more.'

Chris laughed as he continued to weave his way nimbly between the cargo, settling their equipment amidst the boxes of supplies that always filled the Dakota on the way out. 'Now, here's your parachute,' he said, throwing it across. 'I want you to clip it on, just in case. One of the planes took a hit on the way over yesterday. They didn't go down, but it was a close-run thing … At least going this way, you can bail out if you need to …'

She knew Chris's views on the nurses not being allowed to have parachutes on the way home; he hated having to take hers and lock it away, as was instructed. 'I'd be staying with the patients anyway, even if I wasn't ordered to,' she'd told him a number of times, but that didn't stop him having a grumble about it.

As she threaded her way through, finding space for her panniers, she cast an eye over the metal racks and slings that would hold stretchers on the way back. Once the patients were loaded, there would be very little space between each side, so she was preparing herself mentally for that feeling of confinement. The men were often so badly injured, that it took all of her focus to make sure that they had their oxygen, their injections, their intravenous fluids and blood transfusions. It was a fight to make sure they didn't die.

Jo cast her eyes over the cargo, looking for a wooden box to sit on so that she could look out of the window. After the first couple of terrifying flights, she'd discovered that it helped her stay calmer on the way out.

'So, you can see the missile that's going to hit us,' Chris said, with a wry laugh.

'Well, you know what they say, if your number's on it ...'

'Nah, it's pot luck, all random. Wrong place, wrong time. Nothing is pre-ordained,' he replied.

'You're probably right, it would be strange to think that somewhere out there, in some enemy gun, there's a shell that's waiting to come right for us...'

'Thinking a bit too deeply again are we, Corporal Brooks?' He smiled. 'Sit yourself down, I think Alec's about ready to fire up the engines. Tell me about that Officer's party you went to the other night.'

There wasn't much to say about the party. Often she only ever attended out of politeness and would sit at a table sipping one drink that would usually last the whole night. It was always wonderful though to see Miriam and the others dancing and swapping partners, and she picked up on their excitement. But she was also glad to get back in her pyjamas and listen to the stories that flew around the dormitory afterwards. She never found herself embarrassed by them, and naturally, living with a group of women, she heard plenty of details, but still, it felt like that kind of experience would always belong to someone else.

Once they were in the air, it didn't take long for the navigator's voice to crackle through on the intercom — he always gave them a shout when they were flying over the coast. The White Cliffs of Dover shone in the early morning light; on the return journey they were an important landmark for the men, who always wanted to know when they were over the cliffs.

As they got closer to France, Jo heard the first rattle of antiaircraft fire. She was used to it now, after the nerve-wracking first few trips when she'd thought they were all going to die. Sometimes, she'd hear a shell burst close by, but she'd say to herself that it was just flak, that it couldn't reach up high enough, that it was just the Germans sending a warning. She still held her breath though and counted backwards from ten when the stronger bursts felt like they were pounding the sides of the plane. The Dakota was a rattling metal crate that shook and sounded like it might fall apart even at the best of times.

Her hands were stiff and tight from clinging to the box by the time they got through the anti-aircraft fire. They were soon descending, with not far to go, when a huge explosion sounded so close it made her gasp. The Dakota bucked and rolled, but MacNab was a good pilot, and quickly levelled them up. Jo counted backwards from ten, still clinging to her box as Chris, his face tense, swung from a handhold at the side of the plane. They gazed at each other, waiting. Another massive explosion. They lurched, and Chris gasped and Jo screamed as some pieces of shrapnel punched through a rear window, embedding in a box of food supplies. Air was whistling in and Chris was shouting something through to the cockpit.

'Stay calm,' MacNab was calling on the intercom, 'a Dakota can withstand much worse than a bit of shrapnel.'

Jo counted frantically as the plane continued to lurch and Chris seemed to be chanting some kind of prayer.

At last the Dakota started to level up. Jo sighed out the breath that she'd been holding.

'Phew, that was a close shave,' Chris said. He laughed and pointed to the box she was sitting on, he was trying to speak but unable to get the words out. She stood up and looked at the box; it was full of ammunition. 'Oh my God,' she shrieked, 'If that piece of shrapnel had landed in this one...'

'Neither of us would have had time to worry about parachutes.'

Jo could see the wry look on his face; she'd got used to his dark humour and sometimes it seemed the best way to get through.

MacNab crackled through. 'We're coming into land, brace yourselves, it's a brand-new airstrip so we might be in for a bumpy ride.'

'As if it's all been smooth-going so far!' Chris grinned.

MacNab was right, it was a bumpy landing and when Jo clambered down, she could see why — the new runway was no more than a strip of metal that had been hastily laid through the middle of a cornfield. 'It'll probably bed in, once we've landed a few times,' MacNab called as he strode past them in his fur-collared flying jacket and goggles, already lighting up a cigarette.

'Bed in? I swear, if I have another landing like that, I'm going to ask to be transferred to one of those field

229

hospitals,' said Chris, readying himself to assist with the unloading of supplies.

'I might join you,' Jo shouted back, already moving away, needing to go and check on the casualties that were waiting to be loaded. As she walked, she saw a concrete bunker at the edge of the field — there were some discarded rations on the floor and a German helmet lying amongst the grass. 'Crikey, they haven't been gone long.'

It made her feel jumpy, as if someone might be lurking. She'd heard plenty of stories of snipers hiding, ready to pick off the unsuspecting. She surveyed the perimeter of the cornfield carefully before proceeding. All she could see were bright red poppies amongst the corn. The flowers were so colourful and so beautiful.

Entering the camp, she spotted the hospital marquee with the stretchers waiting and immediately she was walking towards a group of wounded who were sitting on the ground. Straightaway, she spotted a little dog, a terrier with a brown patch over one eye. The little fella was running between the men, jumping up and playing, making them all laugh. A big soldier with a tin hat placed jauntily towards the back of his head, scooped the dog up and pushed him inside his tunic; the little puppy looked so happy with his cute head poking out.

'Are all of you men waiting for evacuation?' she asked, crouching down beside them, reaching out a hand to stroke the little dog. 'That's right, Miss, I mean Corporal,' the big fella replied. 'Are you one of the nurses?'

'Yes, I'm air ambulance and I'll be accompanying you on the flight back. Are you all comfortable? Can I get you any drinks or anything now, whilst we're wait-ing?'

'No, that's alright, nurse,' they all replied in unison. The little dog was still sticking his head out. She gave him another stroke. 'You are cute, aren't you? What's your name?' she said.

'I call him Ambrose.' The man's voice seemed sad.

Jo frowned, wondering what might be wrong. The man had a below knee plaster of Paris, but he looked comfortable enough.

'Are you alright?' she asked, sensing there was something on his mind.

'It's just that I was hoping to take Ambrose back with me on the plane, but the Medical Officer, well, he says no dogs allowed, and I'll have to leave him here. We've been together since the week before I got injured, and I don't know who to leave him with.'

The dog looked at her and he whined; his bright little eyes seemed to be pleading.

'Where is this MO?' she said, knowing that she couldn't leave the issue.

'He's there...' The solider pointed. Jo could see a tall, broad-shouldered man in an officer's uniform standing with his back to her, his hands on his hips.

'Leave it with me, I'll see what I can do. And what's your name?'

'Corporal Vince Earnshaw.'

She strode confidently towards the MO. 'Excuse me,' she said, firmly, to the man's back. 'Are you the officer in charge?'

The man turned round instantly. He was wearing sunglasses but she immediately recognised him.

For a split second they stared at each other.

He removed his sunglasses. 'Brooks? Is that you?'

231

'Dunbar! What the heck are you doing here?'

'I could say the same myself,' he replied, slipping his sunglasses into his breast pocket. 'Well, well,' he looked her up and down. 'I would hardly have recognised you, and you seem to have a bit of a tan. I didn't know you'd gone and joined the WAAF — air ambulance is it?' She nodded but couldn't get a word in edgeways. 'The uniform suits you very well.'

Jo didn't care a jot what he thought about her appearance, even though she hadn't seen him since that night at Broadgreen when he'd sutured Mac's forehead. She was already starting to feel mildly irritated with him, and she just wanted to try and secure passage for the little dog.

'You look very well yourself, Dunbar. I trust you're keeping busy.'

'Too bloody right,' he said with a grim smile. 'The casualties never stop coming, and if it wasn't for you lot taking 'em off our hands, we'd be overrun and we wouldn't have room for the buggers.'

'I've just been chatting to that group over there,' she said, trying to sound nonchalant. 'They're a nice bunch, all set to go, and I don't know if you've seen that little dog, but it's so good for morale, isn't it, having a dog as a mascot?' He opened his mouth to speak but she didn't let him. 'And it will all be fine. Our pilot, Sergeant MacNab, he's a real dog lover and I'm sure he won't have any objection to taking the animal, providing his owner can keep him under control.'

Dunbar was opening and closing his mouth, as if he was trying to say something else, but what came out was, 'Yes, of course, I'll leave that with you, after all your team are responsible for the evacuation.'

She smiled, readying herself to move on and do a

round of the stretcher cases. 'I'll come with you,' he offered, walking by her side. 'I can give you a handover as we go.'

As they moved from stretcher to stretcher, Jo was appalled by some of the injuries — men with missing limbs, faces blown away, one struggling to breathe through a tracheotomy, and a number of severe burns cases. One man with a blackened face was a tank commander who had lost the whole of his crew in a blast. Dunbar told her quietly that Captain Greenlees had been unable to speak, probably due to the trauma.

Jo took the Captain's hand and gave it a squeeze. 'I'm an air ambulance nurse, I'll make sure that you get home safe.' He continued to stare at the canvas ceiling of the tent, awake but barely even blinking.

Just as they finished their round, Chris appeared, a little breathless. 'We're going to be delayed for a couple of hours, the ground crew want to check out the plane and repair that window. We should be ok to go, but they just need a bit more time.'

Jo nodded, ready to settle in and assist the army nurses who were tending the wounded in the tent.

'Nurse Brooks, as you have some time to kill, why don't you come with me in the jeep, and I'll give you a tour of the site,' Dunbar declared.

He'd already linked her arm and was steering her away; she seemed to have no choice in the matter. 'Just one moment,' she said, as he led her towards a jeep, 'I need to—'

She could see the soldier with the little dog looking in her direction. Turning her back on Dunbar, she gave him the thumbs up. He whooped with joy.

'I know what you've been up to, Brooks,' Dunbar said as soon as she turned back. 'And now, as punishment, I'm going to bore you with all the detail of our camp, and even if you beg me to stop, I will not be deterred.'

As soon as they set off in the jeep, he placed his hand on her knee. She gasped at his effrontery, removing it immediately and placing it firmly back on his own knee.

He laughed out loud. 'Just wondered if you might want—'

'Stop right there,' she said, 'we've always had a very good professional relationship, I do not want to compromise it.'

He shook his head. 'You're quite something, Brooks, aren't you? How could you turn down a dashing army surgeon like myself?'

She looked at him with her eyes narrowed. 'Oh, quite easily.'

He guffawed with laughter and then, when he knew that she meant what she said, he put on a straight face, 'Alright, Brooks. Understood.'

Jo felt less than comfortable with him now, but she sat dutifully as they careered around every corner. She knew he would be a fast driver but wasn't quite prepared for having to cling on for dear life. As they careered along, she thought she heard the sound of gunfire, in that moment it seemed less worrying than his driving. 'Might be a sniper,' he yelled, above the noise of the engine. 'Keep your head down!'

Once safely returned to the hospital tent, she accepted a swig of brandy from his flask to settle her nerves. Chris was heading towards them, and Jo prayed that he would say they were ready to load. Thankfully, she saw him smile and nod. 'Might not see you next time you land, Brooks,' Dunbar yelled, as she moved swiftly to help with the stretchers. 'I've been posted to support them right up at the front line.'

'Take care,' she yelled, 'stay safe.' She somehow knew that he would be alright. He was a born survivor.

As they bumped their way along the metal runway for take-off, Jo clung to one of the stretchers. Her teeth were gritted, hoping that MacNab would have enough room for acceleration. At the last moment, he hauled the Dakota up into the air and the patients who were well enough all gave a hearty cheer. 'Not long now, boys, you'll all be home soon,' she called out, smiling when she saw the little dog snuggled inside Vince Earnshaw's tunic.

It was cramped between the stretchers as she oversaw the men. After she'd checked every casualty — inspecting dressings, adjusting the flow rate of drips, giving sips of water — she returned to the man with the tracheotomy to give him extra attention. The silver tube through which he breathed had to be checked regularly; if it became blocked, she would need to clear it as otherwise he would suffocate. She'd made sure that another critical patient, who had a chest drain and was receiving oxygen, was on the opposite side so that she could easily switch from one to the other and continue to monitor both.

All seemed well until they hit some turbulence just as her patient's tracheotomy blocked. She whipped out the metal inner tube and cleaned it with swabs and she could hear his breath bubbling inside the tube even as the plane was bumping up and down. The turbulence brought on a wave of nausea. She needed to replace the tube, but she had to take a deep breath or she knew that she would vomit. Thankfully, with the procedure complete, the patient's breathing was much clearer but she still felt sick. She saw Chris give her an anxious look, and he came over with a sip of water for her, and a cool flannel to wipe her face.

'Thank you,' she murmured. 'Whatever would I do without you?'

Feeling refreshed, she turned to the man with the oxygen, who was coughing and increasingly breathless. She stood by, holding his hand, soothing him, making sure that he could get back some control. As he was settling, another patient began groaning further down the plane, so she went over to check if he was in pain. He wasn't making much sense; his face was stricken and his eyes were filled with terror. It was a young pilot, called Sergeant Logan, who'd been shot down and had parachuted out. His chest wound and fractured ankle were both stable, but it was the terror of it all that he seemed to be reliving. 'It's alright,' she said gently, taking his hand, 'we'll be home soon, you're safe now. You're safe.'

'I think it's a good time to bring out the thermos flasks,' Chris called from the opposite end of the plane. 'Now, who wants a cuppa?'

When the intercom crackled to tell them that they were over the coast, the Dakota was filled with the glorious sound of men cheering. Some of them cried, and one started to sing about bluebirds. Jo always cried when the men cheered, and she knew that these homecomings were something that she would never forget, not for the rest of her life.

22

Germany and Belgium, September 1944

Zach sat cramped and sweating in his new Mustang P-51 fighter plane, as much as he'd admired these state-of-the art machines on a practice run, his chest felt tight now and his muscles were screaming in pain, unused to long periods of flying after a lengthy recovery from injury.

Right now he couldn't believe that he'd sat at home in Long Island with his family all around him, and told them that he was going back to war — he could still see the stricken faces of his mom and two younger sisters and his dad standing solemn-faced. He'd made his case, telling them that now he was recovered from the busted shoulder he'd received during a crash landing, he had to get back to the squadron, especially with the allied forces pushing further and further into German territory. But now, alone in his plane, with only his doubts and fears for company, he wasn't so sure. The deafening roar of the B-17 bombers below and the noise of anti-aircraft fire ahead had made him start to wonder if he should have accepted a non-combat posting after all.

He'd been away from the war long enough to forget how alone you felt in a fighter plane. The job on this mission was to escort the bombers and to fend off any enemy attacks and the amount of awareness it took was terrifying. Today, he was flying wingman. He looked over protectively to the young pilot and

237

the plane he was guarding. He'd only known Frank for a week or so, but he was a cheerful, blond-haired fella, seemingly nonchalant before take-off, but Zach knew what was going on beneath all of that; he knew because he'd been there himself. Whenever Frank moved Zach was right there, flying at the side and slightly to the rear, stuck to him like glue, watching his back so that he could concentrate on shooting down the enemy. He needed to be extra-vigilant on this mission as they were heading to the oil refineries, which were always heavily defended, and the new German fighter plane, a Messerschmitt Me 262, was more powerful and quicker than the Mustang.

They were close and, expecting an attack at any minute, he started to sweat; his flying helmet and goggles felt tight on his head. He wished he could throw off the leather gauntlet gloves that were essential to withstand the sub-zero temperatures at this altitude but made his hands feel stiff and awkward on the controls. He glanced at the instruments, quickly checking his rear-view mirror and then looking straight back to Frank. He could feel the buzz of adrenaline, his hands were sure on the controls and he was ready for anything. He forced himself to slow his breathing right down, to improve his focus, a trick that he'd learned from an old hand on his early missions with the Eagles. He sometimes missed his good old Hawker Hurricane — 1941 had been a very special year for him, fighting alongside the Brits, getting to know some quirky English ways.

The radio crackled into life, and he felt a surge of adrenaline. 'Bandits at twelve o'clock,' said a calm voice. He strained his eyes and he could see the black dots ahead.

Two voices screamed, 'Bandits two o'clock!' and 'Bandits at three!' in quick succession. Zach's pulse broke into double time, the black dots were rapidly enlarging. He flicked his gun switch. The plan, as always, was to head into the enemy at full throttle with guns blazing. Frank's voice crackled across the radio, 'Let's go!' and he was already whipping his plane through the air. Zach was on his tail. Frank was firing now, and one enemy fighter plane was trailing smoke and then it was going down. Out of the corner of his eye, Zach saw a B-17 bomber explode, bursting open, tiny human figures falling out — no parachutes opening. He took a deep breath and ploughed after Frank, who had already latched onto another Messerschmitt, diving and twisting to get close. Zach followed just as swiftly, his body drenched in sweat.

Suddenly, there were urgent shouts on the radio, nothing that made sense as more enemy fighters hit the bombers. Frank swooped down below the bomber stream, shooting another enemy plane, driving ahead, relentless, still going, even though the Messerschmitt showed no sign of yielding. Then the German plane exploded and dropped quickly.

Zach saw another enemy plane straight away and shouted a warning to Frank over the radio. Nothing came back. He fired, landing many strikes on the German, and the plane, covered in flame, nose-dived. Frank's plane was lurching, smoke pouring out — he must have been hit. Zach called him urgently on the radio, still receiving no answer. And then he watched as the nose of Frank's plane dropped and the Mustang plummeted in a fatal dive.

Zach cried out in anguish. This wasn't supposed to happen. He clung to the controls, trying to stay alert,

239

still needing to protect the B-17s. He tried to move back up above the bomber stream, sure they must be almost at their target by now, but his plane wouldn't respond and he realised it was losing height.

'Jesus Christ,' he shouted. 'I'm going down!' he called out across the radio. It crackled back at him but there were no answering voices. He grappled with the controls and managed to level up, but he'd definitely lost power. All he could do was try to limp home but, worryingly, there was a strong smell of fuel. It wasn't good. He thought of his mom, who he knew would be praying for his safe return, and he felt terrible about all of this — not for himself, but for her.

He hadn't got all that far when the Mustang spluttered and dropped again. A burst of flame erupted from the engine and started to lap around his legs. The plane was full of smoke now and though he desperately wanted to stay with it, he had no choice. He unbuckled his seat belt and somehow found and clipped on his parachute. With all his strength, he hauled back the plane's canopy, feeling exposed and terrified as the wind whipped overhead. He jumped, remembering to roll forward and down so he didn't get hit by the tail as he fell.

The parachute unfurled, and he prayed he had enough height to slow him down, so he didn't hit the ground too hard. The earth was coming up fast and at the last moment he realised the area below was a ploughed field.

The air was completely knocked out of him as he landed, and he felt his left leg snap beneath him. He lay still for some time, thinking he might be dead. Eventually, as he registered that his leg hurt like the devil, that his face felt seared and raw, he realised he might just be alive. He groaned with pain and rolled over onto his back. He could see the sky above, he could hear a bird twittering. He started to cry; he was alive.

It was growing dark when he came to again and he was aware of voices on the edge of his consciousness. He listened with all his might, not knowing at first if they were German. Someone was close now, a man's voice, and he didn't want to open his eyes in case he was pointing a gun. But then he realised the voice definitely wasn't German and he slumped with relief.

His rescuer was trying to move him. It jarred his leg and he shouted out in pain. The man sounded concerned as he spoke in broken English, 'You are safe now, airman. My name is Emmanuel, I am a friend and I can take you to the nurses.'

'Thank you,' croaked Zach, his whole body was shaking with the shock and pain, but he felt like the luckiest man alive.

★　★　★

The night shift in the tent hospital was busy. Mac was supervising preparation for another move and this time the casualties would be sent back to field hospitals or for evacuation. Winter was coming and their next move would mean setting up within the four walls of some building — no more smell of grass within the tented world that had become so familiar. But it made sense, there was already a nip in the air and Vera had been sleeping with her greatcoat over her bed for weeks.

They would be moving the patients first thing and then they would be taking down the tents and packing up the beds and equipment, a ritual that they'd gone through so many times that no one needed any instruction. Mac's task tonight was to make sure that all the patients were ready for evacuation — wrapped up warm in their blankets, up to date with intravenous infusions, all dressings and bandages clean and intact and, most importantly, those that required morphia had had a good dose and each man had a full pack of cigarettes. They all needed to be ready to load into the lorries and ambulances that would take them back away from the front line. Mac had hoped that she would have seen Jo at least once during the whole of this time — almost a year now since D-Day — but the field hospitals moved relentlessly forward as the allies pushed harder and harder. And beyond hearing a brief story from a passing acquaintance with Angus Dunbar two, or was it three, field hospitals back — about Jo and a little dog that Mac was sure must have been Vince Earnshaw's terrier — she'd heard nothing from or about Jo for ages. And now that they were moving more frequently, the mail never seemed to quite catch up.

Each time they moved, they drove through a ravaged landscape — fields and streets littered with burnt out vehicles, buildings blown apart, lines of refugees walking, always walking, with suitcases and handcarts. Her team always tried to give them food and, if they had time, provide some first aid. Mac had already packed her medical bag in readiness, so that she could jump down off the truck to help. On one trip, she'd nearly got left behind after stopping to treat a little girl with a nasty head wound and she'd had to sprint to catch up.

Mac glanced around the tent, satisfied at what

they'd achieved. It was the early hours of the morning, the trucks would be arriving soon and they would have to help load the stretcher cases. It was time to make sure that Edith and Lucy had a hot drink and something to eat.

An urgent shout from outside the tent stopped her in her tracks. A man's voice in a broken accent said, 'Please, we need help, please.'

She recognised the voice; it was a man they knew only as Emmanuel, a local farmer who'd been a Belgian resistance fighter — he'd brought casualties in before. She grabbed her battledress tunic, pushing pen and scissors into the breast pocket, before racing out of the door, quickly exchanging a few words with the man who, despite now living within allied territory, still, understandably, always appeared eager to be away. The casualty was another pilot who'd bailed out. The farmers were still finding them in their fields or strung up in trees, but now they had no need to follow elaborate plans to find medical treatment and smuggle the fugitives out, they could just bring them straight to the field hospital.

Mac got up on the back of the flat cart that they'd used to transport him, crouching down beside the casualty. 'Hello, hello, can you hear me?'

'He's American, a fighter pilot. We saw the plane come down. It was nearly dark when we found him... He spoke a few words, he said his name is Taylor. Now he is quiet for a long time.'

Since she'd heard the news about Don, every airman that passed through the hospital made her breath catch. Last year, for weeks after the loss, she'd wandered around the camp like a shadow of herself, still going about her work, but empty inside, pretending to smile when she no longer felt any joy. She was better now, but she knew it was still there, waiting to remind her. She steadied herself and placed a gentle hand on the pilot's chest. Thankfully, he was breathing. She felt down his arms and legs — definite fracture of the left lower leg — but nothing else evident.

She shouted for the orderly to bring a stretcher. 'Let's get him inside, and then I want you to go and get the duty surgeon out of bed, tell him left fractured tibia,' she said, and then reached down to shake the farmer's hand. 'Thank you so much for bringing him in, Emmanuel. Another one you've rescued.'

Once they had the casualty in the electric light, Mac could see that he'd been in a fire — his face was red and peeling, all his hair and eyebrows were singed off and the backs of his hands were covered in white blisters. Thankfully, it looked like it might just be superficial damage, and in a few weeks' time, once the swelling had gone and it was healing, he would look human again. She shouted for cold compresses, plenty of them, suspecting, from her knowledge of previous cases, that this fighter pilot might also have burns on his legs. 'And we need to set up a saline drip,' she called to Lucy who was already running for the compresses.

The pilot groaned and tried to open his eyes, 'Lie still. You are safe, you're in a field hospital. I just need to put these cold compresses on your face. There… that's it… that will make it feel better.'

He groaned louder and started to writhe in pain. Mac gestured for Lucy to run and get an injection of morphia. She needed to check his dog tags, try to identify him, but she knew from experience that they would be buried beneath many layers of pilot's clothing and she wouldn't be able to undress him until he was more comfortable. Hopefully, if he had a big enough dose of morphine it would also see him through the setting of the fracture — she hadn't laid eyes on his leg yet, but from what she'd been able to feel through his flight suit, there didn't seem to be any bone protruding so it would just need manipulation back into place and a plaster of Paris. It would be best if he didn't need ether; they'd have to load him up and send him on his way in a few short hours, and she didn't want him to be groggy.

Within five minutes, Taylor went through into theatre still fully clothed, the surgeon and theatre Sister needed to get him sorted so that they could pack up. Mac would have liked to have kept hold of him for a while longer so that she could make sure that he was improving and maybe find out who he was, this stranger with just one single tuft of pale brown hair. But it was impossible, they were about to move the whole camp and the order had been to take no patients whatsoever.

'You're going to be fine,' she said gently as the surgeon and orderly approached to remove the stretcher.

'Good work, Nurse MacDonald,' muttered the grey-faced surgeon.

Mac watched them take him. For some reason she felt like she'd formed a special bond with this one. She shrugged; she probably felt like that about all the wounded airmen, especially those who'd been found alone in some field.

★ ★ ★

The ambulances and lorries were there at first light, side by side, and the red cross flags on the vehicles were fluttering in the breeze. Mac was rushing to do a final check of the patients, so she had no time to get back to the pilot, but from a distance she could see that he had a plaster of Paris on his leg and his burns had been dressed. The poor man, still bleary and recovering from the extra morphia, looked like a mummy with all the white bandage around his face and hands. The duty surgeon had asked for special instruction to be sent with him — the plaster of Paris would need to be opened up in a week's time so that the dressing to the front of his left leg could be checked. The burns on his legs weren't full thickness, but they were nasty enough and they'd needed debriding. Careful attention would be required if they were to prevent sepsis and he would need a course of penicillin injections, just to make sure. But Mac had already given the last of their supply to one of the men waiting for transfer — now, they were all out until new stock was delivered to their next destination. She felt anxious for her patient — thanks to this magical new drug, they were no longer seeing horrendous suppurating infections and gas gangrene, so she didn't want him to miss out on this crucial treatment. She called for Edith, asking her to pin a note to the pilot's jacket, giving the detail of the dressings and to underline the instruction for a course of penicillin. That was as much as she could do. Now, it was simply time to move and two stretcher bearers were already waiting to load him into the back of an ambulance.

Sister Lloyd had insisted that the night shift get some sleep in their dormitory tent whilst the rest made a start with the packing up. 'You know what it's like,' she had said, standing in the middle of the tent with her hands on her hips. 'As soon as we get there,

246

even before the beds are set up, there'll be patients lined up on stretchers, waiting to get in.'

Mac had been reluctant and tried to argue that they could sleep on the journey, but Sister was adamant, so it looked like they'd no choice but to do as they were told. She needed a smoke, so she went to find her spot, whist Lucy and Edith walked on ahead. At this camp she'd been using the remains of a wall to lean against for her smokes and she liked the outlook — a burnt-out tank in the middle of the next field, tipped up on end, with its metal belly blown open and its single barrel pointing hopelessly to the sky. She lit up, gratefully drawing in the smoke and exhaling slowly. This was her life now — work, eat, sleep, work — and some days it exhausted her. But she knew that keeping so busy was about the only way that she could hold the demons at bay — she didn't want to be tormented by the sound of a man's laughter, the warm smell of him, his voice calling Rita, Rita..., but increasingly that was happening. She felt the scar on her fore-head throb, as if in sympathy, she ran a hand over its familiar contours. At least she'd come to terms with her 'distinguishing mark'. Sometimes it helped the men whom she was nursing — those that were facing life-changing injuries — to know that she'd also been through something traumatic and come out the other side.

Straightening up, she took her last drag and stubbed the cigarette out hard against a stone. Still not ready to go back to the dormitory, she rested against the wall, closing her eyes, breathing in the smell of the earth. She heard a sound and when she looked up, she saw four swans flying high, bright white against the blue sky, their long necks at full stretch and their confident-looking heads thrusting forward. They were beautiful and they made her smile. 'Yes, you go, my beauties, you go,' she said out loud.

Edith and Lucy were sound asleep when she got back to the tent, so she undressed silently and slipped onto her camp bed. It was nice lying in her lace knickers and stretching her bare legs against the rough blanket with the canvas gently flapping and the guy ropes creaking and the sound of voices drifting through as the work of packing up the camp went on around them. She turned onto her side, thinking about the new patient again, still worrying about whether he'd get his course of penicillin. *He'll be fine, he'll be just fine*, she murmured to herself as, at last, she drifted off to sleep.

23

Antwerp, Belgium, October 1944

Jo flew up from her seat as the Dakota plunged down. Chris, clinging to a handhold, his face stricken, gasped in terror, but then as they levelled up, he shouted, 'It was just an air pocket!'

'I thought we were goners,' she groaned, pulling herself back up from the deck, checking her arms and legs for broken bones, she had landed so hard.

He laughed and patted the side of the aeroplane. 'Ah, this old crate, she's going to see us through.' Then seeing that Jo was still groaning and sitting slumped forward on her box of supplies, he added, 'Are you still in one piece?'

'I've twisted my knee, but nothing broken,' she reported, giving it a rub through the thick, prickly fabric of her combat trousers. 'I'll live.'

Chris rooted in his pocket for the small flask of whisky that he always carried. 'For medicinal purposes only.' He grinned and handed it over. 'I mean, you must have sustained some damage.'

MacNab's voice crackled over the intercom, 'Sorry about that, an air pocket, hope you're both alive and kicking back there...We're almost over the drop zone, get ready to release the supplies.'

Chris unclipped the wicker baskets of medical supplies from a bar at the side of the plane and rolled them towards the hatch. Jo had offered to assist a number of times, but she'd always been grateful that he declined. Just the thought of standing there by the open door, so far up in the sky... She even found it hard to watch Chris do it, terrified that he would cast himself out with the baskets.

'Go, go!' called the navigator. Chris deftly slid open the door and immediately Jo felt the whoosh of air, and a glimpse of sky made her feel dizzy. She couldn't watch, so she listened to him pushing out the baskets one by one, seeing them through the window, floating gracefully down on their miniature parachutes. She'd noted blood supplies and penicillin stashed in there — these essential supplies would be saving lives.

Glad when the door was closed, she went to stand by Chris at the window. 'Not long to go now,' he said, taking another crafty swig from his flask. 'Let's hope MacNab's got the touchdown in hand, we've never done Antwerp before.'

Jo swallowed hard, she'd got used to the landings and the experience didn't worry her too much now, but like the rest of the Flying Nightingale team, she was acutely aware that one day it could all go horribly wrong. When she'd joined up, she could never have imagined the extent of the risk that they would be taking. Having survived the bombing of a hospital in Liverpool during the blitz, she still marvelled at her decision-making, but it was simple, one day she just wanted to be able to look back and know that she'd done her bit.

'Coming in to land,' MacNab buzzed through.

Jo exchanged a grim smile with Chris and they both braced themselves — whatever kind of airstrip lay waiting for them, they knew that it would have been hastily constructed and the Dakota could be clumsy and unforgiving when she met the ground.

This time, it was even worse than usual. They whacked straight down and then there was an almighty screeching as the plane tilted and scraped along. They veered wildly, Jo clinging to Chris with both hands.

'Jesus Chriiiist!' he screamed, as they lurched to a halt. 'What the hell was that?'

When the plane had come to a stop, MacNab came through to check that they were both alright. They nodded, breathless — Chris mildly hysterical, Jo doubled over, rigid with fear, her teeth still gritted.

'I think we've lost a bloody wheel,' MacNab opened the door, ready to inspect the damage.

Jo took a ragged breath. Her legs felt weak, but she needed to get out there, to see what was happening with the casualties.

'You won't find any patients,' MacNab called after her. 'The hospital staff were waiting for us to land before they sent them out for evacuation. Maybe they knew this was going to be tricky. I'll let them know that we're going to be delayed, probably overnight.'

Jo hoped that this time she wouldn't be required to sleep on the floor of a tiny tent with a single hurricane lamp and no access to any washroom or toilet for women. Having to squat in the bushes was nobody's idea of fun, especially when there was a risk of sniper fire.

Thankfully, there was no fear of sleeping under canvas this time — she was being transferred to a field hospital. And as they approached, she was intrigued to see that it had been constructed within an elegant stone building, its impressive façade indicating that it must have been some grand house before the war. Part of it lay in rubble but its faded glory still shone through.

'That was a doodlebug, one of them flying rocket bombs, that did that last week,' said the red-faced soldier driving the jeep, pointing to the wall that had been destroyed. 'Horrible things, they come screaming like banshees. This one killed a nurse.' Jo felt a stab of sadness for the woman. She was about to offer some words of consolation to the driver, who'd probably known hundreds of comrades who'd died, but he'd already moved onto lighter topics and now he was screeching to a halt.

Making her way through an arched doorway, she felt the scrunch of grit underfoot as she walked into a high-ceilinged entrance hall, complete with a dusty glass chandelier. A nurse in khaki battledress bustled out through a polished wooden doorway. 'Ooh,' she said, looking her up and down, 'I've not seen a woman in blue before.'

'Oh, I'm an air ambulance nurse,' Jo offered. 'We're here for the evacuation but our plane was damaged during landing. I've been told to stay here overnight.'

'Oh, I see,' said the nurse, 'Follow me.'

The ward was full of light from the tall many-paned windows that formed one wall of the huge space that could once have been a ballroom. Now, the wooden floor and the intricately painted walls were crowded out by iron-framed beds and stretchers — the juxtaposition was bizarre. She gazed up to the ceiling — another, even more impressive chandelier hung, dull but magnificent, in the centre of the room, and the domed ceiling was painted with a colourful fresco. Jo was transfixed as she gazed up to pastoral scenes from another age.

'Are you the air ambulance nurse?' Sister approached, her thin lips pursed.

'Oh, hello, sorry,' said Jo, dragging her eyes away from the beautiful ceiling. She stumbled on her words as she started to offer some explanation. Sister held up a hand. 'I've already had all of the detail from your pilot,' she said, 'Nurse Radcliffe will show you to your quarters and then you can come back down to the ward.'

Jo followed Nurse Radcliffe, a lively, smiling young woman who bounded up the marble stairs in front of her. 'Ta da,' she called, opening an ornately carved door that led into a huge room with a vaulted ceiling. 'We're in what used to be the master bedroom, and that's the spare bunk.'

Jo followed where she was pointing and saw a camp bed in the corner of the room. 'You'll find some emergency supplies, all ready and waiting for waifs and strays.'

Jo laughed. 'That's me alright.'

'Well, I'll leave you to freshen up,' said Nurse Radcliffe, taking a moment to inspect her reflection in the heavy wooden mirror above the marble fireplace, tucking some stray wisps of her fluffy blonde hair behind her ears. 'Christ, what I'd give for a powder compact right now.' She laughed, her blue eyes alight with mischief. Just for a split second, Jo saw Mac, laughing, getting ready for a night out. It almost brought tears to her eyes.

'Are you alright? Nurse Radcliffe's voice was full of concern.

Jo nodded, trying to laugh. 'Just tired that's all.'

'We're all run into the ground, aren't we? You get some rest — have a lie down, I can square it with Sister.'

Jo was already shaking her head 'No, I'll come down

to the ward, I want to help. It's the least I can do, what with the change of plan.'

'Well, it's not your fault is it, sunshine, these things happen. But Sister Jemison is having to rearrange and she's never good with disruption, so it might be best if you did show your face, at least for a while.'

Jo gave a sympathetic nod; she'd almost forgotten what it was like to work under a temperamental senior nurse.

'I need to get back or she'll have my guts for garters.'

'Yes, of course,' said Jo, 'I'll see you down there. I'm Jo, by the way.'

'Laura.' She smiled, pointing to herself before diving back out through the door. 'Take your time,' she yelled.

Jo could hear her rapidly descending the marble staircase. She had nothing to unpack so she removed her battledress tunic, dusted it down and laid it carefully on the bottom of the bed. She ran her hands through her short hair and stretched her back before stooping down to examine the army issue overnight supplies: a large, coarse-fabric nightdress, soap and flannel and even a toothbrush. She took the soap and flannel to a large sink in the corner of the room, which had ornate brass taps that even gave hot water and the porcelain basin was shaped like a seashell. She giggled; wait till she told Chris, he was probably going to have to spend the night bunked down on a stretcher in the Dakota.

Back on the ward, she could see Sister at her desk, dealing with a mound of paperwork. Jo saw her look up and give her a stern glance, but then she went straight back to her work. The other nurses were busy with the patients and although there was the usual cease-less activity of a ward, there was something about the quality of the light coming in through the windows and the green of the lawns outside, that made this place seem relatively peaceful.

Some of the men looked like they'd been scooped up off a battlefield, their faces still grimed, bundled up in bed in their dusty, bloodstained uniforms. She was used to it; most of those who they evacuated were moved through so quickly that there was never any time to get them scrubbed up properly and often they had nothing else to wear but their uniforms. The plaster of Paris and the white bandages around the heads, arms and legs of the patients stood out in stark contrast, instantly demarcating every injury. Only one young man was sitting up in bed, seemingly unscathed, his tin hat sitting forlornly on the orange box that served as a bedside table.

Laura appeared by her side. 'That's Private Jones, just nineteen years old, a very bad case of shell shock. He's mute and he can't do anything for himself — if the nurses didn't feed him he'd starve to death. The poor lad just sits up in bed all day long, staring into space.'

'What a shame,' Jo said.

'You go round the ward, get to know some of them — the poorly young man next to Private Jones is a German prisoner of war, we're doing our best for him but he is very badly injured.' Sister was calling for Nurse Radcliffe now, so she quickly said goodbye: 'I'll see you later.'

Jo moved towards Private Jones's bed, racking her brains for anything she could remember from nursing the shell-shocked victims at The Midland in Morecambe. The men there also had physical injuries; she'd never encountered a soldier who was suffering just with shell shock. She was used to making sure her casualties didn't choke or bleed to death on a flight home, so she felt at a bit at a loss as she tried to introduce herself. He continued to stare into space, giving no sign that he had any awareness of her. 'I'll call by and see you later,' she said gently, not knowing what else to say.

The German soldier in the next bed lay propped up on many pillows, sleeping peacefully. Part of his face had been blown away — it had all been bandaged up, but he must have pulled at the dressing or it had slipped, revealing the horror of a missing jawbone. Jo shuddered. Even after all her years of nursing, some of the injuries that these poor men had to endure were truly shocking.

A cheeky chap was sitting up in the next bed, a bandage around the stump of his left arm and a bed cradle over his leg. 'You coming to give me an injection in my bum, new nurse,' he called, grinning.

'Most definitely not,' she retorted, 'I think Matron will want to do that, she's got a special syringe with a very big needle.'

'Ha!' He laughed, fumbling to slip a cigarette out of his pack with one hand. She wanted to go there and help him, do it for him, but one thing she'd learnt from bitter experience was to wait until a soldier asked for help. Never jump in, not unless the situation was unsafe for the patient. With relief, she saw him succeed and he was lighting up, still chuckling to himself.

In the next bed along, a patient with a bandage around his head and a plaster of Paris on his left leg was lying flat on his back and he looked like he was asleep. Jo gazed at him, taking in every detail — his face and the backs of both hands were red, and the skin was peeling; he had extensive burns but they seemed for the most part superficial. She moved closer to find the skin was healing very nicely, but she knew beneath the dressing on his head, there might well be a deeper wound on what would have been his hairline — the only hair he had left was a tuft of pale brown sticking up behind the bandage. She spotted a small book with a dog-eared cover, face down on his bed. She didn't want to pick it up and risk losing his page — knowing how fussy she was herself about that — but she twisted her head and squinted at the title. It was a volume of poetry, by someone called Robert Frost; she'd never heard that name and she didn't know much about poetry, the classics were more her style — Jane Austen, Thomas Hardy, Charles Dickens.

'He's my favourite poet.' The man in the bed spoke with a gentle American voice.

She gave a small gasp in shock, feeling like she'd been caught prying when she shouldn't. But he was smiling and propping himself up on one elbow. He had such a lovely smile and his eyes were bright blue — she almost felt hypnotised — and she had to force herself to speak. 'Oh, I'm sorry, I didn't mean to pry, it's just that I love books.'

'No need to apologise,' he said. There was that smile again, and his voice was like warm caramel. His blue eyes were still shining and she felt captivated. She swallowed hard, to try and stop the warm feeling that was spreading out from the pit of her stomach.

She cleared her throat. 'Well, I'm just going round all the patients, trying to get to know them. I'm an air ambulance nurse and I'll be accompanying those of you who are being evacuated tomorrow.'

'Well, that's me, and I can tell you, for the record, that I have a fractured left tibia, burns to both lower legs, superficial scorching to the backs of my hands and my face — as you can see it looks like a very bad sunburn — oh, and earlier in the year, I had a busted shoulder from a crash landing. In fact, I'd only just got back to my squadron, before all of this happened.'

'Well, you seem to have had your share—' He was still holding her gaze with his very blue eyes and she started to step back, away from the bed, desperate to stop the pink flush that she could feel forming at the base of her throat from spreading up to her face. She cleared her throat again. 'Well, I'll be seeing you tomorrow then… I'm Jo— I mean Corporal Brooks.'

'Pleased to meet you, Jo Corporal Brooks,' he said, his voice polite but still warm. 'I'm Captain Taylor, Zach Taylor, and if you have time later before lights out and want to share some poetry, I'll be right here. I'm not going anywhere.'

'Thank you,' she said, knowing for sure that he would have a beautiful reading voice, but she was completely thrown. She needed to avoid any hint that she might join him to read his poems, didn't she? Wasn't that the right thing to do? She stepped back from his bed. 'I think we'll probably be too busy later, but I do hope you enjoy your reading.'

'You too, Nurse Brooks, you too.'

It made her realise that it was a long, long time since she'd been able to truly enjoy a book — she'd tried to read when she'd been at The Midland but somehow the words only went in so far. The stories were often jumbled and, with all the real-life drama unspooling on a daily basis, it just didn't seem as meaningful any more. The last thing she remembered reading and enjoying must have been *Far from the Madding Crowd*, when she'd been living in the Nurses' Home, and she'd never been able to finish it. It had been lost on the night of the bomb, along with everything else.

Realising that she was standing in the middle of the ward, staring into space, Jo made herself move onto the next patient. So much for helping out, she thought, thankful that Sister was still fully absorbed in her paperwork.

After her ward round she pitched in with the unending nursing tasks and was glad to be directed by Laura to give the routine penicillin injections, renew some dressings, and then at tea-time she volunteered to feed Private Jones.

Fortunately, nothing was required for Captain Taylor, so she didn't even need to go near his bed. Every time she walked by, though, she was aware of him propped up in bed on his pillows, reading his book, and she knew, even though she daren't even look in his direction, that he was smiling at her and his blue eyes were shining.

As the light through the windows began to fade, the ward took on an even slower, more peaceful pace. Sister had gone off for some meeting with the medical officer and the patients were very settled now, probably from the extra bit of morphia they'd had earlier in the day. It was a long time since Jo had felt this kind of end of shift contentment.

'You can go now, get some rest,' Laura murmured. Left in charge by Sister, she was able to issue her own orders.

'No, I can't do that; I can't leave you all still work-

259

ing.'

She saw Zach out of the corner of her eye, beckoning her over.

'Captain Taylor needs something,' Laura said, a twinkle in her eye. 'I've never seen him so awake at this time of day, he seems to be really perking up.'

Jo was glad of the failing light as once again, she felt her face flush bright pink.

'Oh for goodness sake, get yourself over there,' murmured Laura. 'With the times we're living through, nothing's the same any more. Go on, there's a stool by his bed, just go and sit with him, will you.'

She was right, Jo knew that. They all needed to snatch whatever opportunities they could to find some solace. And maybe reading some poetry was exactly what she needed to do right now.

He was smiling as she walked towards him and it was a good job that the stool was ready and waiting because her legs were feeling a little bit weak. 'Choose a poem,' he said, handing her the book, his eyes creasing up at the corners with pleasure. She nodded and started to turn the well-thumbed pages, feeling calmer already just with the feel of the hardback cover in her hand. She looked through, devouring the poems as if she'd been starved of the written word. The words were all sliding into each other.

At last, she said, 'This one: "The Road Not Taken".' She passed the book back to him and he started to read — his gentle American voice making her heart twist with pleasure.

'Two roads diverged in a yellow wood,
And sorry I could not travel both
And be one traveler, long I stood...'

260

She felt as if she was holding her breath as he spoke, and all the while the words seemed to roll deliciously in his mouth. She could hardly speak, and when he asked her if she liked it, 'Yes,' was all that she could say.

He was smiling at her now — his eyes shining beneath his lopsided bandage — and when he reached for her hand she couldn't resist. She smiled back, holding on to him with the overwhelming feeling that she never wanted to let go.

Later, as she stripped off her uniform to don the scratchy linen nightdress, she insisted to herself that she'd been caught up in a brief moment, that that was all it had been, but deep down, she already knew that she was lying to herself. But maybe she was also just tired, feeling the effects of mission after mission. She would sleep this off, she would get Zach Taylor out of her head.

★ ★ ★

Jo slept fitfully, sitting bolt upright as daybreak came, worried that she would be late onto the ward. She tried to go back to sleep but already all of the details of the evacuation were buzzing through her head and she had no choice but to reach for her pad and pen and write them down.

The men were all ready and wrapped in their blankets and the last-minute top ups of morphia were just being administered when Jo and the rest of the day staff walked onto the ward. She'd spruced up with a good wash in the lovely sink, made sure her air force shirt and tie were smooth and straight, and damped down her hair, sweeping it back from her face. Sis-

261

ter looked her up and down as soon as she walked through the door, but Jo was ready for her. She gave an efficient nod and then produced the checklist from her pocket. 'Are we all ready to go, Sister?'

When she saw Zach — wearing a brown flying jacket with a fur collar — wave and smile in her direction, she had no choice but to determinedly turn her back on him. She wished that she could have taken a moment to go over and have a few words, but Sister was watching her like a hawk.

'You might find *this* useful,' said Sister, thrusting a piece of paper in her direction — it was the order of travel for each patient. Jo was relieved to see that Zach was on the final truck, along with Private Jones. She thought it was a good idea that Private Jones would be last, as with such bad shell shock, he might struggle with the move and it would help to ensure the other men were settled in the plane before he arrived.

When she got out of the truck at the airstrip with the first group of patients, Chris was straight there to meet them. He had grey smudges beneath his eyes and he looked like he hadn't slept a wink. He told her that he'd had to bunk up in the Dakota, and he'd been up late into the night playing cards with Mac-Nab and sharing a bottle of Scotch. 'But you look chipper this morning, Corporal Brooks,' he offered with a wry smile.

'Well, I had a comfortable camp bed and access to hot running water in a porcelain sink. It was heaven.'

'I am so jealous,' Chris breathed, running a hand over his bristled chin. 'I feel all itchy inside this uniform.'

'Ugh, don't come near me,' she joked. 'Now, come on, let's get this lot loaded. We've got a young lad with severe shell shock coming through on the final transport, I want all the other men to be settled by then.'

The first stretcher on board was the cheeky chappy with the amputated arm. As they were loading him, Jo noted, with regret, that he'd also lost the leg on that side, above the knee. Her heart went out to the young fella, he was certainly putting a good face on things but who knew what lay beneath all that bravado. He'd been talking about getting home to his fiancée. Jo hoped she was wrong but could see all kinds of trouble that lay ahead for him.

There were also two poorly-looking men with abdominal wounds that would need to be checked for any sudden haemorrhage — she'd seen it happen a number of times in transit and she'd had to apply pressure bandages to contain it. And then sadly, the German prisoner with the missing jaw. His eyes were pleading; he looked afraid. Chris was speaking to him gently, and the poor man was gesturing as if for a drink. Jo could have sobbed — he was asking for a drink because he still had the feeling of thirst and what was left of his mouth was dry. She joined Chris, checking the saline drip that was keeping the man hydrated, and she notched up the rate to help make him less thirsty. She'd be vigilant later and make sure he had extra morphia if he needed it.

As they waited for Zach's truck — the final transport — she could feel her chest tightening and there was that buzz of excitement in her head again. She was glad that as a more able patient he would have to sit in the utility seats against the side of the plane — the area that was attended by Chris.

She glanced at her watch; the truck should have been here by now. Clambering back inside the plane,

263

she did her final checks on the men who were already installed. Chris had pulled out one of the thermos flasks and he was offering tea to all who wanted it. Again, she checked her watch, and she could sense MacNab in the cockpit, already getting impatient.

Then she saw the truck moving at speed towards them, with a large dint in the bonnet and a piece of metal flapping at the side.

Straight away she knew that something was very wrong. She jumped down, ready to receive the casualties, calling for Chris to assist. In the last few seconds that it took for the truck to approach, she felt the adrenaline start to pulse throughout her body — she could hear a man shouting and someone was screaming in pain.

As soon as it ground to a halt, the stretcher bearers leapt down. The wide-eyed driver was shouting something about a doodlebug. She ran to him as he jumped out of the truck, gasping. 'We were hit, the hospital was hit, just as we finished loading. Sister shouted for us to go, just go... There wasn't much left of the hospital.'

Jo had an instant image of Laura, running for her life.

'I've got newly injured men in the back,' said the driver. Jo was already running to the rear, where a man was screaming, shouting out. The stretcher bearers were moving fast, pulling men out.

'Take them straight to the Dakota,' she shouted, her eyes frantically searching for any sign of Zach.

Then turning to Chris, she said, 'The young man screaming, he's William Jones, known as Will, and he has bad shell shock, you take him. Don't board him until you've calmed him down.'

Chris thrust the medical panniers at her and slipped by the stretcher bearers to take hold of Private Jones. 'Right, come on, Will, you're going to be fine, just come with me...'

One of the bearers pointed to the back and said, 'We've managed the minor injuries but there's still one bleeding, we put him on a stretcher.'

With dull certainty, Jo knew straight away who it was.

She climbed straight up inside the truck, clawing her way to the side of the stretcher, 'Zach,' she shouted, 'can you hear me?' He didn't reply, but she could see that he was breathing. 'Zach,' she called again, her voice breaking on his name. He started to rouse and groaned in pain. She opened his flying jacket to find a lot of blood, seeping onto the stretcher. Then, she ripped open his shirt and saw that he'd been hit in the left upper chest.

She wanted to wail and scream out loud, and for someone who was always calm in an emergency, she knew that she was out of kilter. A chest wound was drastic — even if they got him as far as the plane, he might not make it. She pulled up his vest, and there it was, a gaping hole, gushing blood. She gulped in air, needing to steady herself. This was her call and her call only, she had no other medical assistance at hand. Grabbing a handful of swabs, she pressed them firmly to the wound, her hands instantly covered in blood. Despite this, he was still bleeding, and she held back a sob as she grabbed more swabs and pressed them tight to the wound. She thought the bleeding might be starting to slow, but she wasn't sure. Her screaming brain was moving at speed through the protocol for bleeding wounds: she needed to check his colour, breathing and general condition. He looked pale, even with his pink healing face. She picked up his wrist to check his pulse and she was unable to find it, her hand was full of blood and slipping on his skin.

'Get a grip!' she shouted to herself.

When she looked back at the wound, she was reassured that the swabs seemed to be containing the bleeding. And, better still, his breathing wasn't rasping or laboured. With the bleeding stemmed, she'd have to determine the depth of the wound to find out if it was penetrating, and examine for shrapnel. 'I'm just going to check the wound,' she said, her voice steady, 'this might hurt.'

Peeling back the swabs she saw another heavy trickle of blood. Using one hand, she scrabbled in the medical bag for some forceps. She opened up the wound with her fingers, noting that his muscled chest created enough padding to absorb the impact of the injury. He winced as she gently inserted a finger into the wound. She could feel a lump of metal, shrapnel, that needed to come out. She tried to use the forceps, but he gasped in pain, and with metal on metal, the forceps kept slipping off, so she threw them down. 'Hold tight,' she instructed, using her index finger now and digging deeper, hooking her finger beneath the shrapnel, which was slippery with blood and still wouldn't budge. She tried again and this time it came to the surface so she grabbed it with her free hand. Zach shouted out and blood continued to well up from the wound. Quickly, she wrapped the shrapnel in a swab and pushed it in her pocket.

Examining the wound more closely, she could see that although it was deep, it was confined to soft tissue, and at least it hadn't penetrated the chest cavity.

She could have fallen to her knees with relief as she grabbed some clean swabs and pressed them down firmly. He was still scrunching his face in pain, but he managed to open his eyes and look at her. She smiled at him. 'You're going to be fine, Zach, just fine.'

'Just my luck, injured three times in one war,' he groaned. And then he looked at her with such intensity, 'But looking at you now, I'd say that it was all worth it.'

She laughed and then she was in tears. He smiled at her and then she couldn't stop herself, still pressing the swabs tight to his chest, she leant down and kissed him full on the mouth. His lips were firm and he tasted of salt and cigarettes. If he hadn't still been bleeding, she could have carried on kissing him.

'I think I love you,' he murmured, 'and not just because you've saved my life.'

'No, I didn't save your life... you weren't going to die from this one.'

He tried to laugh, his face creased in pain. 'Well, let's hope there isn't a next one, because I've got to tell you, I've found a whole new reason to live.'

She fought the urge to tell him that it was probably just the euphoria after a brush with death — because she knew, really, that he was right. There was something between them, and she could feel it just as surely as she could feel his heart beating beneath her hand.

She heard Chris calling, 'How are you doing?'

'All fine,' she turned, shouting back down to him. 'Can you get me more gauze and some saline? I need to clean up this wound and pack it to control the bleeding. They can stitch him up when we get over to the other side.'

Once Zach was loaded, Jo needed to find a bowl

of water and a clean flannel. Her hands and uniform were covered in blood. 'Even some on your face,' Chris pointed out, taking the end of the flannel to dab at her cheek. 'If I didn't know better, Corporal Brooks, I'd think you'd been kissing a wounded man.'

Jo gasped, her eyes wide. 'It was just a—'

'Don't you worry, if you see love in the midst of a war, it is a very precious thing. My lips are sealed, not a word will pass.'

She knew that she could trust Chris, of course she could, but what she couldn't work out was what she could do about it. Although the allies were pushing on week by week towards Germany and there were whispered conversations about it only being a matter of time now before it was all over, no one really knew. The war was still going on, people were being shot, bombed, taken prisoner, and it was over five years now since this had all started. No one could even remember what life had been like before. It was clear to Jo that there was very little that she could do about this precious thing that had happened with a pilot who would be sent back to the US in due course. She might never see him again. And she needed to carry on with her work; more nurses had undoubtedly been killed today at the evacuation hospital. No nurse could just take herself out of harm's way, they were all desperately needed. She had to keep going.

Once Zach was loaded, they were ready to depart. She was still setting up a saline drip to give him extra fluid and making sure he had an injection of penicillin as the Dakota rattled along the runway. The men cheered as the plane heaved into the air. Out of the corner of her eye, she saw young Will, who seemed to be taking notice of what was going on around him, and she thought he might have given a little cheer as well. Checking Zach's dressing one final time, she patted his arm. 'Do you need something for the pain?' she asked.

He smiled back up at her. 'No, not yet, but could you give it to me just before we land, so I'm ready for the stitches?'

She nodded, struggling to tear herself away from him, but another man was crying out in pain. She went over to his stretcher, pulling the ready-prepared syringe of morphia from her pocket.

As soon as they were over the coast the men gave another hearty cheer. Even though Jo experienced it on every flight, it still always brought tears to her eyes, and some of the men were openly weeping. She knew they were still thinking of the mates they'd left behind, the ones who would never come home. She wiped her tears as she arrived at Zach's stretcher to give his morphia. His face looked tight and he could hardly speak, and she worried at first that he was in more pain. 'I wasn't prepared for this,' he gasped at last. 'You Brits don't show much on the outside, but you sure have a lot of feeling going on.'

She brushed the tears from her face. 'I suppose we do, we're not all stiff upper lip.'

'I think I might need a double dose of that,' he said, nodding towards the syringe in her hand. 'This whole thing has been a hell of an experience.'

She laughed.

'And before you give me the needle, I need to tell you something. I want to meet up with you after the war. I have to see you again...' he whispered.

'Let's not talk about it. You'll be shipped back to America, I'll be carrying on here, this will all pass, you know how it is…' she whispered, already pulling up his blanket to find an injection site.

He was shaking his head. 'It's real, I know it is.'

'No, these are exceptional times,' she insisted.

He winced as she stuck the needle into his thigh.

She knew that it wouldn't help to be thinking about seeing him 'when it was all over'. It was far too much to comprehend. For now, her life was going from one evacuation flight to the next, dealing with things as they came up. It was the only way that she could cope and she couldn't imagine anything else.

'Well, I know your name, and I'm guessing that the Jo is for Josephine, so you're Josephine Brooks.'

'Yes,' she said, feeling sure that once he got back home with his family, he'd barely give her a second thought.

'I want you to know that I will come back to England and I will find you, Jo Brooks. Make no mistake, I will find you.'

24

Louvain, Belgium, March 1945

Mac never would have thought that she'd end up in a convent, but that was exactly where she'd been working for months now. Such a welcome change from the tent hospitals and the temporary set-ups in any kind of large building that the army could find. This was very civilised in comparison — they had hot water, a bath, small shops in the town selling fruit and vegetables, and she'd even managed to buy a new lipstick and some perfume.

For the first time since she'd been posted she was out of her grimy battledress tunic and in the dress uniform of the Queen Alexandra's Nurses. Vera, Lucy and Edith loved the flowing white head dress, the little red cape and the plain grey dress, but it wasn't altogether the best, as far as Mac was concerned. Sometimes she missed the simplicity of her battledress — and she definitely missed driving her jeep. But even though they'd been separated from Sister Lloyd, who'd been sent up to take charge of a hospital in another Belgian town, she could have no real objection to this posting. They were having a fine time — there were officer's dances to attend and they could even go into Brussels for a night out with no end of ever-changing handsome men in uniforms. She was getting ready for one such night right now. At last, she'd managed to get herself a new dress from a local shop — it was cobalt blue, fitted at the waist. She'd just done her hair, brushing it back from her face in her preferred style. She took her bright red lipstick and smoothed it on, top and bottom, smudging her lips together, enjoying the feel of it.

'Are you ready?' called Vera, anxious to be off and make the most of their time. In the autumn and winter of last year, before coming to the convent, they'd worked twelve-hour shifts, constantly attending the men who'd been fighting at Arnhem and along the front — men with horrific injuries, blown to pieces with legs, hands and arms missing. All of them arrived direct from casualty clearing stations with the strong stench of war on them; none of them had medical notes, just an identity disc and the name, date, and time of any administered drug written on their foreheads. Most of the casualties at that time required a blood transfusion or a bottle of plasma and so many men didn't make it through. And the level of shell shock that the poor buggers were experiencing was horrendous — all of it exacerbated by lack of food, water and sleep when they were trapped between German infantry with mortars behind and tanks in front. Men were screaming on the wards all night long, reliving the horrors.

That's why now that Mac and the other nurses had the chance, their nights out were so important. They'd all been working on overdrive. Nobody could sit still when they were off duty, all they wanted was to get out for a few drinks, have a dance with a man in uniform, maybe a kiss and a cuddle, then back to work the next day.

Mac was feeling more herself than she'd done for years and Vera was really coming into her own — from the quiet, conscientious but shy nurse at the beginning of the war, she'd blossomed into a woman who was sure of herself and who wouldn't take any bullshit.

'Come on, we need to get out,' Vera urged.

Just as they reached the top of the stairs there was a shout, 'All nurses to the ward, we have a convoy of wounded coming in.' Mac and Vera ran straight back, stripping off their going-out clothes and scrabbling into their uniforms. Then they ran down the stone stairs that led straight onto the one ward that occupied the ground floor of the convent. Sister Maria-Anselm was already waiting, plump and self-contained in her nun's robe.

'So sorry, I know it's your night off,' she said in perfect English, 'but we are expecting many wounded men, they're coming down from the Siegfried Line — mostly Canadian First Army. I do hope our new surgeon and anaesthetist arrive on time, I've been told they're on their way.'

All the lights were on, the supplies were checked and they were ready and waiting when the door burst open and the first of the stretchers came through. Mac was straight there, directing the stretcher bearers. The scrubbed stone floor was soon littered with badly wounded men and the stench of blood and vomit was overwhelming. Some of the men already had drips in situ and those who had been given injections had the drug and dose scribbled on their foreheads. Other information chalked on uniforms indicated injuries — Mac had long ago learned to read the symbols; there was never any paperwork and she needed to make her own assessments. Edith and Lucy were running around from one stretcher to another, desperately trying to apply pressure dressings to heavily bleeding wounds whilst Vera checked IVs. One man whose mangled leg was barely attached was screaming in agony. She shouted across the room, 'Vera, get him some morphia, even if he's already had all of his doses, he needs more.'

Mac took out her scissors. There was no time to try and undress the men, they would need to cut through their battledress, quickly. She got to work straight away, assessing exactly who needed to be treated first and who could afford to wait.

Crouched by the stretcher of her penultimate patient, she heard a man's voice call, 'Hello, nurses.' It was the new surgeon and he was already shrugging off his great coat and rolling up his sleeves.

Mac jumped up from the stretcher, ready to direct him to the first patient. She knew that Sister Maria-Anselm was waiting in theatre, making last-minute preparations. 'Over there, that man there, the first one,' she shouted, catching her breath when she saw properly who the surgeon was. Angus Dunbar.

'Nurse Mac, we meet again! For some reason we always seem to be rushing; maybe when we've got through this lot we can have a catch up.'

Mac gave a wry laugh. 'We never seem to ever get through all of the patients. It might have to wait till we're back home.'

She worked solidly throughout the night, supplying Dunbar, his anaesthetist and Sister Maria-Anselm with patients and settling those who were coming out of theatre into bed. At least here, in the convent, they had clean army-issue pyjamas for the men, and in due course they would be able to get them all washed and changed.

The spring sunshine was peeking in through the

windows that were set in the thick stone walls of the building by the time the last of the surgical cases had been dealt with. Mac and Vera, their aprons covered in blood and grime, had stayed on till the last.

'That new surgeon's a bit of a character,' murmured Vera, as they stumbled back up the stone stairs, barely able to speak through their exhaustion.

'Yes, he is, and he's the one who did the needle-work on my forehead.'

'Really? How come?'

'He was a surgeon at Mill Road, the night the bomb fell, so...'

'Oh, yes of course. How strange that you should meet him again here though,' she said, stifling a yawn.

'Yes,' Mac sighed, 'but I don't think I'm surprised by anything any more. We already met briefly when we were in Normandy and I've heard of all kinds of strange coincidences in this war. If people are destined to meet, it happens I suppose.'

25

May 7, 1945

Above the English Channel, Jo was flying home with a group of paratroopers who'd been prisoners of war. For the most part they were subdued, but some were still wearing their red berets and had a bit of spark about them. There was only one man, Phil, who'd suffered an injury — his arm was in a plaster cast after he'd broken it falling from a fence, trying to escape just a few days before liberation. The men were undernourished, but on the whole, it looked like they hadn't been too badly treated. A German doctor had reset Phil's arm, making sure that it was in the correct position. Jo had started to get used to these trips with prisoners, which were quieter and calmer as there were hardly any acute injuries coming through now.

The last lot of wounded that they'd flown home were battle-weary — sons who'd been away from home far too long, fathers who hadn't been able to see their children grow up — and all they wanted was to be back home with their families; they were sick of war.

Jo collected up the cups after the final drink. They were almost home. She knew that the men would rally just as soon as they knew they were flying over the British coast. MacNab's voice crackled through on the intercom, 'We've just been informed of a BBC newsflash.' Jo saw Chris frown. They exchanged a glance. MacNab cleared his throat and when his voice came, he was choked: 'The war is over.'

Jo and Chris gazed at each other, open mouthed.

The intercom crackled again and this time he sounded like he was crying, 'I repeat: the war is over.'

One of the paratroopers leapt up from his seat. He cheered loudly and pulled off his beret, tossing it into the air and jumping up and down. 'Do you hear that? The war is over!'

The joy caught like wildfire. All the men were animated now, some were laughing, some were crying. Jo and Chris hugged each other, laughing uproariously as MacNab repeated over and over again, 'The war is over, the war is over…'

Another paratrooper grabbed Jo and smacked a kiss on her cheek. 'That's for you and all of the nurses, you've served us so well!'

Jo burst into tears, the para still holding onto her, and laughing as he hugged her.

'We're going home!' someone shouted — it was like a champagne cork popping; the cabin was alive.

Jo clung to Chris's arm with tears streaming down her face as silently, the British coast slipped by beneath the Dakota. Her chest was aching, and she pressed a hand over her heart to try and ease the pain. She thought about her mum and dad and wondered if they'd heard the broadcast. She knew that they would cry with joy. And what about Mac? Where was she? Wherever she was, she'd be celebrating. And Zach, the American who had won her heart in one single night; and who she would probably never see again — was he at home with his family, was he thinking of her?

★ ★ ★

277

Mac and Vera were just finishing off a series of tricky dressings on a soldier whom they'd nursed long term through terrible burns to both legs, when Sister Maria came running onto the ward, her round face red with delight, so breathless that she could hardly speak.

'It's over,' she gasped.

Mac and Vera exchanged a glance, 'What?'

'The war is over,' Sister Maria said, sobbing and laughing all at the same time.

Mac looked at Vera again and back towards Sister. She still couldn't quite grasp what Sister had just said.

'Did you hear what I said?' cried Sister Maria, to the whole ward. 'I've just heard it on the radio, there's been a BBC news flash — the Germans have surrendered unconditionally!'

Mac grabbed her patient's hand, 'The war's over, it's over!' she cried. He stared back up at her, his eyes wide, and then he burst into tears.

'We're going home,' Vera said, from the other side of the bed, and then covered her face and started to cry.

The news spread among the patients and they were all cheering and laughing and crying as Sister Maria stood in the middle of the ward, beaming. 'Tomorrow, Mr Churchill will make a formal announcement at three o'clock. The whole day will be known as Victory in Europe Day.'

The soldiers cheered.

As the windows and the doors stood wide open, letting in the last of the light from the streets of Louvain, Mac and Vera headed out to celebrate. Sister Maria had said that she would take care of the ward, and the numbers of patients were reduced now anyway.

The church bells were ringing as they stepped out

and Belgian, British and American flags were flying from the windows. Mac and Vera grabbed each other and ran screeching with laughter down the street. Vera was shouting, 'The war's over, the war's over, I'm going home to Newcastle!'

Out of breath, they slowed to a walk and linked arms, just as a jeep came by, right up close. 'Do you ladies want to come into Brussels?' called an American GI. 'My name's Steve, I'm going in for a few hours but I'm on duty in the morning, so I'll have to come back this way.'

'Yes, we do!' cried Mac, and the two jumped up into the jeep.

Vera sat up front. 'Hi Steve, where are you from?'

The chat in front continued, punctuated by Vera's hearty laugh, and Mac sat quietly in the back as they rattled along in the jeep. It had all come as a shock in the end, even though they'd been expecting it for weeks. And she wasn't sure how she felt now that the initial surge of joy had subsided. It was more of an absence of feeling really, it was all over and she wasn't quite sure what she was going to do with herself.

Brussels was alive with singing and dancing and the whole city was lit up by searchlights, rockets and flares. They drove through crowds of laughing people, car horns sounding around them and the trams clanking along with people on their roofs. Mac lay back against the seat of the jeep, gazing up to the sky, with jumbled thoughts of the war and home flashing through her mind. It was starting to feel a bit overwhelming. Vera glanced over her shoulder at Mac, laughing at something Steve had just said. She wanted to join in wholeheartedly but there was a niggle of something stuck deep inside her, something that was holding her back. It was no shock when it came to her: it was Don. There he was again, his dark eyes burning as she stood in the pub doorway, and she felt that heavy ache in the pit of her stomach. Tears sprung to her eyes, making her gasp, and she did what she always had to: she swallowed hard, forcing it all down inside until it made her chest hurt.

When Steve was unable to nudge the jeep any further along the busy street, he parked up outside a bar that was packed out with British and American military. Loud music everywhere, there was a brass band in the street and a piano inside the bar and people were singing along to all tunes, any tune, all at the same time. Steve had one arm around Vera and one arm around Mac, leading them towards the bar. He was a real gentleman, and good-looking in that big-boned way that some men had. He and the other GIs were perfect companions for what was the biggest celebration in a lifetime.

After at least two hours of drinking, singing and dancing, Mac found herself sitting quietly on a low wall that ran down the side of the bar, smoking a cigarette. As she exhaled, through the fug of smoke she saw the familiar shape of someone down the alley. The city was bright with light, so it was easy to make out that it was the little tousle-haired girl. Mac hadn't seen her since she'd been posted abroad, but now she was there, smiling and waving.

Mac stood up from the wall and took a pace towards her. The girl stood for a few moments with her eyes wide, taking in every detail. Mac held her breath, not wanting her to leave, feeling like she wanted to put her arms around her, to hold her close. She took another step towards her, but the girl smiled, raised a hand in goodbye and turned away. Mac felt tears springing to her eyes. She had no choice but to let her go.

'Mac!' Vera's voice broke through, making her gasp, 'come and see this trick that Steve can do.'

'Coming,' she replied, turning towards Vera for a second. When she looked back a firework burst into silver stars overhead, and she could see that the girl was gone. 'Goodbye,' she breathed, looking up to the sky to catch the last of the stars above.

As they drove back to the convent, Mac slipped her arm around Vera, who was drunkenly falling asleep on her shoulder. Steve was a little wobbly at the wheel of the jeep, but he seemed safe enough and he was driving slowly. Mac relaxed back, pulling Vera in close beside her. The sound of an explosion startled her, taking her breath, but it was just more fireworks bursting in the sky. She knew that she would always remember this day, for the rest of her life. She wondered what she would be in ten, twenty years, when the war had become something marked by a memorial, like they had each November for the last one. She laughed quietly to herself; probably some crabby spinster, a senior nurse like Matron Jenkins at Mill Road.

But at least she'd be alive. She now knew that, despite it all, she would come out of this alive.

Epilogue

Liverpool, July 1945

The clock on Lime Street station clearly showed twelve as Mac waited beneath it while chaotic passengers and so many men in uniform streamed by. She'd already had several admiring glances as she stood in her cobalt blue dress with her hair stylishly pinned beneath a black pillar box hat. She lit up a cigarette and breathed in the smoke, feeling the cigarette paper gently adhere to her bright red lipstick.

She'd only been back in Liverpool three days, but she'd managed to secure an interview for a Sister's post at the Liverpool Royal Infirmary. It helped that Amy Goodwin and Ruth Lee were firmly established there, but Matron was a tough cookie, so if she hadn't come with top notch credentials, she wouldn't have stood a chance. She'd applied to work in Casualty — a natural choice given her war experience — and she knew that she could cope with anything now. And only yesterday, Vera had sent word. She was already back to work at the Infirmary in Newcastle; she'd gone for Female Medical, claiming that never in her whole life did she want to see another surgical wound.

Mac knew by now that the train must be running late, she would have time for a browse through the magazine stall after all. She needed to distract herself, she hadn't realised how much she'd missed Jo until she'd rung her at the farm. Just the sound of her voice had brought tears to her eyes. It seemed strange that

282

she was the one waiting for her; in all the time that they'd known each other, it had always been the other way round.

★ ★ ★

Jo snapped her book shut, sitting back against the seat, feeling the coarse material prickle through her white cotton blouse. It was so hot in the compartment and the woman opposite had smoked one cigarette after another and even though the ventilation windows were fully open, she still felt like she could hardly breathe. She tried to stop herself from continually checking her wristwatch, it wouldn't make the train move any faster and they were already late. She thought about Mac waiting for her. Hopefully she'd be her characteristic ten minutes behind time, but maybe not, given all the time they had been apart. She glanced at her watch again, her head jangled by the noise of the jovial people jammed in the passage outside the compartment and the two giggling children who were squashed into the luggage rack above. It seemed that the train had slowed down even more now; she felt like she'd never get into Lime Street station.

Exasperated, she grabbed her bag and fought her way out of the compartment and then along the passage, squeezing her way between people to get to the door so that she could feel some breeze and be ready to get off. As she waited, she felt a trickle of sweat run down between her shoulder blades. She loved the high-waisted slacks that she always wore now, but maybe she would have been cooler in a skirt.

At last, the guard was opening the door and she pushed her way through. Two soldiers in uniform stood back to let her through, they had packs on their backs and big smiles on their faces: they were returning home. One was slightly drunk but their joyful banter was pleasant. A sandy-haired woman was waiting on the platform with a baby in her arms. Jo saw her frowning, glancing frantically down the line of carriages. One of the soldiers shouted, 'Marion!' as Jo stepped down from the train. Just the timbre of his voice brought tears to her eyes. She stepped aside as he almost fell from the carriage, grabbing the woman, the baby between them, sobbing his heart out. The man settled the baby in his arms, a tender look on his face. Jo slipped a handkerchief out of her pocket and dabbed at her eyes.

And then she saw Mac waiting beneath the clock. She felt a surge of pure joy go right through her body and she started to run towards her. Jo shouted out, calling her name — she couldn't help herself. Mac was jumping up and down, shrieking with laughter, and when they grabbed each other, they held on so tight they both gasped for air.

Jo pulled a clean hankie out of her pocket and wiped her own eyes and then passed it to Mac. 'I think your eye make-up is smudged a bit,' she said, putting her arms around her again and holding her tight.

'We have so much to catch up on,' sobbed Mac, waving the hankie away; there was no chance of rescuing her make-up now.

As they walked away, arm in arm, they chatted as if the time apart had slipped away without a second thought. Mostly it was Mac doing the talking but Jo didn't mind, she was happy to hold onto her, to feel the warmth of her and to hear her stories. They walked and chatted with little sense of direction until Jo realised that they seemed to be heading in the direction of Mill Road.

'We might as well go and have a look,' Jo said, 'given that we've come so close.'

The ruined part of the hospital had been demolished long ago, and what stood there now was empty, windows blown out, exposed to the elements. 'I wonder if they're going to rebuild,' murmured Jo, as she stood with her arm firmly linked through Mac's.

'Well, I've heard that they might be planning a Maternity hospital, which I suppose after what happened is—' Mac didn't seem to be able to find the words. 'I also heard that they took all of the rubble up to Crosby beach, along with the rest from the city, to build some kind of sea defence. Apparently, if you go for a walk you can look at bits of brick and tile and even chunks of carved stone from the old buildings.'

'How strange,' said Jo, still holding tight to Mac, 'I don't know how I'd feel about that, it sounds like a graveyard.'

'And another thing ...' Mac's voice was so sombre that Jo felt a shiver go through her. 'Some of the bodies of those killed that night... they were buried so deep down in the rubble that the rescue team never managed to recover them, so they had to seal them in with concrete ... See, there, I think that's where they might be.'

'That must be where Casualty was ...' Jo said. Her heart felt like it was twisting in her chest. She still couldn't believe what had happened that night.

'We were lucky to come out of that lot weren't we, Jojo?'

Jo couldn't speak. There didn't seem to be any words. She just stood silently beside Mac, thinking of Myfanwy and all the other lives that had been lost that night.

As they walked away, Mac turned to Jo with a smile. 'But we did have some good times here, though, didn't we? When we were probationers and then even just after the war had started...'

'You were out every night — dancing, meeting men, driving me crazy.'

'And then I met Don.'

'Yes, you did,' said Jo, pulling Mac closer. 'I was so sorry to hear about what happened; I never did get that letter you sent.'

'That's alright, I'm OK now, I think. Life goes on, doesn't it, and by the time I got to my last posting, near Brussels, I was able to have some nights out again and enjoy myself. I even saw Dunbar at the hospital, he worked with us there for a week or two.'

'Do you know that cheeky devil once put his hand on my knee.'

'What! You didn't tell me that.'

As they walked, Jo told the story and they both started to cackle with laughter.

'You know what, Jo, I've got another hour to burn before I'm due at the hospital for my interview, why don't we go to the old pub, the one around the corner, and have a quick drink. I think it might settle my nerves.'

'Why not,' said Jo, 'I seem to have become partial to a nip of rum, even in the middle of the afternoon.'

'Oh my God, you were tee total at the start of the war!'

As they pushed open the battered door of The Crown, the smell of beer and cigarette smoke hit them full in the face. Just walking in took Jo back to a night before the May Blitz when Mac had persuaded her, for once, to come out for a drink. The old pub had stood throughout, worse for wear with chunks of ceiling plaster missing and a big crack down one of the walls. But beyond that it was very much the same: the curtains were still dusty and almost threadbare, the tables and chairs were in need of a coat of varnish, and there was the same cranky landlord.

Jo saw a man with broad shoulders in a demob suit leaning on the bar cradling a pint, and something about him made her alert. When another man, somewhere in the pub, gave a low wolf whistle, the man at the bar turned. He had a lock of dark hair falling onto his forehead and he was staring at Mac. Jo heard her gasp and the man was still looking directly at her. Mac was stock still, a hand pressed to her chest. She reached out, mumbling, 'It's not him, it's not…' and then she gave a small sob and pulled Jo with her as she turned on her heel. Jo knew instantly what had happened, the man had a longer face, but he looked like Don, there was no mistake there.

As they walked, Jo could see that Mac was fighting to hold back tears, so she gave her arm a squeeze, knowing that if she started to speak about what had just happened it would only make things worse. Jo was annoyed with herself, she should have insisted that they go somewhere else, made sure that they didn't take any risks. But the fact was, this city was packed with reminders of their 'before' time, especially for Mac, who had lived here her whole life. It didn't help that the streets were lined with the bombed-out remains of buildings — roofs without slates, empty windows, iron girders on display — as if the skeleton of the city lay exposed. There was so much relief, so much joy amongst the people, but behind that lay the tragedy of what had happened and all the lives that had been lost.

They stopped — even Mac was struggling to get her bearings, the city was so changed. 'Ah that's it, we need to go that way,' she said, turning to Jo with a smile, 'Sorry, about that, it's just I got the heebie-jeebies when we were in that pub...'

'I know, I know,' Jo replied. 'No need to apologise.'

'It's only round the corner, I'll just have a smoke to steady my nerves.' Jo watched as she slipped out a cigarette and lit up. They were in front of yet another broken building, which had moss growing up over the red bricks and rubble that lay discarded inside while a tangle of goosegrass and nettles had claimed the rest.

'There's something painted there, on that wall inside,' said Mac, walking towards the blown-out window, leaning through, her face wreathed in smoke. 'It says, "We'll meet again" and there's a huge heart with an arrow through it and "Tony and Marion 1942". I hope they both made it through...'

She drew back, her eyes glinting with unshed tears. Then, glancing at her watch, she said, 'Bloody hell, I'm due at the hospital in ten minutes... Do I look alright?'

'You look more than alright,' said Jo, 'You look great.'

'Right, so, there's a pub, just up the road, can you see it?'

Jo nodded in response.

'I'll meet you there when I'm done. Wish me luck.'

'Good luck!' Jo smiled, leaning in to give her a kiss on the cheek. 'You're going to be just fine.'

She watched Mac go and in that moment she felt

alone, deserted. She walked away aimlessly at first, but then she realised that she could put the time that she had to kill to good use. She remembered there'd been a bookshop somewhere around here, maybe it was still there. It was nice to have the luxury of wandering down the street with nothing to do. She'd been busy helping on the farm ever since she'd got back — since Len had gone back to Salford, Henry had been struggling to manage. She'd been driving the tractor, mucking out, picking up eggs — the work was never-ending. But some good news had come, just that morning. Young Len, who was now a gangly teenager, was coming back to the farm. He'd run away from the father Henry referred to as 'that violent bastard' and he'd gone to the authorities, asking to be placed permanently at Bracken Farm. When she headed out, she'd left her parents delighted, already making plans to convert Michael's room into a place that would be more suitable for a growing teenager.

Smiling to herself and distracted, she wandered past the bookshop and then had to retrace her steps. She peered in through the window, not sure now whether she should go in or not. She still hadn't properly got back to her reading, and she was trying to save up as much money as she could. She had some work lined up with the District Nursing service in Lancaster, but she'd have to make sure that Len was back at the farm before she could even think about a start date.

There were lots of books in the shop window and she was sorely tempted. She noticed a copy of *Far from the Madding Crowd*, still in its dust cover — exactly the same edition that she'd lost that night of the bomb. Maybe it was time for her to go right back to the start, read through the whole lot this time. That was it, her mind was made up: she was going in.

As she pushed open the door, a tall man in a smart suit was waiting to come out. 'Sorry,' she said, apologising automatically, and waiting for him to slip by, so she could get into the shop. But he was still standing in her way, and when she looked up, he was staring at her, his eyes were blue, very blue.

'Corporal Brooks?' he said.

As soon as she heard his voice, she knew, it was him.

'Zach?'

She was flustered, not knowing what to say, as they stood in the shop doorway.

'I'm just here in Liverpool to meet up with a friend of mine, someone I know from the start of the war.'

'Me too,' she said, feeling her skin prickle with sensation.

'I got into Liverpool last night, I was going to come and find you...' he said.

'No, honestly, that's alright, you don't have to say that. I know how things are in war...'

'No, that's the reason I've come back to England — to find you.'

She shook her head.

'Your address, I know your address, it's Bracken Farm.'

'Yes, but...' This felt like it should be happening to someone else. Her head was reeling.

'I'm meeting my friend today and then I was going to find you, I was going to knock on your door!'

This was all too much; she didn't know what to say, and she was backing out through the door, with him following.

Out on the street, she could see the remains of the

scar from the burn on his forehead, his hair had grown back but it was still patchy. And he had eyebrows now — probably why she didn't recognise him. He was gazing at her so intently that she couldn't speak.

'Jo, I can't believe that...' He seemed unable to form the words, and instead he leant in to kiss her on the cheek. She put her arms around him, pulling him close, reaching up to kiss him on the mouth. She could feel the warmth of his body and it sent a shiver of excitement right through her.

'I never stopped thinking about you,' he murmured. 'I drove my family crazy going on and on about it but there was so much turmoil, so much information jumbled up in those weeks after the end of the war that even when I rang, and I rang many times, no one could tell me anything. And then, one day, I got an address out of someone, they said they weren't sure, but it was enough. It was easier to find my friend — he had a forwarding address in Liverpool, so I thought I'd see him first and then I'd come to find you, up in the mountains, or wherever it is that you live. I wouldn't have stopped till I found you. When I was rescued from that field in Belgium, I felt like the luckiest man alive, and then I met you and I spent a lot of time back home, staring up to the sky, just thinking about you.'

She shook her head; this was unreal. She reached up to kiss him again, never wanting to let him go. Every day she'd thought about him and by night she'd dreamt of his slow smile and his blue eyes. She'd had to keep telling herself to get things in perspective, to accept that what they'd had was a passing thing.

'I thought about you as well, Zach.' At last, she gave voice to how she had felt, allowing the pleasure of it to flow through her. 'How could I not, how often do you meet a man who reads poetry?'

'Ha, maybe we should thank Robert Frost for all this,' he said.

'Maybe we should, but if it hadn't been for the war, how would I ever have met a man from Long Island? And the war isn't really something that we can thank is it?'

'Not really, but it's part of us, now, just like all the GIs and their brides.'

'Hold on, slow down!' Jo laughed. 'I think we should start with a cup of tea and a chat first, don't you? Come on, let's go, we've got a lot to talk about.'

When the time came for Zach to go and meet his friend and Jo knew that she really ought to be going to wait for Mac, it was hard to separate. Zach didn't seem to want to let her go, as if he was scared of losing her again. He walked her to the pub, still holding onto her. 'Look, why don't you meet up with your friend and then bring him here, I'm sure my friend won't mind, she's very easy going. And it might help me explain exactly what's happened.'

'OK. I can do that. But promise me you won't move on anywhere, not until I come back.'

'I promise. And besides, you've got my home address, there's no way I can escape.'

There was no sign of Mac, so Jo got herself a rum and black and found a quiet corner. Her mind was still reeling and she had to keep telling herself it was him, it really was, and he had come back to find her.

Mac burst through the door. 'I got the job!'

Jo stood up from her seat to congratulate her. 'Well done!'

'What the heck have you been up to?' Mac said, as

she approached the table. 'Your cheeks are all pink.'

'I... well... I've just bumped into someone,' she said, breathy with her news. 'You know that American pilot I told you about, the one who was injured? Well, I've just seen him in a bookshop. He said he'd come back from America to look for me, he'd got my home address and everything.'

'Are you sure it's the same guy?' Mac's eyes were wide.

Jo was nodding and she was grinning. 'He's just gone to meet up with a mate, and then he's coming here.'

'Oh my God!' gasped Mac. 'I need to sit down, this is unbelievable... You must have been destined to meet, that's all I can say.'

'I don't know about that, and there might even be a logical explanation. The reason we got talking in the first place, when he was in the hospital, was because we both like reading, and today we were in bookshop, so...'

'Jo! You met in Antwerp and he's from Long Island, New York! He's come all this way to find you?'

'Yes,' Jo said simply, she couldn't stop smiling.

'I need a drink, I'll get you another to celebrate!' Mac unpinned her hat, shook her hair loose and headed towards the bar.

* * *

As Mac stood at the bar with her back turned, the door opened, and she heard the tinkle of the bell. She turned out of curiosity, just in case it was Jo's pilot.

It had to be him; he was tall and handsome, with short-cropped hair and, yes, he was looking right over at Jo. It was him. And coming into the pub behind him was a thin fella with broad shoulders. He had dark hair and he looked a bit like Clark Gable. Mac's breath caught and her eyes widened. He was looking at her now, and there was no mistake: it was Don.

She saw him step back, clasping a hand to his chest as if he'd been shot. But when he looked up again his eyes were burning into her and he strode towards her. She could see that he had tears streaming down his face and she couldn't help but move urgently towards him.

He pulled her close, crushing her against his body, and then he kissed her full on the mouth. She wanted the moment to go on forever, the smell of him, the feel of his lips forcing the years to melt away. She felt it through her whole body; she could have sobbed with it.

'I thought you were dead,' she cried, when at last he drew back, 'I thought you were dead...'

'Everybody thought that, even my family,' he gasped, 'But I was lucky, I managed to hide my parachute and then keep out of sight until I got picked up by the Belgian resistance. I fought with them for a while, but then I was captured and ended up in a prison camp.'

Mac couldn't believe it, she felt dazed and in shock. 'But why didn't you let me know that you were still alive, after you got back... why?'

He glanced down at himself in his baggy suit. 'I had to go to Ireland, stay with my dad for a bit, I was in a bad way. I've only just got back to Liverpool... and I was going to come and find you... Look...' He pulled a magazine clipping from his inside pocket, the image was almost worn away, but you could still make out the face of Rita Hayworth. 'This was in my inside pocket on every mission, I carried it with me all the way through the war.'

Mac took the clipping, her hand shaking.

'My love for you never faltered, Mac, you were right there in this photograph, next to my heart.'

She reached up to brush the tears from his cheeks and wipe her lipstick from his mouth, and she smiled. 'I see you've still got your crying and kissing moles.'

Jo was beside them, with Zach by her side. 'I don't know if you remember me, Don, but I saw you at the hospital and you came up to the farm, when Mac stayed with my family.' He was still crying but he managed to mumble, 'Yes, of course I remember you. Of course.'

Mac took a deep breath and swallowed hard. 'And, Zach, you were with Don that night he came into the hospital to find me, and then we met in that pub.'

He was nodding. 'I remember,' he said, smiling.

'How could this have happened?' Mac asked, looking from one to another, not able to stop the buzzing in her brain.

'I suppose it's what you were saying before… destiny?' Jo said, her eyes wide.

'This is beyond any destiny I've ever heard of,' Mac replied, wiping her eyes, smudging her mascara. 'I need that drink.'

'I'll get them,' said Jo, 'you all go and sit down. What are you having, Don, Zach?'

★ ★ ★

As she stood waiting for Don's pint and Zach's Scotch to be added to the order, Jo turned to look at the three

295

of them at the table. Mac was in the middle, talking non-stop, one arm linked through Don's, pulling him close to the side of her body. Zach looked up and gave her a smile that made her breath catch.

'Scuse me, Miss,' said the landlord.

Jo turned to pay, flustered now, fishing in her pocket for some money. Her fingers caught something else in there, a shard of metal — it was the piece of shrapnel that she'd scrubbed clean so she could carry it as a reminder of the American pilot who'd shared his poetry. She wouldn't tell him just yet, this was all strange enough already, but somehow she knew that there would be time for all their stories.

As she walked back to their table with a glass in either hand, all three of them looked up and smiled. She found herself grinning and then laughing as she placed the drinks down.

'What you laughing at, Brooks?' Mac asked.

She was going to say, *oh nothing*, but how could she? 'I'm laughing at everything, all of this, it is absolutely perfect.'

'Here's to us,' called Don, lifting his glass and then turning to kiss Mac on the cheek. Zach reached for Jo's hand and she slipped onto the bench, moving right up next to him so that she could feel the warmth of his body. So much had happened, it was difficult to take it all in. But as she felt Zach put his arm around her and pull her close, she knew that they would all grasp this life that they'd been offered with both hands and, whatever happened, they would be there for each other, for the rest of their days.

A Letter From Kate

I want to say a huge thank you for choosing to read *An Angel's Work*. If you enjoyed it and want to keep up to date with all my latest releases, just sign up at the following link. Your email address will never be shared and you can unsubscribe at any time:

www.bookouture.com/kate-eastham

I remember nursing a Spitfire pilot. A dapper, articulate man who told stories of night flights over the British coast, drinking sprees after a mission, and the sadness of the empty bunks of those who didn't return. We got on well and I had the privilege to help guide him through the final phase of a long and very full life. It turned out that he was to be one of my last patients before I needed to leave nursing and become a full-time carer.

His story added to many others that I'd been told over the years by men and women who served in the forces, worked in munitions, the ATS, or as land girls, and one woman who laughed uproariously when she told us of dancing the night away with American GIs at the Tower Ballroom in Blackpool.

My Spitfire pilot refused to leave any memoir — even though I tried to persuade him many times — he didn't want to be seen as having done anything out of the ordinary. I've known many others like him — unassuming, stoic people who'd often say, 'we're not the heroes… The ones who didn't come back are the heroes.'

'You write it down, if you want to,' the pilot had said, not thinking that I ever would. But here I am, writing away, inspired by stories of the past and the lives of ordinary yet very extraordinary people.

I hope you loved *An Angel's Work*. If you did, I would be very grateful if you could write a review. I'd love to hear what you think, and it makes such a difference in helping new readers discover my books for the first time.

I love hearing from my readers. You can get in touch on Twitter. Thank you!

All best wishes to you and yours,
Kate Eastham

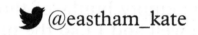 @eastham_kate

Acknowledgements

I'm indebted to the stories that inspire me. From the very start of the research for *An Angel's Work*, I was captivated by accounts and diaries of the Flying Nightingales, army nurses, fighter pilots and bomber crews; and, the people of Liverpool who endured the Blitz and the bombing of Mill Road Hospital. I'm also grateful for all the stories that have been shared with me, during the course of my work as a nurse, by so many war veterans.

I'd like to thank my agent, Judith Murdoch, for her unwavering support and sound advice. Kathryn Taussig and the wonderful team at Bookouture for their warm welcome and very attentive approach.

And, of course, I would also like to thank my family for their love, enthusiasm and for always believing in me.